OTHER BOOKS BY EOIN COLFER

Airman

Benny and Omar

Benny and Babe

Half Moon Investigations

The Supernaturalist

The Wish List

Iron Man: The Gauntlet

ARTEMIS FOWL

Artemis Fowl

Artemis Fowl: The Arctic Incident

Artemis Fowl: The Eternity Code

Artemis Fowl: The Opal Deception

Artemis Fowl: The Lost Colony

Artemis Fowl: The Time Paradox

Artemis Fowl: The Atlantis Complex

Artemis Fowl: The Last Guardian

EOIN COLFER

Disney • HYPERION
Los Angeles   New York

First Hardcover Edition, November 2019
First Paperback Edition, July 2020

1 3 5 7 9 10 8 6 4 2
FAC-025438-20143
Printed in the United States of America

This book is set in American Typewriter ITC Pro, Courier New, DIN Next LT Pro, ITC Novarese Pro, Perpetua MT Pro/Monotype; Neutraface Condensed/House Industries
Designed by Tyler Nevins

Library of Congress Cataloging-in-Publication Control
Number for Hardcover Edition: 2019005479
ISBN 978-1-368-05256-6
Visit www.DisneyBooks.com

SUSTAINABLE
FORESTRY
INITIATIVE

Certified Sourcing

www.sfiprogram.org
SFI-01054
The SFI label applies to the text stock

For my sons, Finn & Seán,
who are neither twins nor foul

PROLOGUE

There are things to know about the world.

Surely you realize that what *you* know is not everything there is to know. In spite of humankind's ingenuity, there are shadows too dark for your species to fully illuminate. The very mantle of our planet is one example; the ocean floor is another. And in these shadows we live. The Hidden Ones. The magical creatures who have removed ourselves from the destructive human orbit. Once, we fairies ruled the surface as humans do currently, as bacteria will in the future, but for now, we are content for the most part to exist in our underground civilization. For ten thousand years, fairies have used our magic and technology to shield ourselves from prying eyes, and to heal the beleaguered Earth mother, Danu. We fairies have a saying that is writ large in golden tiles on the altar mosaic of the Hey Hey Temple, and the saying is this: WE DIG DEEP AND WE ENDURE.

But there is always one maverick who does not care a fig for fairy mosaics and is hell-bent on reaching the surface. Usually this maverick is a troll. And specifically in this case, the maverick is a troll who will shortly and for a ridiculous reason be named Whistle Blower.

For here begins the second documented cycle of Fowl Adventures.

CHAPTER 1

MEET THE ANTAGONISTS

The Baddie: Lord Teddy Bleedham-Drye
The Duke of Scilly

If a person wants to murder any member of a family, then it is very important that the entire family also be done away with, or the distraught survivors might very well decide to take bloody revenge, or at least make a detailed report at the local police station. There is, in fact, an entire chapter on this exact subject in *The Criminal Mastermind's Almanac*, an infamous guidebook for aspiring ruthless criminals by Professor Wulf Bane, which was turned down by every reputable publisher but is available on demand from the author. The actual chapter name is "Kill Them All. Even the Pets." A gruesome title that would put most normal people off reading it, but Lord Teddy Bleedham-Drye, Duke of Scilly, was not a normal person, and the juiciest phrases in his copy of *The Criminal Mastermind's Almanac* were marked in pink highlighter, and the book itself was dedicated as follows:

To Teddy

From one criminal mastermind to another

Don't be a stranger

Wulfy

Lord Bleedham-Drye had dedicated most of his one hundred and fifty plus years on this green earth to staying *on* this green earth as long as possible, as opposed to being buried beneath it. In television interviews he credited his youthful appearance to yoga and fish oil, but in actual fact, Lord Teddy had spent much of his inherited fortune traveling the globe in search of any potions and pills, legal or not, that would extend his life span. As a roving ambassador for the Crown, Lord Teddy could easily find an excuse to visit the most far-flung corners of the planet in the name of culture, when in fact he was keeping his eyes open for anything that grew, swam, waddled, or crawled that would help him stay alive for even a minute longer than his allotted three score and ten.

So far in his quest, Lord Teddy had tried every so-called *eternal-youth therapy* for which there was even the flimsiest of supporting evidence. He had, among other things, ingested tons of willow-bark extract, swallowed millions of antioxidant tablets, slurped gallons of therapeutic arsenic, injected the cerebrospinal fluid of the endangered Madagascan lemur, devoured countless helpings of Southeast Asian liver-fluke spaghetti, and spent almost a month suspended over an active volcanic rift in Iceland, funneling the restorative volcanic gas up the leg holes of his linen shorts. These and other extreme practices—never ever to be tried at home—had indeed kept Bleedham-Drye breathing and vital thus far, but there had been side effects. The lemur fluid had caused his forearms to elongate so that his hands dangled below his knees. The arsenic had paralyzed the left corner of his mouth so that it was forever curled in a sardonic sneer, and the volcanic embers had scalded his bottom, forcing Teddy to walk in a slightly bowlegged manner as though trying to keep his balance in rough seas. Bleedham-Drye considered these secondary effects a small price to pay for his wrinkle-free complexion, luxuriant mane of hair, and spade of black beard, and of course the vigor that helped him endure lengthy treks and safaris in the hunt for any rumored life-extenders.

But Lord Teddy was all too aware that he had yet to hit the jackpot, therapeutically speaking, in regard to his quest for an unreasonably extended life. It was true that he had eked out a few extra decades, but what was that in the face of eternity? There were jellyfish that, as a matter of course, lived longer than he had. Jellyfish! They didn't even have brains, for heaven's sake.

Teddy found himself frustrated, which he hated, because stress gave a fellow wrinkles.

A new direction was called for.

No more penny-ante half measures, cribbing a year here and a season there.

I must find the fountain of youth, he resolved one evening while lying in his brass tub of electric eels, which he had heard did wonders for a chap's circulation.

As it turned out, Lord Bleedham-Drye *did* find the fountain of youth, but it was not a fountain in the traditional sense of the word, as the life-giving liquid was contained in the venom of a mythological creature. And the family he would possibly have to murder to access it was none other than the Fowls of Dublin, Ireland, who were not overly fond of being murdered.

This is how the entire regrettable episode kicked off:

Lord Teddy Bleedham-Drye reasoned that the time-honored way of doing a thing was to ask the fellows who had already done the thing how they had managed to do it, and so he set out to interview the oldest people on earth. This was not as easy as it might sound, even in the era of worldwide-webbery and marvelous miniature communication devices, for many aged folks do not advertise the fact that they have passed the century mark lest they be plagued by health-magazine journalists or telegrams from various queens. But nevertheless, over the course of five years, Lord Teddy managed to track down several of these elusive oldsters, finding them all to be either tediously virtuous, which was of little use to him, or lucky, which could neither be counted on nor stolen. And such was the way of it until he located an Irish monk who was working in an elephant sanctuary in California, of all places, having long since given up on helping humans. Brother Colman looked not a day over fifty, and was, in fact, in remarkable shape for a man who claimed to be almost five hundred years old.

Once Lord Teddy had slipped a liberal dose of sodium Pentothal into the Irishman's tea, Brother Colman told a very interesting story of how the holy well on Dalkey Island had come by its healing waters when he was a monk there in the fifteenth century.

Teddy did not believe a word of it, but the name *Dalkey* did sound an alarm bell somewhere in the back of his mind. A bell he muted for the present.

The fool is raving, he thought. I gave him too much truth serum.

With the so-called monk in a chemical daze, Bleedham-Drye performed a couple of simple verification checks, not really expecting anything exciting.

First he unbuttoned the man's shirt, and found to his surprise that Brother Colman's chest was latticed with ugly scars, which would be consistent with the man's story but was not exactly proof.

The idiot might have been gored by one of his own elephants, Teddy realized. But Lord Bleedham-Drye had seen many wounds in his time and never anything this dreadful on a living body.

There ain't no fooling my second test, thought Teddy, and with a flash of his pruning shears he snipped off Brother Colman's left pinky. After all, radiocarbon dating never lied.

It would be several weeks before the results came

8

back from the Advanced Accelerator Mass Spectrometer
Laboratory, and by that time Teddy was back in England
once again, lounging dejectedly in his bath of electric eels
in the family seat: Childerblaine House, on the island of St.
George in the Scilly Isles. Interestingly enough, the island
had been so named because in one of the various versions
of the Saint George legend, the beheaded dragon's body had
been dumped into Cornish waters and drifted out to the
Scilly Isles, where it settled on a submerged rock and fossilized, which provided a romantic explanation for the small
island's curved spine of ridges.

When Lord Teddy came upon the envelope from AAMSL
in his pile of mail, he sliced it open listlessly, fully expecting
that the Brother Colman excursion had been a bally waste
of precious time and shrinking fortune.

But the results on that single page made Teddy sit up so
quickly that several eels were slopped from the tub.

"Good heavens!" he exclaimed, his halo of dark hair
curled and vibrating from the eel charge. "I'm off to Dalkey
Island, begorra."

The laboratory report was brief and cursory in the way
of scientists:

The supplied specimen, it read, *is in the four-hundred- to five-
hundred-year-old age range.*

Lord Teddy outfitted himself in his standard apparel of
high boots, riding breeches, and a tweed hunting jacket, all
topped off with his old commando beret. And he loaded up
his wooden speedboat for what the police these days like to

call a stakeout. It was only when he was halfway across the Irish Sea in the Juventas that Lord Teddy realized why the name *Dalkey* sounded so familiar. The Fowl fellow hung his hat there.

Artemis Fowl.

A force to be reckoned with. Teddy had heard a few stories about Artemis Fowl, and even more about his son Artemis the Second.

Rumors, he told himself. Rumors, hearsay, and balderdash.

And even if the stories were true, the Duke of Scilly's determination never wavered.

I shall have that troll's venom, he thought, opening the V-12 throttles wide. And I shall live forever.

The Goodies (relatively speaking)
Dalkey Island, Dublin, Ireland
Three Weeks Later

Behold Myles and Beckett Fowl, passing a late-summer evening on the family's private beach. If you look past the superficial differences—wardrobe, spectacles, hairstyles, and so on—you notice that the boys' facial features are very similar but not absolutely identical. This is because they are dizygotic twins, and were, in fact, the first recorded nonidentical twins to be born conjoined, albeit only from wrist to little finger. The attending surgeon separated them with a flash of her scalpel, and neither twin suffered any ill effects, apart from matching pink scars that ran along the outside of their palms. Myles and Beckett often touched scars to comfort each other. It was their version of a high five, which they called a wrist bump. This habit was both touching and slightly gross.

Apart from their features, the fraternal twins were, as one tutor noted, "very different animals." Myles had an IQ of 170 and was fanatically neat, while Beckett's IQ was a mystery, because he chewed the test into pulpy blobs from which he made a sculpture of a hamster in a bad mood, which he titled *Angry Hamster*.

Also, Beckett was far from neat. In fact, his parents were forced to take up Mindfulness just to calm themselves down whenever they attempted to put some order on his cata-strophically untidy side of the bedroom.

It was obvious from their early days in a double cradle that the twins did not share similar personalities. When they were teething, Beckett would chew pacifiers ragged, while Myles chose to nibble thoughtfully on the eraser end of a pencil. As a toddler, Myles liked to emulate his big brother, Artemis, by wearing tiny black suits that had to be custom-made. Beckett preferred to run free as nature intended, and when he finally did agree to wear something, it was plastic training pants, in which he stored supplies, including his pet goldfish, Gloop (named for the sound it made, or at least the sound the goldfish was blamed for).

As the brothers grew older, the differences between them became more obvious. Myles became ever more fastidious, 3-D-printing a fresh suit every day and taming his wild jet-black Fowl hair with a seaweed-based gel that both moisturized the scalp and nourished the brain, while Beckett made zero attempt to tame the blond curls that he had inherited from his mother's side of the family, and continued to sulk when he was forced to wear any clothes, with the exception of the only article he never removed—a golden necktie that had once been Gloop. Myles had cured and laminated the goldfish when it passed away, and Beckett wore it always as a keepsake. This habit was both touching and extremely gross.

Perhaps you have heard of the Fowl family of Ireland? They are quite notorious in certain shadowy circles. The twins' father was once the world's preeminent crime lord, but he had a change of heart and reinvented himself as a champion of the environment. Myles and Beckett's older brother, Artemis the Second, had also been quite the criminal virtuoso, hatching schemes involving massive amounts of gold bullion, fairy police forces, and time travel, to name but a few. Fortunately for more or less everyone except aliens, Artemis had recently turned his attention to outer space, and was currently six months into a five-year mission to Mars in a revolutionary self-winding rocket ship that he had built in the family barn. By the time the world's various authorities, including NASA, APSCO, ALR, CNSA, and UKSA, had caught wind of the project and begun to marshal their objections, Artemis had already passed the moon.

The twins themselves were to have many adventures,

some of which would kill them (though not permanently), but this particular episode began a week after their eleventh birthday. Myles and Beckett were walking along the stony beach of a small island off the picturesque coast of South Dublin, where the Fowl family had recently moved to Villa Éco, a newly built, state-of-the-art, environmentally friendly house. The twins' father had donated Fowl Manor, their rambling ancestral home, to a cooperative of organic farmers, declaring, "It is time for the Fowls to embrace planet Earth."

Villa Éco was a stunning achievement, not least because of all the hoops the county council had made Artemis Senior jump through just for planning permission. Indeed, the Fowl patriarch had on several occasions considered using a few of his old criminal-mastermind methods of persuasion just to cut through the miles of red tape, but eventually he managed to satisfy the local councillors and push ahead with the building.

And what a building it was. Totally self-sufficient, thanks to super-efficient solar panels and a dozen geothermal screws that not only extracted power from the earth but also acted as the building's foundation. The frame was built from the recycled steel yielded by six compacted automobiles and had already withstood a hurricane during construction. The cast-in-place concrete walls were insulated by layers of plant-based polyurethane rigid foam. The windows were bulletproof, naturally, and coated with metallic oxide to keep the heat where it should be throughout the seasons. The design was modern but utilitarian, with a nod to the island's monastic heritage in the curved walls of its outbuildings, which were constructed with straw bales.

But the real marvels of Villa Éco were discreetly hidden until they were called upon. Artemis Senior, Artemis Junior, and Myles Fowl had collaborated on a security system that would bamboozle even the most technically minded home invader, and an array of defense mechanisms that could repel a small army.

There was, however, an Achilles' heel in this system, as the twins were about to discover. This Achilles' heel was the twins' own decency and their reluctance to unleash the villa's defenses on anyone.

On this summer evening, the twins' mother was delivering a lecture at New York University with her husband in attendance. Some years previously, Angeline had suffered from what Shakespeare called "the grief that does not speak," and, in an effort to understand her depression, had completed a mental-health doctorate at Trinity College and now spoke at conferences around the world. The twins were being watched over by the house itself, which had an Artemis-designed Nano Artificial Neural Network Intelligence system, or NANNI, to keep an electronic eye on them.

Myles was collecting seaweed for his homemade hair gel fermentation silo, and Beckett was attempting to learn seal language from a dolphin just offshore.

"We must be away, brother," Myles said. "Bedtime. Our

young bodies require ten hours of sleep to ensure proper brain development."

Beckett lay on a rock and clapped his hands. *"Arf,"* he said. *"Arf."*

Myles tugged at his suit jacket and frowned behind the frames of his thick-rimmed glasses. "Beck, are you attempting to speak in seal language?"

"Arf," said Beckett, who was wearing knee-length cargo shorts and his gold necktie.

"That is not even a seal. That is a dolphin."

"Dolphins are smart," said Beckett. "They know things."

"That is true, brother, but a dolphin's vocal cords make it impossible for them to speak in the language of a seal. Why don't you simply learn the dolphin's language?"

Beckett beamed. "Yes! You are a genius, brother. Step one, swap barks for whistles."

Myles sighed. Now his twin was whistling at a dolphin, and they would once again fail to get to bed on time.

Myles stuffed a handful of seaweed into his bucket. "Please, Beck. My brain will never reach optimum productivity if we don't leave now." He tapped the right arm of his black plastic spectacle frames, activating the built-in microphone. "NANNI, help me out. Please send a drobot to carry my brother home."

"Negative," said the house system in the strangely accented female voice that Artemis had selected to represent the AI. It was a voice that both twins instinctively trusted for some reason.

Myles could hear NANNI through bone-conduction speakers concealed in the arms of his glasses.

"Absolutely no flying Beckett home, unless it's an emergency," said NANNI. "Mother's orders, so don't bother arguing."

Myles was surprised that NANNI's sentences were unnecessarily convoluted. It seemed as though the AI was developing a personality, which he supposed was the point. When Artemis had first plugged NANNI into the system, so to speak, her responses were usually limited to one-word answers. Now she was telling him not to bother arguing. It would be fascinating to see how her personality would develop.

Providing NANNI doesn't become too human, thought Myles, because most humans are irritating.

At any rate, it was ridiculous that his mother refused to authorize short-range flights for Beckett. In tests, the drone/robots had only dropped the dummy Becketts twice, but his mother insisted the drobots were for urgent situations only.

"Beckett!" he called. "If you agree to come back to the house, I will tell you a story before bed."

Beckett flipped over on the rock. "Which story?" he asked.

"How about the thrilling discovery of the Schwarzschild radius, which led directly to the identification of black holes?" suggested Myles.

Beckett was not impressed. "How about the adventures

of Gloop and Angry Hamster in the Dimension of Fire?"

Now it was Myles's turn to be unimpressed. "Beck, that's preposterous. Fish and hamsters do not even share the same environment. And neither could survive in a dimension of fire."

"*You're* preposterous," said Beckett, and went back to his whistling.

The crown of Beck's head will be burned by the evening UV rays, thought Myles.

"Very well," he said. "Gloop and Angry Hamster it is."

"And Dolphin," said Beckett. "He wants to be in the story, too."

Myles sighed. "Dolphin, too."

"Hooray!" said Beckett, skipping across the rocks. "Story time. Wrist bump?"

Myles raised his palm for a bump and wondered, If I'm the smart one, why do we always do exactly what Beck wants us to?

Myles asked himself this question a lot.

"Now, brother," he said, "please say good night to your friend, and let us be off."

Beckett turned to do as he was told, but only because it suited him.

If Beckett had not turned to bid the dolphin farewell, then perhaps the entire series of increasingly bizarre events that followed might have been avoided. There would have been no nefarious villain, no ridiculously named trolls, no shadowy organizations, no interrogations by a nun (which are known in the intelligence community as *nunterrogations*, believe it or not), and a definite lack of head lice. But Beckett did turn, precisely two seconds after a troll had surged upward through the loose shale at the water's edge and collapsed onto the beach.

Fairies are defined as being "small, humanoid, supernatural creatures possessed of magical powers," a definition that applies neatly to elves, gnomes, sprites, and pixies. It is, however, a human definition, and therefore as incomplete as human knowledge on the subject. The fairies' definition of themselves is more concise and can be found in the Fairy Book, which is their constitution, so to speak, the original of which is behind crystal in the Hey Hey Temple in Haven City, the subterranean fairy capital. It states:

```
Fairy, faerie, or faery: A creature of
the earth. Often magical. Never will-
fully destructive.
```

No mention of *small* or *humanoid*. It may surprise humans to know that they themselves were once considered fairies and did indeed possess some magic, until many of them stepped off the path and became extremely willfully destructive, and so magic was bred out of humans over the centuries, until there was nothing left but an empath here and there, and the occasional telekinetic.

Trolls are classed as fairies by fairies themselves, but

would not be so categorized by the human definition, as they are not magical—unless their longevity can be considered supernatural. They are, however, quite feral and only slightly more sentient than the average hound. Another interesting point about trolls is that fairy scholars of their pathologies have realized that trolls are highly susceptible to chemically induced psychosis while also tending to nest in chemically polluted sites, in much the same way as humans are attracted to the sugar that poisons them. This chemical poisoning often results in uncharacteristically aggressive behavior and uncontrollable rage. Again, similar to how humans behave when experiencing sugar deprivation.

But this troll was not sick, sluggish, or aggressive—in fact, he was in remarkable physical health, all pumping limbs and scything tusks, as he followed his second most powerful instinct:

REACH THE SURFACE.

Trolls' most powerful instinct being EAT, GOBBLE, DEVOUR.

This particular troll's bloodstream was clear because he had never swum across a chromium-saturated lake and he had never carved out his burrow in mercury-rich soil. Nevertheless, healthy or not, this specimen would never have made it to the surface had the Earth's crust under Dalkey Island not been exceptionally thin, a mere two miles and a quarter, in fact. This troll was able to squeeze himself into fissures that would have made a claustrophobe faint, and he wriggled his way to the open air. It took the creature four sun cycles of agonizingly slow progress to break through, and you might think the cosmos would grant the fellow a little good fortune after such Herculean efforts, but no, he had to pop out right between the Fowl Twins and Lord Teddy Bleedham-Drye, who was lurking on a mainland balcony and spying on Dalkey Island through a telescopic monocular, thus providing the third corner of an irresistible triangular vortex of fate.

So the troll emerged, joint by joint, reborn to the atmosphere, gnashing and clawing. And in spite of his almost utter exhaustion, some spark of triumph drove him to his feet for a celebratory howl, which was when Lord Teddy, for diabolical reasons that shall presently be further explored, shot him.

Once the shot had been fired, the entire troll-related rigmarole really got rigmarolling, because the microsecond that NANNI's sensors detected the bullet's sonic boom, she dispensed with her convoluted sentences and without a word upgraded the villa's alert status from beige to red, sounded the alarm Klaxon, and set the security system to Siege mode. Two armored drobots were dispatched from their charging plates to extract the twins, and forty decoy flares were launched from mini mortar ports in the roof as countermeasures to any infrared guided missiles that may or may not be inbound.

This left the twins with approximately twenty seconds of earthbound liberty before they would be whisked into the evening sky and secured in the eco-house's ultrasecret safe room, blueprints of which did not appear on any set of plans.

A lot can happen in twenty seconds. And a lot did happen.

Firstly, let us discuss the marksman. When I say Lord Teddy shot the troll, this is possibly misleading, even though it is accurate. He did shoot the troll, but not with the usual explosive variety of bullet, which would have penetrated the troll's hide and quite possibly killed the beast through sheer shock trauma. That was the absolute last thing Lord Teddy wanted, as it would void his entire plan. This particular bullet was a cellophane virus slug that was being developed by the Japanese munitions company Myishi and was not yet officially on the market. In fact, Myishi products rarely went into mass production, as Ishi Myishi, the founder and CEO, made quite a lot of tax-free dollars giving a technological edge to the world's criminal masterminds. The Duke of Scilly was a personal friend and possibly his best customer and had most of his kit sponsored by Ishi Myishi so long as the duke agreed to endorse the products on the dark web. The CV bullets were known as "shrink-wrappers" by the development team, and they released their viruses on impact, effectively wrapping the target in a coating of cellophane that was porous enough to allow shallow breathing but had been known to crack a rib or two.

And then there is the physicality of the troll itself. There are many breeds of troll. From the ten-foot-tall behemoth

Antarctic Blue, to the silent jungle killer the Amazon Heel Claw. The troll on Dalkey Island beach was a one-in-a-million anomaly. In form and proportion he was the perfect Ridgeback, with the distinctive thick comb of spiked hair that ran from brow to tailbone, and the blue-veined gray fur on his chest and arms all present and correct. But this creature was no massive predator. In fact, he was a rather tiny one. Standing at barely eight inches high, the troll was one of a relatively new variety that had begun to pop up in recent millennia since fairies were forced deep in the earth's mantle. Much in the same way as schnauzer dogs had miniature counterparts known as toy schnauzers, some troll breeds also had their shrunken varieties, and this troll was one of perhaps half a dozen toy Ridgebacks in existence and the first to ever reach the surface.

Not at all what Lord Teddy had been expecting. Having seen Brother Colman's scars, the duke had imagined his quarry to be somewhat larger.

When the little troll's heat signature had popped up in his eyepiece like an oversized gummy bear, the duke had exclaimed, "Good heavens! Could that little fellow be my troll?"

It certainly matched Brother Colman's description, except for the dimensions. In truth, the duke couldn't help feeling a little let down. He had been expecting something more substantial. That diminutive creature didn't look like it could manufacture enough venom to extend the life span of a gerbil.

"Nevertheless," muttered the duke, "since I've come all this way . . ."

And he squeezed the trigger on his sniper's rifle.

The supersonic cellophane slug made a distinctive yodeling noise as it sped through the air, and impacted the toy Ridgeback square in the solar plexus, releasing its payload in a sparkling globule that quickly sprawled over the tiny creature, wrapping it in a restrictive layer of cellophane before it could do much more than squeak in indignation.

Beckett Fowl spotted the cartwheeling toy troll, and his first impressions were of fur and teeth, and so, consequently, his first thought was *Angry Hamster!*

But the boy chided himself, remembering that *Angry Hamster* was a sculpture that he himself had constructed from chewed paper and bodily fluids and therefore not a living thing, and so he would have to revise his guess as to what this tumbling figure might be.

But by this time the troll had come to rest at his feet, and Beckett was able to snatch it up and scrutinize it closely, so there was no need for guessing.

Not alive, he realized then. Doll, maybe.

Beckett had thought the figure moved of its own accord, perhaps even made a squealing noise of some kind, but now he could see it was a fantasy action figure with a protective plastic coating.

"I shall call you Whistle Blower," he whispered into the troll's pointed ear. The boy had chosen this name after barely a second's consideration, because he had seen on Myles's preferred news channel that people who squealed were sometimes called whistle-blowers. Also, Beckett was not the kind of fellow who wasted time on decisions.

Beckett turned to show Myles his beach salvage, though his brother had always been a little snooty when it came to toys, claiming they were for children even though he was patently himself a child and would be for a few more years.

"Look, brother," he called, waggling the action figure. "I found a new friend."

Myles sneered as expected, and opened his mouth to pass a derogatory remark along the lines of *Honestly, Beck. We are eleven years old now. Time to leave childish things behind.*

But his scorn was interrupted by a deafening series of honks.

The emergency Klaxon.

It is true to say that there is hardly a more alarming sound than an alarm Klaxon, heralding as it does the arrival of some form of disaster. Most people do not react positively to this sound. Some scream, some faint. There are those who run in circles wringing their hands, which is also pointless. And, of course, there are people who have involuntary purges, which shall not be elaborated upon here.

The reactions of the Fowl Twins could seem strange to a casual observer, for Myles discarded his seaweed bucket and uttered a single word: "Finally."

While Beckett spoke to his new toy. "Do you hear that, Whistle Blower?" he asked. "We're going flying!"

To explain: Designing the security system had been a fun bonding project for Myles, Artemis, and their father, so Myles had a scientific interest in putting the extraction drobots through their paces, as thus far they had only been tested with crash dummies. Beckett, on the other hand, was just dying to be yanked backward into the air at a high speed and dumped down a security chute, and he fervently hoped the ride would last much longer than the projected half a minute.

Myles forgot all about getting to bed on time. He was in action mode now as the countermeasure flares fanned out behind his head like fireworks, painting the undersides of passing cumuli. NANNI broadcast a message to his glasses, and Myles repeated it aloud to Beckett in melodramatic tones that he knew his brother would respond to, as it made him feel like he was on an adventure. And also because Myles had a weakness for melodrama, which he was aware he should at least attempt to control, as drama is the enemy of science.

"Red alert!" he called. "Extraction position."

The twins had been drilled on this particular position so often that Beckett reacted to the command with prompt obedience—two words that he would never find written on any of his school report cards.

Extraction position was as follows: chin tucked low, arms stretched overhead, and jaw relaxed to avoid cracked teeth.

"Ten seconds," said Myles, slipping his spectacles into a jacket pocket. "Nine, eight . . ."

Beckett also slipped something into his pocket before assuming the position: Whistle Blower.

"Three," said Myles. "Two . . ."

Then the boy allowed his jaw to relax and spoke no more.

The two drobots shot from under the villa's eaves and sped unerringly toward the twins. They maintained an altitude of six feet from the ground by dipping their rotors and adjusting their course as they flew, communicating with each other through coded clicks and beeps. With their gears retracted, the drobots resembled nothing more than old propeller hats that children used to wear in simpler times as they rode their bicycles.

The drobots barely slowed as they approached the twins, lowering micro-servo-cable arms that lassoed the boys' waists, then inflated impact bags to avoid injuring their cargo.

"Cable loop in place," said Myles, lowering his arms. "Bags inflated. Most efficient."

In theory, the ride should be so smooth that his suit would not suffer one wrinkle.

"No more science talk!" shouted Beckett impatiently. "Let's go!"

And go they did.

The servo cables retracted smoothly to winch the twins into the air. Myles noted that there had been no discernible impact on his spine, and while acceleration was rapid— zero to sixty miles an hour in four seconds according to his smartwatch—the ride was not jarring.

"So far so good," he said into the wind. He glanced sideways to see Beckett ignoring the flight instructions, waving his arms around as though he were on a roller coaster.

"Arms folded, Beck!" he called sternly to his brother. "Feet crossed at the ankles. You are increasing your own drag."

It was possible that Beckett could not hear the instructions, but it was probable that he simply ignored them and continued to treat their emergency extraction like a theme park ride.

The journey was over almost as soon as it began, and the twins found themselves deposited in two small chimney-like padded tubes toward the rear of the house. The drobots lowered them to the safe room, then sealed the tubes with their own shells.

NANNI's face appeared in a free-floating liquid speaker ball, which was held in shape by an electric charge. "Perhaps this would be a good time to activate the EMP? I know you've been dying to try it."

Myles considered this as he unclipped the servo cable. Villa Éco was outfitted with a localized electromagnetic-pulse generator, which would knock out any electronic systems in the island's airspace. The Fowls' main electronics would not be affected, as the entire villa had a Faraday cage embedded in its walls, and the Fowl systems had backups that ran on optical cable. A little old-school, but should the cage fail, the cable would keep systems ticking until the danger was past.

"Hmm," said Myles. "That seems a bit drastic. What is the nature of the emergency?"

"Sonic boom detected," said NANNI. "I would guess from a high-powered rifle."

NANNI is guessing now, thought Myles. She really is developing.

"Guessing is of little use to me, madam," said Myles. "Scientists do not guess."

"Oh yes, that's right. Scientists *hypothesize,*" said NANNI. "In that case, I hypothesize that the sonic boom was caused by a rifle shot."

"That's better," said Myles. "How certain are you?"

"Reasonably," replied NANNI. "If I had to offer a percentage, I would say seventy percent."

A sonic boom could be caused by many things, and the majority of those things were harmless. Still, Myles now had a valid excuse to employ the EMP, something he had been forbidden to do unless absolutely necessary.

It was, in fact, a judgment call.

Beckett, who had somehow become inverted in the delivery chute, tumbled onto the floor and asked, "Will the EMP hurt my insects?"

Beckett kept his extensive bug collection in the safe room so it would be *safe.*

"No," said Myles. "Unless some of them are robot insects."

Beckett pressed his nose to the terrarium's glass and made some chittering noises.

"No robots," he pronounced. "So activate the EMP."

For once Myles found himself in agreement with his brother. While the sonic boom could possibly be the by-product of a harmless event, it also might herald the arrival of an attack force hell-bent on wreaking vengeance on one Artemis or the other. Better to press the button and survive than regret not pressing it just before you died.

So, thought Myles, I should activate the EMP. But before I do . . .

Myles rooted in the steel trash can until he found some aluminum foil that he had been using for target practice with one of his many lasers. He used it to quickly wrap his spectacles, then stuffed them down to the bottom of the trash can. This would protect the lite version of NANNI that lived in the eyeglasses in the event that both his safeguards failed.

"I concur," said Myles. "Activate the EMP, NANNI. Tight radius, low intensity. No need to knock out the mainland."

"Activating EMP," said NANNI, and promptly collapsed in a puddle on the floor, as her own electronics had not yet been converted to optical cable.

"See, Beck?" said Myles, lifting one black loafer from a glistening wet patch. "That is what we scientists call a design flaw."

* * *

Lord Bleedham-Drye was doubly miffed and thrice surprised by the developments on Dalkey Island.

Surprise number one: Brother Colman spoke the truth, and trolls did indeed walk the earth.

Surprise the second: The troll was tiny. Who ever heard of a tiny troll?

Surprise the last (for the moment): Flying boys had sequestered his prey.

"What on earth is going on?" he asked no one in particular.

The duke muttered to himself, "These Fowl people seem prepared for full-scale invasion. They have flare countermeasures. Drones flying off with children. Who knows what else? Antitank guns and trained bears, I shouldn't wonder. Even Churchill couldn't take that beach."

It occurred to Lord Teddy that he could blow up the entire island for spite. He was partial to a spot of spite, after all. But after a moment's consideration, he dismissed the idea. It was a cheery notion, but the person he would ultimately be spiting was none other than the Duke of Scilly, i.e., his noble self. He would hold his fire for now, but when those boys reemerged from their fortified house, he would be ready with his trusty rifle. After all, he was quite excellent with a gun, as his last shot had proven. Off the battlefield, it was unseemly to shoot anything except pheasant, unless one were engaged in a duel. Pistols at dawn, that sort of thing. But he would make an exception for a troll, and for those blooming Fowl boys.

Lord Teddy loaded the rifle with traditional bullets and set it on the balcony floor, muzzle pointed toward the island.

You can't stay in that blasted house forever, my boys, he thought. And the moment you poke your noses from cover, Lord Teddy Bleedham-Drye shall be prepared.

He could wait.

He was prepared to put in the hours. As the duke often said to himself: One must spend time to make time.

Teddy lay sandwiched between a yoga mat and a veil of camouflage that had served as a hide of sorts for almost a month now, and ran a sweep of the island through his night-vision monocular. The whole place was lit up like a fairground with roaming spotlights and massive halogen lamps. There was not a square inch of space for an intruder to hide.

Clever chappies, these Fowls, thought the duke. The father must have a lot of enemies.

Teddy sat up, fished a boar-bristle brush from his duffel bag, and began his evening ritual of one hundred brushes of his beard. The beard rippled and glistened as he brushed, like the pelt of an otter, and Teddy could not help but congratulate himself. A beard required a lot of maintenance, but, by heaven, it was worth it.

He had only reached stroke seven when the duke's peripheral vision registered that something had changed. It was suddenly darker. He looked up, expecting to find that the lights had been shut off on Dalkey Island, but the truth was more drastic.

The island itself had disappeared.

Lord Teddy checked all the way to the horizon with his trusty monocular. In the blink of an eye the entirety of Dalkey Island had vanished with only an abandoned stretch of wooden jetty to hint that the Fowl residence might ever have existed at the end of it.

Lord Bleedham-Drye was surprised to the point of stupefaction, but his manners and breeding would not allow him to show it.

"I say," he said mildly. "That's hardly cricket, is it? What has the world come to when a chap can't bag himself a troll without entire land masses disappearing?"

Lord Teddy Bleedham-Drye's bottom lip drooped. Quite the sulky expression for a hundred-and-fifty-year-old. But the duke did not allow himself to wallow for long. Instead, he set his mind to the puzzle of the disappearing island.

"One can't help but wonder, Teddy old boy," mused the duke to the mirror on the flat side of his brush, "if all this troll malarkey is indeed true, then is the rest also true? What Brother Colman said vis-à-vis elves, pixies, and gnomes all hanging around for centuries? Is there, in fact, magic in the world?"

He would, Lord Teddy decided, proceed under the assumption that magic did exist, and therefore, by logical extension, magical creatures.

"And so it is only reasonable to assume," Teddy said, "that these fairy chaps will wish to protect their own, and perhaps send their version of the cavalry to rescue the little troll. Perhaps the cavalry has already arrived, and this disappearing-island trick is actually some class of a magical spell cast by a wizard."

The duke was right about the cavalry. The fairy cavalry had already arrived.

One fairy, at least.

But he was dead wrong about a *wizard* casting a spell. The fairy responsible for the disappearing-island trick was a far cry indeed from being a wizard, and could no more cast a spell than a frog could turn itself into a prince. She had made a split-second decision to use the only piece of equipment available to her, and was now pretty certain that her decision was absolutely the wrong one.

CHAPTER 2

MIRROR BALL

THE gnome professor Dr. Jerbal Argon once presented a theory, dubbed the Law of Diminishing Probabilities, to the fairy Psych Brotherhood. Argon's law states that the more unusual the subjects involved in a conflict, the more improbable the resolution to that conflict will be. It is possibly the vaguest behavioral theory ever to make it into a journal, and it is really more of a notion than a law. But in the case of the Fowl Twins' first magical adventure, it would certainly prove to be accurate, as we will see from the hugely improbable finale to this tale.

The law's requirements were certainly fulfilled, as this day was, without doubt, one for unusual individuals:

An immortalist duke . . .

A miniature troll . . .

And a set of fraternal human twins: the first a certified genius with a criminal leaning lurking in his prefrontal cortex, and the second possessed of a singular talent that has been hinted at but not fully explored as yet.

There are two additional unusual individuals still to join the tale. The nunterrogator, to whom we have already alluded, will presently make one of her trademark theatrical entrances. But the next unusual individual to join our cast of protagonists is more than simply unusual—she is biologically unique. And she made her appearance from above, hovering thirty feet over Dalkey Island.

This unusual individual was Lower Elements Police Specialist Lazuli Heitz, who, **Five Minutes Earlier**, entered the island's airspace to complete a training maneuver in the Fowl safe zone. Usually such safe zones were in remote areas, but in rare cases where there was a special arrangement with the human occupants, a zone could be closer to civilization and provide more of a challenge for the specialists. A case in point being Dalkey Island, where Artemis Fowl the Second, friend to the LEP, had guaranteed safe passage for fairies.

From a human perspective, Lazuli was unusual simply by virtue of being an invisible flying fairy, but from a fairy perspective, LEP Specialist Heitz was unusual because she was a hybrid, that is to say a crossbreed. Hybrids are common enough among the fairy folk, especially since the families were forced into close quarters underground, but even so, they are each and every one idiosyncratic, for all hybrids are as unique as snowflakes and the manifestation of their magical abilities is unpredictable.

In Lazuli Heitz's case, her magic had resolutely refused to manifest itself in any shape or form. Lazuli's particular category of hybrid was known as a *pixel*, that being a pixie-elf cross. There were other species in the ancestral DNA mix, too, but pixie and elf accounted for over ninety-five percent of her total number of nucleotides. And even though both pixies and elves are magical creatures, not a single spark of power seemed to have survived the crossbreeding. In height, Specialist Heitz followed the pixie type at barely thirty-two inches tall, but her head adhered to the elfin model and was smaller than one might expect to see on a pixie's shoulders, with the customary elfin sharp planes of cheekbone, jaw, and pointed ear. This was enough to give her away as a hybrid to any fairy who cared to look. And just in case there was any lingering doubt, Lazuli's skin and eyes were the aquamarine blue of Atlantean pixies, but her hair was the fine flaxen blond associated with Amazonian elves. Scattered across her neck and shoulders was a mottling of yellow arrowhead markings, which, according to paleofatumologists, had once made Amazonian elves look like sunflowers to airborne predators.

Unless that elf is a hybrid with blue skin, Lazuli often thought, which ruins the effect.

All this paleofatumological knowledge only meant one thing to Lazuli, and that was that her parents had probably met on vacation, which was about the sum total of her knowledge on that subject, aside from the fact that one or both of them had deserted her on the north corner of a public square, after which the orphanage administrator had named her Lazuli Heights.

"I changed the spelling, and there you have it," the administrator had told her. "It's my little game, which worked out well for you, not so much for Walter Kooler or Vishtar Restrume."

The sprite administrator had a human streak and often made barbed remarks along the lines of *The lapis lazuli is a semiprecious stone. Semiprecious, hybrid. I think your parents must have been thinking along those lines, or you wouldn't have ended up here.*

The administrator chuckled dryly at his own tasteless joke every single time he cracked it. Lazuli never even smiled.

It was exceedingly exasperating for a pixel not to possess the magical phenotypic trait, especially since her driving ambition was to achieve the rank of captain in the LEPrecon, a post where abilities such as the *mesmer*, invisibility, and healing powers would most certainly prove to be boons. Fortunately for Heitz, her obdurate streak, sharp mind, and dead eye with an oxalis pistol had so far carried her through two years of intense training in the LEP Academy and now to specialist duty in a safe zone. Lazuli did suspect that her Academy application might have been bolstered by the LEP's minority-inclusion policy.

And Lazuli certainly was a minority. Her DNA profile breakdown was forty-two percent elf, fifty-three percent pixie, and five percent undeterminable. Unique.

The evening's exercise was straightforward: Fairies were secreted around the island, and it was her mission to track them down. These were not real fairies, of course. They were virtual avatars that could be tagged by passing a gloved hand through holograms projected by her helmet camera. There would be clues to follow: chromatographic reactions, tracks, faint scents, and a learned knowledge of the species' habits. Once she punched in, Specialist Heitz would have thirty minutes to tag as many virtual fugitives as she could.

Before Lazuli could so much as repeat the mantra that had sustained her for many years and through several personal crises, which happened to be *Small equals motivated*, a pulsating purple blob blossomed on her visor's display.

This was most unusual. Purple was usually reserved for live trolls. Perhaps her helmet was glitching. This would not be in the least surprising, as Academy equipment was always bottom of the priority list when the budget was being carved up between departments. Lazuli's suit was threadbare and ill-fitting, and packed with weapons that hadn't been standard issue in decades.

She blinked at the purple blob to enlarge it and realized that there was indeed a troll on the beach, albeit a tiny one. The poor fellow was smaller than her, though he did not seem as intimidated by the human world as she was.

I must rescue him, Lazuli told herself. This was undoubtedly the correct action, unless this troll was involved somehow in a live maneuver. Lazuli's angel mentor, who directed the exercise from Haven City, had explicitly and repeatedly ordered her never to poke her nose into an operation.

"There are two types of fast track, Specialist Heitz," the angel had said only this morning. "The fast track to the top, and the fast track out the door. Poke your nose into an operation where it doesn't belong, and guess which track you'll be on."

Lazuli didn't need to guess.

A thought occurred to her: Could it be that the coincidental appearance of a troll on this island was her stinkworm?

This was very possible, as LEP instructors were a sneaky bunch.

A specialist's mettle was often stress-tested by mocking up an emergency and observing how the cadet coped. Rookies referred to this testing as *being thrown a stinkworm*, because, as every fairy knew, if a person was thrown an actual stinkworm and they mishandled it, there would be an explosive, viscous, and foul-smelling outcome. There was a legend in the Academy about how one specialist had been dropped into the crater of an apparently active volcano to see how he would handle the crisis. The specialist in question did not respond with the required fortitude and was now wanding registration chips in the traffic department.

Lazuli had no intention of wanding chips in traffic.

This could be my stinkworm, she thought.

In which case she should simply observe, as her angel would be keeping a close eye.

Or it could be a genuine operation.

In which case she should most definitely steer clear, as there would be LEP agents in play.

But there was a third option.

Option C: Was it possible that the Fowls were running an operation of their own here? The human Artemis Fowl had a checkered history with the People.

If that were the case, then she should rescue the toy troll, who was perhaps six feet away from two children her facial-recognition software labeled as Myles and Beckett Fowl.

Lazuli hung in the air while she mulled over her options. Her angel had mentioned the name Artemis before the Dalkey Island exercise.

"If you ever meet Artemis Fowl, he is to be trusted," she'd said literally minutes before Lazuli boarded her magma pod. "His instructions are to be followed without question."

But her comrades in the locker room told a different story.

"That entire family is poison," one Recon sprite had told her. "I saw some of the sealed files before a mission. That Fowl guy kidnapped one of our captains and made off with the ransom fund. Take it from me, once a human family gets a taste of fairy gold, it's only a matter of time before they come back for more, so watch out up there."

Lazuli had no option but to trust her angel, but maybe she would keep a close eye on the twins. Should she do more than that?

Observe, steer clear, or engage?

How was a specialist supposed to tell a convincingly staged emergency from an actual one?

All this speculation took Lazuli perhaps three seconds, thanks to her sharp mind. After the third second, the emergency graduated to a full-blown crisis when a shot echoed across the sound and the little troll was sent tumbling with the force of the impact, landing squarely at the rowdy child's feet. Beckett Fowl immediately grabbed and restrained the toy troll.

This effectively removed Specialist Heitz's dilemma. It was just as her comrades had foretold:

The Fowls were kidnapping a fairy!

An LEP operative's first responsibility was to protect life, prioritizing fairy life, and so now Lazuli was duty bound and morally obliged to rescue the toy troll.

The prospect both terrified and thrilled her.

The first thing to do was inform her angel of the developing situation, even though radio silence was protocol during exercises.

"Specialist Heitz to Haven. Priority-one transmission . . ."

If anyone was on the other end of that transmission, they would have been left curious, because at that moment dozens of flares were launched from the house, and Specialist Heitz was forced to take evasive action to avoid being clipped. She had barely gotten her rig under control when there came a rumbling series of booms and Lazuli felt a wave of crackles pass through her body. The crackles were not particularly painful, but they did have the effect of shorting out her communicator along with every circuit and sensor in her shimmer suit. Lazuli watched in horror as her own limbs speckled into view.

"Oh . . ." she said, then fell out of the sky.

Not all the way down, fortunately, as Specialist Heitz's suit launched its backup operational system, which ran like clockwork, because it *was* clockwork: a complicated hub of sealed gears and cogs ingeniously interlinked in a series of planetary epicyclic mechanisms that fed directly into a motor in Lazuli's wing mounts.

Lazuli felt the legs of her jumpsuit stiffen and instinctively began to pedal before she hit earth like an injured bird. The gears were phenomenally efficient, with barely a joule of energy loss thanks to the sealed hub, and so Specialist Heitz was able to reclaim her previous altitude with a steady midair pedal. But she was still quite plainly in the visible spectrum, looking for all the world like she was riding an invisible unicycle.

Though Lazuli's spine had not been compacted by a high-speed impact with Dalkey Island, she still had the problem of how to effectively engage a sniper when she was operating under pedal power. If Lazuli attempted to approach the sniper, he could take potshots at his leisure.

Visibility was the problem.

So become invisible, Heitz.

But how to become invisible without any magic or even an operational shimmer suit?

There was a way, but it was neither foolproof nor field-tested, though it had been tried in somewhat raucous conditions, those being the communal area of the cadets' locker room—inside lockers 28 and 29, to be precise. Lazuli knew this because she had witnessed the bullying, and lost ten grade points for repeating the experiment on the bully.

Lazuli reached into one of the myriad pockets in her suit and drew out a pressurized pod of chromophoric camouflage filaments held together by reinforced spider silk. The Filabuster, as it was known by LEP operatives, was rarely deployed, and in fact was due to be removed from duty kits in the next few months because of the unpredictability of its range, but now it was the only weapon in Lazuli's arsenal that was actually of any use, as it had no electronic parts and came pre-primed.

The Filabuster operated on the same system that certain plants employ to disperse their seeds. The fibers inside the dried egg pulled against each other to create tension, and when the silken cowl was ruptured, the reflective filaments exploded with considerable force, creating a visual distortion that could provide enough cover to cause momentary confusion.

But I need more than momentary confusion, Lazuli thought. I need to be invisible.

Which was where the locker-room antics came in. When a hulking demon cadet had forced a tiny pixie into his own locker and then tossed in an armed Filabuster, the pixie had emerged coated in filaments and practically invisible, and also, it turned out later, battered and bruised.

Perhaps this is not a good idea, thought Lazuli; then she pulled the spider silk ripcord before she could change her mind. Now there were approximately ten seconds before the silk surrendered to the internal pressure and exploded in a dense fountain of chromophoric filaments that would adjust to the region's dominant color, which ought to be the blue-black of the early evening Irish Sea.

"D'Arvit," swore Lazuli in Gnommish, knowing that this experience was going to be, at the very least, quite unpleasant. "D'Arvit."

But what were a few cuts and bruises in the face of a troll's life?

Specialist Heitz hugged the Filabuster close to her body and went to her happy place, which was the cubicle apartment she'd recently rented on Booshka that she shared with one single plant and absolutely no people.

"See you soon, Fern," she said, and then the Filabuster exploded with approximately ten times more force than the locker model.

The sensation was more kinetic than Specialist Heitz had anticipated, and she instantly had more respect for the locker pixie who'd borne the torment without complaint. Lazuli felt as though she had been dropped into a nest of extremely irritable wasps that were not overly fond of hybrid fairies. The filaments clawed at every inch of her suit, more than a few managing to wiggle inside and tear her skin. This laceration was accompanied by a tremendous concussive force, which sent *pedaling* to the bottom of Lazuli's list of priorities and sent the pixel herself tumbling to earth, with only the drag of doubledex wings to slow her down.

As she fell, Lazuli had the presence of mind to notice a ragged shroud of Filabuster filaments assemble around the small island, rendering it invisible to anyone outside the field.

Good, she thought. If I survive the fall, the camouflage filaments should hang around long enough to facilitate a toy-troll rescue.

Though perhaps her thoughts were not so lucid. Perhaps they were more as follows: Aaaargh! Sky! Rescue! D'Arvit!

Whichever the case, Specialist Heitz was correct: If she survived—which was a gargantuan *if* for a fairy without magic—then the Filabuster drape should afford her time to rescue the toy troll.

And it *would* have afforded her time if left undisturbed. Unfortunately, mere moments later, an army helicopter thundered over Sorrento Point, the downdraft from its rotors scattering the Filabuster curtain to the four winds. And just as suddenly as Dalkey Island had disappeared, it returned to view.

Specialist Lazuli Heitz hit the earth hard. Technically she did not hit the earth itself, but something perched on top of it. Something soft and slimy that popped like Bubble Wrap as she sank through its layers.

Lazuli could have no way of knowing that her life had been saved by Myles Fowl's seaweed fermentation silo. She plowed her way through several slick levels before coming to a stop in the bottom third of the giant barrel, and in the moment before the seaweed covered her entirely, she watched the lead helicopter hover above and noticed a black-clad figure standing right out on the landing skid, her skirt flapping in the rotor-generated wind.

Is that what the humans call a ninja? Lazuli wondered, trying to remember her human studies. But *ninja* was not the right word. What had come after ninja on the *human occupations* chart?

Not a ninja, she realized. It's a nun.

Then the seaweed slid over Lazuli's small frame, and, because the universe likes its little jokes, this felt almost exactly the same as being submerged in a brass tub of eels.

CHAPTER 3
JERONIMA, NOT GERONIMO

INSIDE Villa Éco's safe room, Myles and Beckett Fowl were experiencing a shared emotion—that emotion being confusion. Confusion was nothing new to either boy, but this was the first occasion on which they had felt it simultaneously.

To explain: As the twins were so dissimilar in everything except for physiognomy, it was not unusual for the actions of the one to confound the mind of the other. Myles had lost count of how many times Beckett's attempted conversations with wildlife had bewildered his logical brain, and Beckett, for his part, was flummoxed on an hourly basis by his brother's scientific lectures.

So, generally, one twin was lucid while the other was confused, but on this occasion, they were mystified as a unit.

"What's happening, Myles?" asked Beckett.

Myles did not answer the question, reluctant to admit

that he couldn't quite fathom what exactly was going on.

"Just a moment, brother," he said. "I am processing."

Myles was indeed processing, almost as quickly as the safe room's processors were processing. NANNI's gel incarnation may have been a puddle on the floor, but the AI itself was safe inside Villa Éco's protected systems and was now replaying footage from a network of cameras slung underneath a weather balloon. These cameras were outside the Faraday cage and, unfortunately, had succumbed to the EMP, but before then they had managed to transmit the video to the Fowl server. NANNI had zeroed in on two points of interest. First, the AI located a dissipating bullet vapor trace and followed it back to the mainland to find that there was a camouflaged sniper there, a hirsute chap with an antique Russian Mosin-Nagant rifle, which would be over eighty years old, if NANNI was correct.

"There's the culprit," she said from a wall speaker. "A sneaky sniper near the harbor."

This was not the source of Myles's confusion, as the sonic boom had to have come from somewhere, and after all, the Fowl family had many enemies from the bad old days. The fact that one enemy would employ an antique weapon could relate back to some decades-old vendetta having to do with any number of the twins' ancestors, most probably Artemis Senior, who had once attempted to muscle in on the Russian mafia's Murmansk market. This sniper might simply be on a revenge mission, and what better way to hurt the father than to target the sons?

The second point of interest, and the cause of Myles's bewilderment, was another, much smaller figure that had been captured by one camera. The tiny creature had appeared out of thin air, pedaled to keep herself aloft, and then plummeted into the seaweed silo.

Beckett's confusion was more general in nature, but he did have one question as the brothers reviewed the balloon footage. "A pedaling fairy," he said. "But where's her bicycle?"

Myles was not inclined to answer but *was* inclined to disagree. "There's no bicycle, brother mine," he snapped. "And I do not happen to believe in fairies or wizards or demigods or vampires. This is either photo manipulation or interference from a satellite system."

He rewound the footage and froze the figure in the sky, stepping closer for a decent squint.

"Magnify," he told his spectacles, which Myles had augmented with various lenses pillaged from his big brother's sealed laboratory. Artemis had set a twenty-two-digit security code on his door that he did not realize Myles had suggested to him subliminally by whispering into his ear every night for a week as he slept. To add further insult, the numbers Myles had chosen could be decoded using a simple letter-to-number cipher to spell out the Latin phrase *Stultus Diana Ephesiorum,* which translated to *Diana is stupid,* Diana being the Roman version of the Greek goddess Artemis, for whom Artemis had been named. It was a very complicated and time-consuming prank, which, in Myles's opinion, was the best kind.

"Yes," said Beckett. "Magnify."

And the blond twin accomplished his magnification simply by taking a step closer to the screen, which, in truth, was both more efficient and cost-effective.

Myles studied the suspended creature. It seemed clear that there was, at the very least, a possibility it was not human.

Beckett jabbed the wall screen with his finger, daubing it with whatever gunk was coating his hand at the time.

"Myles, that's a fairy on an invisible heli-bike. I am one million percent sure."

"There is no such animal as a heli-bike and you can't have a million percent, Beck," said Myles absently. "Anyway, how can you be so sure?"

"Remember Artemis's stories?" asked Beckett. "He told us all about the fairies."

This was true. Their older brother had often tucked in the twins with stories of the Fairy People who lived deep in the earth. The tales always ended with the same lines:

The fairies dig deep and they endure, but if ever they need to breathe fresh air or gaze upon the moon, they know that we will keep their secrets, for the Fowls have ever been friends to the People. Fowl and fairy, fairy and Fowl, as it is now and will ever be.

"Those were stories," said Myles. "How can you be certain there is a drop of truth to them?"

"I just am," said Beckett, which was an often-employed phrase guaranteed to drive Myles into paroxysms of indignant rage.

"You just are? *You just are?*" he squeaked. "That is not a valid argument."

"Your voice is squeaky," Beckett pointed out. "Like a little piggie."

"That is because I am enraged," said Myles. "I am enraged because you are presenting your opinion as fact, brother. How is one supposed to unravel this mystery when you insist on babbling inanities?"

Beckett reached into the pocket of his cargo shorts and pulled out a piece of gummy candy.

"Here," he said, wiggling the worm at Myles as though it were alive. "This gummy is red and you need red, because your face is too white."

"My face is white because my fight-or-flight response has been activated," said Myles, glad to have something he was in a position to explain. "Red blood cells have been shunted to my limbs in case I need to either do battle or flee."

"That is soooo interesting," said Beckett, winking at his brother to nail home the sarcasm.

"So the last thing I shall do is eat that gummy worm," declared Myles. "One of us has to be a grown-up eleven-year-old, and that one will be me, as usual. So, whatever I do in the immediate future, gummy-eating will not be a part of it. Do you understand me, brother?"

By which time Myles had actually popped the worm in his mouth and was sucking it noisily.

He had always been a sucker when it came to gummy candy. In this case, he was a sucker for the gummy he was sucking.

Beckett gave him a few seconds to unwind, then asked, "Better?"

"Yes," admitted Myles. "Much better."

For, although he was a certified genius, Myles was also anxious by nature and tended to stress over the least little thing.

Beckett smiled. "Good, because a squeaky genius is a stupid genius. I dreamed that one time."

"That is a crude but accurate statement, Beck," said Myles. "When a person's vocal register rises more than an octave, it is usually a result of panic, and panic leads to a certain rashness of behavior untypical of that individual."

But Myles was more or less talking to himself at this point, because Beckett had wandered away, as he often did during his twin's lectures, and was peering through the safe room's panoramic periscope's eyepiece.

"That's nice, Myles. But you'd better stop explaining things I don't care about."

"And why is that?" asked Myles a little crossly.

"Because," said Beckett. "Helicopter."

"I know, Beck," said Myles, softening. "Helicopter."

It was true that Beckett didn't seem to either know or

care about very many things, but there were certain sub-jects he was most informed about—insects being one of those subjects. Trumpets was another. And also, helicopters. Beckett loved helicopters. In times of stress he sometimes mentioned favorite items, but there was little significance to his helicopter references unless he added the model number.

"Helicopter," insisted Beckett, making room for his brother at the mechanical periscope. "Army model AgustaWestland AW139."

Time to pay attention, thought Myles.

Myles propped his spectacles on his forehead and stud-ied the periscope view briefly for visual confirmation that there was, in fact, a helicopter cresting the mainland ridge. The chopper bore Irish Army markings and therefore would not need warrants to land on the island, if that were the army's intention.

And I cannot and will not fire on an Irish army heli-copter, Myles thought, even though it seemed inevitable that the army was about to place the twins in some form of custody. For most people this knowledge would be a source of great comfort, but, historically, incarceration did not end well for members of the Fowl family, and so Father had always advised Myles to take certain precautions should arrest or even protective custody seem inevitable.

Give yourself a way out, son, Artemis Senior had said. *You're a twin, remember?*

Myles always took what his father said seriously, and so

he regularly updated his Ways Out of Incarceration folder.

This calls for a classic, he thought, and said to his brother, "Beck, I need to tell you something."

"Is it story time?" asked Beckett brightly.

"Yes," said Myles. "That's precisely it. Story time."

"Is it one of Artemis's? *The Arctic Incident* or *The Eternity Code?*"

Myles shook his head. "No, brother, this is a very important story, so you will need to concentrate. Can you achieve a high level of focus?"

Beckett was dubious, for Myles often declared things to be important when he himself regarded them as peripheral at best.

For example, some of the many things Myles considered important:

1. Science
2. Inventing
3. Literature
4. The world economy

And things Beckett considered hugely important, if not vital:

1. Gloop
2. Talking to animals
3. Peanut butter
4. Expelling wind, however necessary, before bed

Rarely did these lists overlap.

"Is this important to me, or just big brainy Myles?" Beckett asked with considerable suspicion. This was a most exciting day, and it would be just like Myles to ruin it with common sense.

"Both of us, I promise."

"Wrist-bump promise?" said Beckett.

"Wrist-bump promise," said Myles, holding up the heel of his hand.

They bumped and Beckett, satisfied that a wrist-bump promise could never be broken, plonked himself down on the giant beanbag.

"Before I tell you the story," said Myles, "we must become human transports for some very special passengers."

"What passengers?" asked Beckett. "They must be teeny-tiny if we're going to be the transports."

"They *are* teeny-tiny," said Myles, not entirely comfortable using such a subjective unit of measurement as *teeny-tiny*, but Beckett had to be kept calm. He opened the Plexiglas door on top of the insect hotel and scooped out a handful of tiny jumping creatures. "I would even go so far as to say teeny-weeny."

"I thought we weren't supposed to touch these guys," said Beckett.

"We're not," said Myles, dividing the insects between them. "Except in an emergency. And this is most definitely an emergency."

It took a mere two minutes for Myles to relate his story,

which was, in fact, an escape plan, and an additional six minutes for him to repeat it three times so Beckett could absorb all the particulars.

Once Beckett had repeated the details back to him, Myles persuaded his twin to don some clothing, namely a white T-shirt printed with the word UH-OH!, a phrase often employed both by Beckett himself upon breaking something valuable, and also by people who knew Beckett when they saw him approach. Myles even had time to disable the villa's more aggressive defenses, which might decide to blow the helicopter out of the sky with some surface-to-air missiles, before the knock came on the door.

Here comes the cavalry, thought Myles.

In this rare instance, Myles Fowl was incorrect. The woman at the door would never be mistaken for an officer of the cavalry.

She was, in fact, a nun.

"It's a nun," said Beckett, checking the intercom camera.

Myles confirmed this with a glance at the screen. It was indeed a nun who appeared to have been winched down in a basket from the hovering helicopter.

If we do nothing, she might go away, thought Myles. After all, perhaps this person doesn't even know we're here.

Myles should have voiced this thought instead of thinking it, for, quick as a flash, Beckett pressed the TALK button and said, "Hi, mysterious nun. This is Myles Fowl speaking, one of the Fowl Twins. My brother Beckett is here, too, and we're home alone. We'll be with you in a minute—we're down in the safe room because of the sonic boom. I'm so glad the EMP didn't kill your helicopter."

Beckett's statement contained basically every scrap of information that Myles had wanted to keep secret.

"Gracias," said the unexpected nun. "I shall await your arrival."

Beckett was hopping with excitement. "Myles, it's a nun with a helicopter! You hardly ever see that. This is the start of our first real adventure. It has to be—I can feel it in my elbows."

Beckett often felt things in his elbows, which he claimed were psychic. He sometimes pointed them at cookie jars to see if there were cookies inside, which Myles had never considered much of a challenge, as one of NANNI's robot arms filled the kitchen containers as soon as their smart sensors informed the network they were empty.

"Beck, with no disrespect to your extrasensory elbows," said Myles, "why don't we stay calm and stick to the plan? If we can stay, we stay, but if we go, remember the story."

Beckett tapped his forehead. "It's all in here, brother. Angry Hamster in the Dimension of Fire."

"No, Beck!" snapped Myles. "Not *that* story."

"Ha!" said Beckett. "You snapped at me. I win."

Myles counted up to ninety-seven in prime numbers to calm himself. One of Beckett's pleasures in life was teasing his brother until he snapped. It was unfair, really, as it was very difficult to tell the difference between a Beckett who genuinely didn't know something and a Beckett who was pretending not to know something.

"Ha-ha," said Myles, without a shred of humor. "You got me. You're the big comedian, and I'm just Myles the dunce. But, in my defense, I am trying to keep us alive and out of an army cell."

Beckett relented and hugged his brother. "Okay, Myles. I'll lay off this time, because you have no sense of humor when you're stressed. Let's go upstairs and you can lecture this nun."

Myles had to admit that sounded wonderful.

A new person to lecture.

As eager as Myles Fowl was to debate, argue with, and deliver a monologue to the mysterious nun, he was determined to take his time reaching the front door. It is always a good idea to keep potential enemies waiting, he knew, as they are more likely to expose their real selves if they become impatient. Beckett was not aware of this tactic, and so Myles had to literally hold him back by hanging on to his belt loops. And thus Beckett dragged his brother along in his wake as a mule might drag a cart.

They passed through the reinforced steel door and climbed the narrow stairwell of polished concrete to the main living area, an open-plan quadrangle marked on three sides with glass walls that were threaded with a conductive mesh, which served both to maintain the integrity of the Faraday cage and reinforce the windows. The reclaimed wooden floors were strewn with rugs, the placement of which might seem random to the untrained eye, but they were actually carefully laid out in accordance with the Ba Zhi school of feng shui. The space was dominated by a driftwood table and a rough stone fireplace that ran on recycled pellets. But the main feature of the villa was the panoramic view of Dublin Bay that it afforded the residents. Myles could remember visiting the island with his father before construction of the villa began.

"Criminal masterminds are always drawn to islands," Artemis Fowl Senior had said. "All the greats have them. Colonel Hootencamp had Flint Island. Hans Hørteknut had Spider Island, which was more of a glacier, I suppose. Ishi Myishi, the malignant inventor, has an island in the Japanese archipelago. And now we have Dalkey Island."

And Myles had asked, "Are we criminal masterminds, Father?"

His father did not answer for half a minute, and Myles got the feeling that he was choosing his words carefully.

"No, son," he said eventually. "But sometimes you have to fight fire with fire."

This, Myles knew, was a metaphor, and as a scientist he felt obliged to dissect it.

"Fire being analogous of crime," he said. "So, if I take your meaning correctly, you are saying that on occasion the only way to defeat a criminal is to turn his own methods against him."

Artemis Senior had laughed and tousled his son's hair.

"I'm just thinking out loud, son. The Fowls are out of that game. Now why don't we forget I ever mentioned criminal masterminds and just enjoy the view?"

A view that was utterly ignored by Myles now, as he attempted to slow his energetic brother's trip to their front door. He felt confident that once they reached the door he would be able to argue legal precedent through the intercom for hours with the waiting nun until the cows came home—or at least until he could fill in his parents on the situation. The problem would be how to contain Beckett.

As it happened, this problem never materialized. When they reached the front door, it was already open. The nun had stepped from the rescue basket and was closing her fingers over a hockey-puck-size device strapped to her palm.

"There you are, chicos," said the nun. "The door simply opened of its own accord. Increíble, no?"

Incredible indeed, thought Myles. This nun may not be as virtuous as her clothing suggests.

The woman at Villa Éco's front door was indeed a nun, but her habit was a little more stylish than one would usually associate with the various religious orders. She was dressed in a simple black linen smock that could have indicated that she liked Star Wars films or had just discovered an amazing young designer. The smock was cinched with a wide satin belt that nodded toward ancient Japanese culture. Her hair was too golden to be natural and was arranged in that bouffant style known in salons as 1980s News Anchor, on top of which perched a veil of black polyester secured with a jeweled hat pin.

"Buenas tardes, chicos," she said. "I am Sister Jeronima Gonzalez-Ramos de Zárate of Bilbao."

Beckett didn't hear anything after the first name.

"Geronimo-o-o!" he cried enthusiastically, throwing up his arms.

"No, niño," said the nun patiently. "Jeronima, not Geronimo."

Beckett altered his cry appropriately—"Jeronima-a-ah!"— and segued into a couple of blunt questions: "Sister, why are you red? And why do you smell funny?"

Jeronima smiled indulgently. These were the questions that most people wished to ask but would not. "You see, chico, my skin has the slight tinge because of my order: the Sisters of the Rose. We stain our flesh red with a nontoxic aniline dye solution to demonstrate our devotion to Mary, the rose without thorns. And the odor is from the dye. It is like the almonds, no?"

"It is like the almonds, yes!" said Beckett. "I love it. Can I stain my skin, Myles?"

"No, brother," said Myles, smiling. "Not until you are eighteen."

Myles was less smiley in his attitude toward the nun.

"Sister Jeronima," he said, "it would seem that you have broken into our home."

Jeronima joined her hands as though she might pray. "I am a nun. I would never do this. As I think I said, the door was open. Perhaps your EMP affected the locks, no?"

Myles was glad the rose-colored nun had lied. At least he knew where they stood now.

"You are, at the very least, trespassing on private property," he countered.

Jeronima waved his point away as though it were a pesky mosquito. "I do not answer to your country's estúpido laws."

"I see," said Myles. "You obey a higher power, I suppose."

"Sí, absolutamente, if you like."

"A higher power in the helicopter?" said Beckett.

Jeronima smiled tightly. "Not exactly, niño. Let us simply say that I am not bound by the rules of your government."

"That's very nice," said Myles. "But we are not donating today. Can you please call again when my parents are home?"

"But I am not here for donations, Myles Fowl," said Jeronima. "I am here to rescue you."

Myles feigned surprise. "Rescue us, you say, Sister? But we are in the safest facility on Earth. In fact, I am disobeying my parents' instructions by speaking with you. So, if you don't mind . . ."

He attempted to close the aforementioned door but was thwarted by the nun's left knee-high leather boot, which she had jammed between door and frame.

"But I *do* mind, niño," she said, pushing the door open. "You are unsupervised minors under attack from an unknown assailant. It is my duty to escort you to a place of safety."

"I would like to be escorted in a helicopter, Myles," said Beckett. "Can we go? Can we, please?"

"Sí, Myles," said Jeronima. "Can we go, please? Make your brother happy."

Myles raised a stiff finger and cried, "Not so fast!"

It was undeniable that this was a touch melodramatic, but Myles felt justified in indulging his weakness, as there was a rappelling nun at the front door. "How would you know we are under attack, Sister Jeronima?"

"My organization has eyes everywhere," said Jeronima with what Myles would come to know as her customary vagueness.

"That sounds suspiciously illegal, Sister," said Myles, thinking he could stall her for several minutes while he winkled out more information about this mysterious "organization" they were supposed to simply hand themselves over to. "That sounds as though you are infringing on my rights, which is unusual for a woman of the cloth."

Jeronima crossed her arms. "I *am* unusual for a woman of the cloth. Also, I am a trauma nurse, and I once threw knives in the circo—that is to say, circus. But I am not important now. *You* are important, and it is true what they say about you, chico. You are the smart one."

"And I am the one who can climb!" said Beckett, blowing his brother's stalling plan to smithereens by vaulting into the helicopter's rescue basket and scrambling up the winch cable faster than a macaque scaling a fruit tree.

"And he *is* the one who can climb," said Sister Jeronima.

"And most quickly, too." She stepped back and opened the basket's gate. "Shall we follow, chico?"

Myles had little choice in the matter now that Beckett had taken the lead.

"I suppose we should," he said, a bit miffed that his fact-finding mission had been cut short. "But only if you desist with the fake endearments. *Chico*, indeed. I am eleven years old now and hardly a child."

"Very well, Myles Fowl," said Sister Jeronima. "From now on you shall be tried as an adult."

The gate was already closed behind Myles when this comment registered. "Tried? I am to be tried?"

Jeronima fake-laughed. "Oh, forgive me, that was—How do you say?—a slip of the tongue. I meant, of course, to say *treated*. You will be *treated* as an adult."

"Hmmm," said Myles, unconvinced. There was some form of trial ahead, he felt sure of it.

Jeronima made a circling motion with her index finger and the winch was activated. As the basket rose into the night sky, Myles glanced downward, appreciating the aerial view of Villa Éco, which, when seen from above, formed the shape of an uppercase F.

F for Fowl.

Still a little of the criminal mastermind in you, eh, Papa? he thought, and wondered how much of that particular characteristic there was in himself.

However much there needs to be in order to keep Beckett safe, he decided.

With a tap to the temple of his spectacles, Myles activated the infrared filter in his lenses and noticed that, across the bay, the sniper was packing up his gear.

We were not the target, he realized now. A sniper with even one functioning eyeball could have easily picked us off on the beach. So, what were you after, Mr. Beardy Man?

He committed this puzzle to his subconscious, to be worked on in the background while he dealt with Sister Jeronima and the other mysterious player in their drama. A player who was now emerging from the seaweed silo— not that anyone but Myles would notice, for the creature, whatever it proved to be exactly, was more or less invisible.

Invisible, thought the Fowl twin. How mysterious.

And as his father often said: *A mystery is simply an advanced puzzle. Thunder was once a mystery. A wise man learns from the unknown by making it known.*

And the wise boy, Father, thought Myles now. He magnified his view of the silo creature and saw that a single body part was visible even without the infrared. Its right ear, which was pointed. Somewhere in Myles's brain, a lightbulb flashed.

A pointed ear.

And then the pointy-eared creature began to pedal, and it lifted off after the ascending rescue basket.

Beck was right, thought Myles, glancing upward at his brother, who was already boarding the helicopter.

It was indeed a fairy on an invisible bicycle.

"D'Arvit," he blurted, shocked that Artemis's stories had been, in fact, historical rather than fictional.

Sister Jeronima mistook the blurt for a sneeze. "Bless you, chico," she said. "The night air is cool."

Myles did not bother to correct her, because an explanation would be difficult, considering that the word *D'Arvit* was a fairy swearword, according to Artemis's fairy tales.

Myles silently vowed not to use it again, at least not until he knew what it meant exactly.

Lord Teddy Bleedham-Drye was surprised to find his mood brightening somewhat. This would have been a bombshell to anyone who knew him, as the duke was notorious for throwing royal tantrums when things did not go his way. He'd had an emotional hair trigger since childhood, when he would heave his toys from the stroller if refused a treat. At family gatherings, his father often embarrassed him with the story of how five-year-old Teddy had hurled his wooden horse over the St. George cliffs when the nanny served him lukewarm lemonade. And how Teddy had been so antisocial that it had become necessary to send him to Charterhouse boarding school at age five instead of seven, which was more traditional among those of the upper class. Now, one and a half centuries later, the duke's general mood had not improved much, though he tended to take out his frustrations on other people's property rather than his own and let his irritation fester in his stomach acid. Good form at all times.

And so Lord Teddy was surprised to find himself whistling as he packed his gear.

Whistling, Teddy old boy? Surely you ought to be sinking into your usual vengeful funk.

But no, he was verging on the exuberant.

And why would that be?

It would be, Teddy old fellow, because there is something afoot here.

I take a single shot and suddenly the army is swooping in for an extraction? The Fowls were an important family, but not *that* important.

The island was obviously under the surveillance of some agency or other.

This confirms my growing certainty that Brother Colman's lead was sound.

Now Teddy had a choice: He could continue to stake out the island and wait for another troll, or he could follow the Fowl children and find the one he had wrapped earlier.

Lord Bleedham-Drye knew that, logically, he should maintain his surveillance on the soon-to-be-unguarded Dalkey Island, but his instinct said *Follow the Fowls*.

The duke trusted his instinct; it had kept him alive this long.

After all, it would be child's play to follow the troll, for each Myishi CV round was radioactively coded, and Teddy had programmed the individual codes into his marvelous Myishi Drye wristwatch, which had over a thousand functions, including geo-pinned news alerts and actually telling the time. The Drye series was *the* gold standard in criminal appliances. It included watches, exercise machines, a gorgeous porcelain handgun, a line of lightweight bullet-proof apparel, a light aircraft, and a range of communication devices. Each item was embossed with a copy of the famous Modigliani line portrait of the duke from 1915. In return for his sponsorship, Teddy had a yearly credit of five million US dollars with the company, and a fifty percent discount on anything above that amount. The slogan for the Drye range was *Stay Drye in any situation with Myishi*. It had been a most successful arrangement for both parties. And, in truth, Lord Teddy would have long since declared bankruptcy without the Myishi Corp sponsorship deal. For his part, Ishi Myishi had the seal of approval from one of the most respected criminal masterminds/mad scientists in the community, which shifted enough units to easily pay the duke's tab.

Good old Myishi, thought Lord Teddy now, and his marvelous gadgets.

The duke and Ishi Myishi had been associates as man and boy. Or, more accurately, since Myishi was a boy who had lied about his age to join the Japanese army and Teddy Bleedham-Drye was a British army officer. The duke had discovered young Myishi breaking out of a prison shed in Burma, defending himself with a shotgun the lad had cobbled together from the frame and springs of his cot. Teddy recognized genius when he saw it and instead of turning the boy in, he'd arranged for him to study engineering in

Cambridge. The rest, as they say, was history, albeit a secret one. By Teddy's reckoning, Myishi had repaid his debt a hundred times over.

Make that a hundred and one, Teddy thought, for one of the duke's sponsorship perks was a hunter-tracker system that could be bounced off several private satellites. And so, wherever in a several-hundred-mile radius that troll went, Teddy could easily follow.

The Fowls will never hear me coming, he thought. And they will never hear the bullets that kill them.

The Army Helicopter

Lazuli Heitz could not figure out the black-haired Fowl boy.

He just sat there smiling at her as though she were absolutely visible to him. But that could not be, for the other occupants of the chopper were completely ignoring her. The second boy was making bird noises at passing seagulls, while the woman in black plied the bespectacled kid with questions that he blithely ignored, maintaining both his eye contact with Lazuli and a broad grin.

That child radiates smugness, Lazuli thought. I don't like him already. At the first opportunity, I shall retrieve the troll and get far away from these people.

In truth, she was beginning to regret her decision to board the helicopter in the first place. Perhaps she should have simply waited for LEPrecon to show up. But the decision was made now, and there was no point regretting it.

Plus, her pedaling mechanism had been injured by the fall and she had barely managed to make it to the helicopter. Her wings had folded themselves into their rig as a sign that there would be no more flying until her suit regenerated. So now she needed to concentrate on her next step.

As her angel had told her: *There is no future in the past.*

Which meant that obsessively second-guessing your own decisions was a waste of time. At least, that's what she took it to mean.

And so Lazuli had, minutes before, dragged herself from the seaweed, feeling like she had endured a severe beating due to the effects of the Filabuster, and pedaled her way to the chopper's altitude. The ad hoc plan had been to clamp herself on to the skids, but there were already armed soldiers occupying those spots, so Lazuli had no choice but to slip between the troops, careful not to nudge against the automatic weapons, for it was a universal truth that warriors of any species do not like their guns being touched. She crawled under the jump seat, hoping the filaments did not drop off and expose her. Although it felt like the chromophoric camouflage strands were embedded in the fabric of her jumpsuit, not to mention patches of her blue skin, and would never wash off. Which was currently a good thing.

Lazuli hunkered under there in the shadows trying to take stock.

Learn as much as you can, Specialist.

More advice from her angel.

A friend once told me that gold is power. But he was wrong for once. Information is power.

Information. Lazuli had precious little of that currency.

And after more than a minute she hadn't picked up much more, aside from the fact that the bespectacled boy was still looking right at her.

If he's looking, why isn't he telling?

Lazuli sincerely wished she could have done a little homework on this family before embarking on her exercise, but the Fowl file was locked up tighter than a dwarf's wallet.

The strange boy's smile is not a friendly one, she realized. *It is the smile of a boy who has a secret.*

As for the second child, he was apparently a simpleton who cawed and screeched down at seagulls as the chopper *whupp*ed overhead.

Perhaps three minutes later, Lazuli had picked up two potentially useful nuggets.

One: They were headed southeast toward mainland Europe.

And two: As a magic-free zone herself, Lazuli had been forced to study hard just to barely pass the gift of tongues exam, and so she realized that the human child squealing at seagulls was not as simple as she had assumed he was.

Her train of thought was derailed by the bespectacled boy, who cleared his throat noisily.

"Are you ill, *chico*?" the nun asked, to which he replied:

"I am perfectly fine, Sister Jeronima," he said. "There

is no need to shout into my *right ear*. It's here beside you. *Perfectly visible*."

It took Lazuli a moment to realize that his comments were aimed at her and not at the nun. When the lightbulb went on, she hurriedly clamped a hand over her right ear.

D'Arvit, she swore internally, which defeated the venting purpose of swearing. Does this mean I owe the human boy a favor?

CHAPTER 4
OPERATION FOWL SWOOP

Amsterdam, the Netherlands

Commander Diavolo Conroy of the Irish Ranger team assigned to assist Sister Jeronima in whatever manner she wished to be assisted, considered this particular assignment, i.e., to escort twin boys to a black-site facility in the Netherlands, the second-lowest point of his career.

The absolute lowest point being the time a brigadier general ordered the entire squad to dress as manga clowns and fly a pony to his daughter's birthday party. The pony's name was Buckles, and it was, to put it delicately, a nervous flyer. Commander Conroy still shuddered when he thought back on that day.

But at least he had understood the objective of Operation Buckles: Deliver a pony to a child. This assignment—Operation Fowl Swoop, as it had been dubbed—was an altogether more mysterious and unsavory affair. Two months ago, the Spanish nun had simply driven into the Curragh army camp, swiping her way through several locked gates with that infernal black plastic card of hers, and basically made herself at home in her semitruckload of high-tech tricks.

That ink-black card was the first thing about Sister Jeronima to give Conroy the creeps. When Conroy had flashed his ID at the nun and asked her to explain herself, she had simply tapped his badge with her card and the black color had somehow flowed across from her ID to his. While he was still gazing at his altered card in slack-jawed amazement, he received a terse call from the minister of defense himself, who summarily informed Conroy that his squad had been deputized by a top secret intergovernmental organization and he was to follow Sister Jeronima's orders to the letter until his ID returned to its original color.

"And if I don't, Minister?" Conroy had brazenly asked.

"If you don't," the minister had spluttered, "you will find yourself changing the blue latrine blocks in an Antarctic research facility."

This was a most specific threat, and it helped Diavolo Conroy decide to follow orders.

And so now he and his highly trained men were delivering a pair of Irish twins to an industrial park near Schiphol airport so they could be transported to a black site.

Children in a black site?

Sometimes Commander Conroy couldn't help wondering if he was still one of the good guys, if indeed there even were good guys anymore these days.

"That will be all, Commander Conroy," Jeronima told him as soon as the chopper skids touched down. "My people will take it from here."

Sister Jeronima's people emerged from two SUVs, not of any make Conroy could identify. Two four-man teams just to transport a couple of sleeping eleven-year-old children.

Overkill, surely, thought Conroy, and for a moment he entertained the crazy notion of defying the minister and pulling the chopper out of there before the payload could be transferred to the vehicles.

But he didn't, because he was a soldier, after all, and soldiers obeyed orders from the chief. Still, it didn't sit well with Conroy as, after the passengers disembarked, he gave the command to lift off, and he decided to ask some hard questions when he landed back in the Curragh.

The only positive in this entire operation was that Conroy noticed that his ID had shed its skin of black and was back to its original color. As if the black sheen—or the nun herself—had never been there.

On a side note, Conroy was true to his word and asked several hard questions of the minister upon his return to Ireland, but the answers were wishy-washy at best, so Diavolo handed in his resignation and carried around the guilt for what he considered an abduction until, almost two years later, he got the unexpected opportunity to both set things right with the twins and explain the origins of his unusual first name.

But that is another story, which is, incidentally, even more surprising than this one.

The first rule of interrogation is to question captives separately with the hope that their stories might contradict each other. Sister Jeronima had handled scores of prisoners, suspects, and detainees in the span of her long career and had literally written a handbook on the subject, which was entitled *Todo el mundo habla finalmente*, or *Everyone in the World Talks Eventually*, in which Jeronima laid out her interrogation philosophy.

The thing to remember, she wrote in the foreword, *is that everyone is guilty of something.*

If pressed on the matter, Jeronima would say that the strangest subject she had ever questioned was Gary Grayfeather, an African parrot that knew the combination to a Cockney gang lord's safe. It had taken her a few hours and a bucket of nuts, but eventually Gary had spilled the numbers.

The parrot was about to be demoted to second place on the strange-subject list after the Fowl Twins.

Jeronima's plan was as follows: She would place the twins in adjacent rooms and pose questions to both until some disparity appeared, and then she would use the difference in their stories to drive a wedge between them. Jeronima was aware that Myles was a smart one, but she felt confident that he would crumble quickly in an interview situation.

* * *

Myles awoke, and quickly realized that all was not right in the Fowl world. For one thing, he was in a chair, which was most unusual for him. Not being in a chair, per se, but waking from slumber in a chair, for Myles was not the type of boy to simply nod off; he had not once, since the age of two, fallen asleep in a chair, sofa, or recliner.

To explain: Myles's brain was so active that he was obliged to perform a nightly relaxation routine in order to disengage his synapses. This routine involved first inserting his nighttime mouth guard and then completing self-hypnosis exercises while focusing on Beckett's unusually musical snores. Beckett's snores, technically speaking, were not snores at all but a trio of whistles that he exhaled through both of his nostrils and his mouth. This triple exhale was unusual enough in itself, but the really extraordinary thing was that each orifice played a different note. Notes that combined to form a perfect C-major chord, which never failed to remind Myles of Beethoven's Mass.

Myles could not hear the chord now and knew that he been separated from his twin. He looked around to find himself in an underground room with stone columns and vaulted arches. There were no visual cues to suggest that he was underground, but Myles could tell instinctively—something perhaps about the heaviness of the air or a pressure he felt in his skull—that he was below sea level. Myles's skull was very sensitive, and the least change in atmospherics could precipitate a migraine.

Sister Jeronima was seated across a table from him.

Bizarrely enough, the nun was absently polishing a throwing knife with a chamois cloth.

Sad, thought Myles. Such a pathetic attempt to intimidate me.

Jeronima expects me to reference the knife, he realized, thus giving her the upper hand.

"Buenas tardes, Myles Fowl," said the nun without looking up from her knife. "You must have so many questions."

It was true that there were things Myles needed to know, but he had answers, too, should anyone care to pose the corresponding questions.

He could have asked: *Where am I precisely?*

Or indeed: *Who exactly do you represent?*

Or certainly: *What do you want with us?*

Myles knew that should he pretend to pass himself off as a frightened, witless youth to learn these things, Jeronima would see right through him; after all, his intellect was well-documented.

So, instead of firing off a barrage of questions, Myles said, "You sedated us with the helicopter's oxygen masks. That was a despicable trick, Sister."

Jeronima was not in the least abashed. "The levels are delicate. Sometimes people fall asleep."

"And then you are free to smuggle them into your subterranean base without fuss. I would guess we are in Amsterdam. Or perhaps Rotterdam, but I imagine Amsterdam. I do love Amsterdam. The NEMO science museum is a marvel, though I do worry about the EYE theater, architecturally. I have written letters to the board."

Jeronima gave Myles her full attention. "Very good. How did you know we were in Amsterdam?"

This would usually have been a simple question for the NANNI chip embedded in Myles's spectacles to answer. The map of their trip was displayed for his eyes only on the inside of his lenses. Unfortunately, NANNI had lost network outside Schiphol airport, so Myles had been forced to make an educated guess.

"Never mind that," said Myles. "I'm sure you must have questions."

"Oh, sí," said Jeronima. "I have questions, but perhaps some answers, too. I can tell you where your brother is."

Myles rubbed the scar on his wrist. "No need. Beckett is in the next room."

"You can sense your twin?"

"Our scars twinge like a form of spiritual radar," said Myles. "Usually I can see him, too."

"Do not worry, chico," said Jeronima. "You will be together soon. It was necessary to separate you for a short time, considering your peculiar situation."

"And which peculiar situation is that?"

This was a genuine question from Myles. The Fowls had, over the years, been involved in a great many peculiar situations.

"The fairy situation," said Jeronima, and she placed a black plastic card on the table.

Myles did not touch the card and he made no attempt

to scan it with his augmented spectacles. Even basic credit cards had photon technology now. Jeronima had presented her card with such a flourish that Myles felt sure it was packed with advanced sensors and would detect a scan. Then he would lose his precious spectacles and he would have no contact with NANNI, as his watch and smartphone were still beside his bed in Villa Éco.

"Don't worry, niño," said Jeronima, sensing Myles's hesitation. "It is nothing but a card. We are very old-school down here. There is not even the internet."

Myles engaged his organic scanners, those being his eyes. At first glance the card seemed blank, but then Myles noticed seven embossed letters.

"ACRONYM," he read. "I presume ACRONYM is an acronym."

"Sí, correcto, Myles," said Jeronima. "ACRONYM stands for: Asociación para el Control, la Regulación, y la Observación de los No-humanos y la Magia."

"You're telling me that the acronym for ACRONYM is ACRONYM?" asked Myles. "That sounds a little forced, if you don't mind me saying. And it only works in Spanish, though the agency name itself is English."

"I suppose you could do the better acronym, chico," said Jeronima, which was unfortunate, for Myles Fowl had always been a whiz at wordplay.

"Most certainly I could do better," said the bespectacled twin. "Let me see. . . . Off the top of my head, what about IMP? Imaginary Monster Patrol. I have added a second layer to the acronym there by linking the word itself to the organization."

Jeronima smiled thinly. "Most amusing. But also insulting, no?"

"I take your point. Let's try another one: ELF. Excellent Leprechaun Force. I could do a few in Spanish if you like?"

Jeronima shrugged. "English, Spanish, it does not matter. The name is no importante—it is our actions that count. We are an international intergovernmental organization charged with monitoring fairy activity."

"Los no-humanos," said Myles, not bothering to suppress a smirk. "So tell me, Sister, if I ignore the ridiculous premise for your group's very existence, what does your ACRONYM want with us?"

"Nada. We do not want anything," said Jeronima, wide-eyed. "We are merely protecting you."

Myles laughed. "From a gunshot? Why would fairy-hunters care about a shot from a human gun? We had a *close shave*, that is all."

"We do not care about this gunshot, but we are most interested in the disappearing island."

"There you have me at a disadvantage," said Myles. "I genuinely have no idea what you are talking about."

Which was not the whole truth.

The nun's eyes narrowed and she began twirling the throwing knife on the table. "After the gunshot, Villa Éco simply disappeared, momentarily, then came back into view. We do not have such technology. So it must be magic."

Myles laughed. "Really, Sister? Magic is your first port of call? Why not aliens? Why not alternative dimensions? Your reasoning is fatally flawed, I'm afraid."

Jeronima *thunk*ed the knife into the tabletop, where it quivered and sang. "Listen to me, niño. There is another race under our feet with superior weapons and advanced technology. Some years ago, there was an event that shut down the entire world. Airports, hospitals, everything. It took months for civilization to recover, and it cost billions. Several governments collapsed."

Myles sighed, not at all perturbed by the knifeplay. "That is old news, Sister. Five years old, to be precise. Everyone knows about the Big Dark."

"Sí, the Big Dark. A catchy name, no?"

Myles couldn't help saying, "Better than ACRONYM."

Jeronima ignored the jibe. "Earth was thrown back to the Dark Ages. And all over the world there were reports of strange creatures with pointed ears suddenly appearing, and, almost as quickly, disappearing. Fowl Manor was ground zero for this event. And since then we have been watching you and waiting for an excuse to go in. These fairies could appear again at any moment. And next time they might decide not to disappear."

"And now Villa Éco has disappeared and reappeared?"

"Exactly, so it seems as though the fairies want to keep you chicos safe for their own reasons."

"And if they saved us once, they might save us again," reasoned Myles, scratching his crown vigorously. "So, we are to be bait?"

"If you like," said Jeronima. "On Dalkey Island, the environment is yours, but here, I am in control."

"And you can hold two minors who have had a *close shave* without counsel or supervision?"

Jeronima smiled. "But you are not minors in the sight of the law."

Myles caught on quickly. "I see. We activated an EMP, so we are terrorists."

"Exactamente," said Jeronima, bowing slightly in her chair.

Myles appreciated the neatness of Jeronima's plan. "And as terrorists we can be held indefinitely."

"Do not worry, chico. We will release you as soon as we have a fairy in custody."

Myles looked into Jeronima's eyes and saw a zealot's enthusiasm for her task.

We must escape, he realized. Things do not generally end so well for bait. Just ask a worm on the hook.

"When can I see my brother?" he asked, scratching behind one ear.

"Soon," said Jeronima, slipping the knife into a discreet pocket in her sleeve. "First I will speak with him. Perhaps Beckett will share some of the Fowl secrets."

Myles almost felt sorry for Sister Jeronima. Beckett had a way of making even the most steadfast people doubt their very core principles. Sister Jeronima would emerge from a meeting with Beckett more confused than she went in.

Follow the plan, brother, he broadcast through the wall. Remember our way out.

Beckett Fowl had awoken bleary-eyed, which was most unusual for him. Generally, he exploded into consciousness, eager to embrace another day of possibilities. But on this evening he was overtired and grumpy. This had only happened once before—when he'd contracted mumps as an eight-year-old and had developed a frightening case of bullfrog neck, which he absolutely loved once he got used to it. He even gave the lump a name: Bertram.

But, as the naming of Bertram demonstrated, Beckett was too irrepressible to dawdle in the dumps for long, and when he noticed the throwing knife in Sister Jeronima's hands, his mood took a rapid upswing.

"Shiny knife, Sister," he said, reaching across the table between them to touch the wickedly glittering blade of death.

"Yes, Beckett," said Jeronima. "This particular knife you are reaching for with your soft pink finger is coated with deadly nightshade. A horrible poison."

"Why do you even have a knife?" Beckett asked, reluctantly withdrawing his soft pink finger.

Jeronima's gaze was almost as sharp as her knife. "Zombies, Beckett Fowl. Did you ever hear of those creatures? When the apocalypse comes, this nun is going to be prepared."

A very good answer, Beckett decided. Jeronima was indeed a wise woman. "Do you know any zombies?"

"A person cannot really know a zombie, Master Fowl. They are only interested in the eating of brains. Deadly nightshade is very effective for stopping a zombie from eating your brain."

"Eating my brain," said Beckett. "Cool."

"I may not know a zombie," continued the nun, segueing neatly into her area of interest, "but I do know other creatures who are not human."

"Me, too," said Beckett.

Jeronima played it calm. "Really, chico? What creatures do you know?"

Beckett strayed infuriatingly from the point. He pulled up his left T-shirt sleeve, revealing a red mark.

"This is my pet birthmark," he explained. "We call it Infinity because Myles says it looks like the infinity symbol, but that's because he's stupid about real-life things. It actually looks like my pet goldfish, Gloop, who died. But two Gloops is too many Gloops." He pointed to his tie. "This is the real Gloop, if you want to compare."

Sister Jeronima had heard about Beckett's infinity birthmark. It was well-known, and she had an enlarged photograph of it in her file, scanned from hospital records.

"Oh, chico," she said. "That is such a lovely way to remember dear Gloop, even though he was not human. And do you remember when I was asking whether you knew any other creatures who were not human, and you said that sí, you did?"

"Of course I remember," said Beckett. "Because I know a dolphin."

"Ah," said Jeronima, disappointed.

"And some creatures with wings."

Jeronima was interested again. "Yes?"

"I met some seagulls on the way over here."

More disappointment. "I see."

"And there are crows on the island." Beckett jumped up on the chair. "Sometimes I call to them. *Caw! Caw!* It is I, Beckett. *Caw!* I'm their king."

"Very well, Beckett. You can sit down now, niño."

Beckett did not sit. Instead, he made binoculars of his fingers and studied the stone arches. "This is like a church or a dungeon."

"Actually, it is a little of both," said Jeronima. "This was a hidden church from the times when Catholicism was actually illegal. My group uses the underground space as a black site. I mean as a *safe space*."

Beckett's eyes glazed over. "That is so boring, Geronimo."

"Jeronima," corrected the nun.

"That is so boring, Jeronima," said Beckett. "Why do you care about history when there are fairies flying around on invisible bicycles?"

Jeronima coughed twice and was glad there was no water in her mouth. "Fairies, chico?"

"Well, one fairy," said Beckett. "Myles and me know all about fairies. Artemis told us stories. Artemis is our big brother—he's in space."

"What stories?"

Beckett inverted himself on the chair, resting on his shoulders, legs in the air. He made his position even more tenuous by pushing the chair back on two legs with his foot.

"One about the time-traveling lemur, which is not a monkey, in case you don't know. And one about the ghost warrior who took over my body, which tickled, for your information. And my favorite is the one about the dwarf who poops mud, which is actually very good for the environment. And there are demons who live in another dimension. And the angry pixie who blows herself up in a nuclear tube."

We are, Jeronima thought, getting a little off-topic.

"Tell me about the invisible fairy," said the nun.

Beckett righted himself. "I will," he said. "But first, Myles."

"Myles is asleep," said Jeronima.

Beckett was shocked. "That's a lie, Sister. My brother said never to lie unless it's to your own advantage."

"Which brother?" asked Jeronima.

Beckett actually thought before answering. His expression while thinking was one of surprise, as though he couldn't believe it was happening.

"Both of them," he said. "And my father."

Jeronima played it innocent. "Myles *is* sleeping. My soldiers assured me that he was sound asleep."

"Nope," said Beckett. "He's in the next room wide-awake and thinking."

"What is Myles thinking about, niño?" asked Jeronima, wondering just how strong this bond between the twins was.

"The same thing as me," said Beckett, rubbing his scalp against the chair. "Why is my head so itchy?"

Sister Jeronima escorted Beckett next door and the twins were reunited. They shook hands formally before hugging, so both boys' sensibilities were satisfied.

Myles looked Beckett up and down. "Brother. You are unharmed, I see."

"I do have a pain in my neck from this place," said Beckett.

"Now, now," admonished his twin. "We don't use expressions like *pain in my neck*. They are colloquialisms."

"Can I say *This place stinks*?"

"Again, factually inaccurate. There is a certain musk, but that is virtually unavoidable in an underground crypt."

"Underground," said Beckett. "I knew that. Because of the fat air."

"That phrase is satisfactory," said Myles approvingly. "Because gas can be compressed, its density depends on both pressure and temperature, so in actual fact the subterranean air is, on an atomic level, fatter."

Beckett groaned. "I said that already. Why do you take everything I say and make it boring?"

Myles raised his lecturing finger. "Education leads to knowledge, which in turn leads to power."

Jeronima was beginning to sympathize with Beckett.

"No one likes a sabelotodo, Myles. A—how do you say it?—*know-it-all*."

Myles was offended. "But I am not a know-it-all, Sister. There aren't any know-it-alls. It would take an infinity of lifetimes to know even the tiniest fraction of everything. And the more we learn—"

"—the less we know. ¿Correcto?" Sister Jeronima completed the maxim with the hope of cutting off the Fowl boy's lecture.

"The more we learn, the less we know?" asked Myles, aghast. "What kind of infantile babbling is that? How can one learn more and know less? Obviously, I was going to say: 'The more we learn, the more we know.' Honestly, is this what passes for intelligence in the intelligence community?"

"That is not what I meant, precisamente."

Myles shrugged. "I cannot help what you thought you meant, Sister. I merely interpret your words and draw inferences from the movements of your eyeballs, your limbs, and general deportment. I am not a mind reader."

Jeronima was beginning to suspect that perhaps she was not the only expert interrogator in the room.

"Muy bien, Myles Fowl," she said. "You have made your point. I will be less casual with my use of proverbs in the future."

Myles was still in shock. "'The more we learn, the less

we know,' indeed. If that were actually th[...]
life would be without meaning or purpose. [...]
knowledge at all speed. Humans can but scrat[...]
face in this life and hope for total recall with each [...]
nation."

Beckett heard the word *scratch* and was reminded t[...]
scratch, which he did. And since scratching is almost as
contagious as yawning, Myles was soon engaged in the same
activity.

"Madre de Dios," said Jeronima, irritated at yet another
distraction from her line of questioning. "But what is this
scratching?"

"Obviously, our heads are pruritic, Sister," snapped
Myles.

"He probably means itchy," said Beckett.

"Yes, I do mean itchy. It started in the helicopter. I had
suspected some form of allergic reaction, but now I am
leaning toward parasitic infestation."

Sister Jeronima recoiled. "¿Los parásitos? No, I will not
permit it."

Myles snorted. "Your *permiso* is entirely irrelevant to
parasites, Sister. Parasites tend not to speak English. Or
Spanish, for that matter."

"The sleepy mask was itchy," said Beckett, who was by
now knuckling his hairline.

Jeronima was skeptical. After all, were these not the
brothers of Artemis Fowl, one of the world's premier
schemers?

...aid to Beckett, who immediately

...needing a translation of the

...na should have picked up on,

...e boy's file—but she was focused

...nsense.

...e said, raking manicured nails

...re is nothing. . . ."

Little white bugs, which popped like minuscule blisters under her nails.

"¡Madre de Dios!" she cried, stepping back. "¡Los piojos! The lice."

And while it was true that Sister Jeronima Gonzalez-Ramos de Zárate had been in the intelligence business for many decades and had not once flinched in the face of death, there are very few individuals on this earth who can behold a scalp crawling with head lice and not feel a shudder of revulsion. In Jeronima's case, the shudder was so strong that for a moment she seemed to be dancing.

"Oh, for heaven's sake," snapped Myles. "If we are, as I suspect, being feasted upon by *Pediculus humanus capitis*, there is no cause for panic. All that is required is a series of treatments with medicated shampoo."

"Noooo!" said Beckett. "I like my insect friends."

Sister Jeronima composed herself. "Apologies, children. Have no fear, I will chastise the helicopter team for this infection, but we are not having the luxury of time. There will be no series of medical shampoos-ings."

"*Shampooing*," corrected Myles. "And if there is to be no shampooing, then what do you suggest? Something barbaric, no doubt."

A phrase popped into Jeronima's head. A phrase that had been planted by Myles during his solo interrogation.

"No. Nothing barbaric. You shall both have the *close shave*."

Myles pretended to be appalled. "You would shave our heads? This is how you treat your guests?"

"That is how I treat my guests who are infectado," said Jeronima with a nunly firmness. And she raised one hand and snapped her fingers. Obviously, someone was watching, because seconds later two burly figures entered the room wearing lemon-yellow hazmat suits with beekeeper-style headpieces.

"For heaven's sake," said Myles. "That's a little much, don't you think? We are two boys with head lice, not radioactive aliens."

"You are not simply two boys," countered Sister Jeronima. "You are two *Fowl* boys. There is the big difference."

Myles accepted this backhanded compliment with a nod. It was true. Fowl boys were exceptional, even more so than their captor suspected.

"Take them away," said Jeronima to the burly figures. "Shave these niños. Make them both totalmente without the hairs and also burn the clothing. Every stitch."

"No hairs!" exulted Beckett. "A new thing!"

"I am somewhat less enthusiastic about our imminent shearing than my brother," said Myles. "But I am not fond of having bloodsucking insects so near to my brain, where it is conceivable they could somehow corrupt my cerebrospinal fluid, which could, in theory, arrest my thought processes somewhat. So, I suppose an all-over shave is practically foolproof."

"Practically," said Jeronima. "But to be fully certain, also use the steam lances."

"Lances!" crowed Beckett, over the moon.

Lances and shaving! Surely this was a prince among days.

"At least forty degrees," advised Myles. "Otherwise, it's pointless."

"Precisamente," said Sister Jeronima. "First the lance, then the shave. And then the lance once more for the good measures."

Both hazmat guys nodded, but if a person happened to be a student of kinesics, that is to say body language, that person might notice that one of the hazmat people seemed to find the notion of an *all-over shave* quite upsetting in spite of his nod. There was an audible crackle from the material of his suit as he flinched. Perhaps this was because the fellow was imagining the forced shaving of his own beard, which he had proudly brushed a hundred strokes per day for the past one hundred and thirty-two years.

For, as you have no doubt deduced, the second hazmat guy was, in fact, our villain, Lord Teddy Bleedham-Drye, who would actually appreciate being referred to as *a guy*. Guy Fawkes, who had planned the infamous Gunpowder Plot to blow up the Parliament, was one of Teddy's heroes, as he himself had considered a similar course of action some years previously when the House of Commons had banned foxhunting. It really irked the Duke of Scilly that commoners should be allowed to dictate to a fellow what he may or may not chase on his own plot.

But how on earth had Teddy managed to infiltrate ACRONYM's black site? This is a reasonable question and deserves an answer. And the answer is perhaps more straightforward than one might think, given the effectiveness of modern security systems. The problem with these security systems is that somewhere in the chain there is a human link. And humans are invariably fallible, often inexpert, and occasionally dull-witted. The human whom Lord Teddy had encountered was all three.

To rewind, as they say:

Almost three hours earlier, you may remember that Lord Teddy's Myishi CV bullet had coated the mini troll in radiation-infused cellophane in case his prey somehow removed itself from the shooting zone. Once this had come to pass with the aid of an army helicopter, the duke nipped down to the jetty and unzipped the tarpaulin covering a collapsible ultra-light aircraft that he habitually towed behind his yacht like a Jet Ski. He used a fob to fold out the wings, which bore his personal insignia, climbed into the tight two-seater cockpit, and took off in pursuit of the Westland helicopter.

Lord Bleedham-Drye had purchased the seaplane

from his old pal, Ishi Myishi, who claimed to supply the majority of the world's more discerning criminals. Myishi's actual company slogan was: *Ninety percent of the planet's criminal masterminds can't be wrong, and the other ten percent are incarcerated.*

Teddy smiled whenever he thought of that slogan. Myishi certainly was a marketing genius, not to mention a technical one.

The Myishi Skyblade was indeed a wonderful craft, and it came with certain features tailored to the discerning poacher's needs. Features such as an aluminum fuselage wrapped in quantum stealth material, so that the craft was virtually invisible to the naked or electronic eye at night, and a weighted hunter's net that could transport large animals several hundred miles. The duke adored his little plane and had already preordered a Myishi flying car, which would roll off the line five years before any police force in the world got their hands on one. Borders really wouldn't exist for a chap with a long-range flying motor.

Lord Teddy's smartphone synced with the Skyblade's onboard navigation, quickly extrapolating the most likely destination for the army helicopter, and so, two hours later, the Skyblade swooped into late-night Dutch airspace before the Fowl Twins even arrived. Teddy set down illegally in the Western Docks opposite the old Palace of Justice, which he thought a pleasing irony, and dawdled in the shadows of a moored party barge while the troll-nappers made their way into the city.

Amsterdam was winding down for the evening, but there were still a few clusters of bed-shy stragglers ambling along the dockside, though none had noticed his light aircraft slicing like a tailor's scissors through the green silk of the canal's surface. Lord Teddy found himself humming along with the strains of "You'll Never Walk Alone," which was being drunkenly mangled by a bunch of lurching soccer fans. The duke did consider wrapping the bunch in cellophane for a spot of target practice but quickly dismissed the idea.

Business before fun, Ted, he told himself. Keep your eyes on the prize, don't you know.

He did know.

If there was one thing the Duke of Scilly had learned over the decades, it was focus.

Teddy did not have long to wait. As the Skyblade's computer had predicted, the army helicopter landed in the Schiphol region—not quite in the regular airport, but in the adjacent industrial park. This slight deviation by the tracker bleep both infuriated Lord Bleedham-Drye and established that his adversaries had serious political clout. He himself had been forced, by pernickety international law, to sneak into the Netherlands literally under the radar, while this helicopter was given leave to land *near* the airport, where passport controls would not be exercised. Most convenient for them.

Having said that, Teddy could not fume for long, because the troll's bleep required his full attention as it pulsed directly toward the city center. The duke lowered the Skyblade's wings to pontoon position and prepared to discreetly tail his enemies wherever they might be going in the city of water. He was rewarded twenty minutes later by the sight of a mini convoy passing by onshore. Two custom-built SUVs, super-stealthy. They were, Teddy thought, reminiscent of panthers prowling near a watering hole.

Very nice, thought the duke, wondering briefly if Myishi was supplying governments these days.

Unlikely, he thought. Criminals pay more promptly than governments.

Lord Teddy shadowed the black automobiles, sticking to the far side of the canal, availing of the shelter provided by the hulking keels of barges and houseboats. By incredible good fortune, the duke's landing spot was less than a mile from the convoy's destination, which appeared to be a rowdy café on the corner of Prinsengracht.

A café, thought Teddy, allowing the Skyblade to drift behind the gunwales of a houseboat. Now, why would security types pick the only busy spot on the blasted street?

It occurred to Teddy that perhaps one of the Fowl urchins needed a bathroom break.

But no, the entire company dismounted and shuffled inside, grouped in an irregular cluster that might be mistaken for random by members of the general public but Lord Teddy recognized as a shielding formation.

The twins are inside that bunch. I'd bet my electric eels on it.

And where the twins went, the duke must follow——his foreseeable and unforeseeable future depended on it.

Teddy was reluctant to abandon the Skyblade in a public dock, but the craft's antitheft systems were considerably more punitive than the legal versions. Any thief possessed of the temerity to lay a finger on the seaplane's bio-coded handle would find himself with ten thousand extra volts of electricity coursing through his system, so the duke felt reasonably confident that the Skyblade would be safe from ne'er-do-wells and good-for-naughts.

He stepped smartly across the humpbacked bridge toward the café, rubber-soled boots squeaking on the cobblestones as though the duke were squashing a church mouse with each step.

Amsterdam never changes, he thought, as the familiar aromas of stale beer and dank sweat rode the raucous music through the open door. Still a town of sailors frittering away their wages.

Frittering was not in Lord Teddy's nature, especially when it came to time, and so he compartmentalized any doubts he might have had about leaving his smashing flying machine out in the open and double-timed a quick reconnoiter around the building, which, like so many of Amsterdam's stilted houses, was leaning heavily against its neighbor like a drunken companion.

The tracking contraption integrated into his wristwatch informed Teddy with a teardrop alert that his quarry were now below sea level.

They have descended into some kind of basement, the duke thought. That is an unwelcome development.

Unwelcome because subterranean strongholds were notoriously difficult to crack, which was why guerrilla fighters often used tunnels to hide themselves away from enemy forces. And Teddy had rather uncomfortable memories of tussling with a wiry South African Boer in a dusty catacomb under the veld.

The blighter had the nerve to tug on my beard, Teddy thought now, which is simply not done.

Teddy had almost resigned himself to yet another period of surveillance when he came upon a narrow stairwell that led down to a doorway daubed in shadow. The steps had been compressed by centuries of pressure from the adjacent building and were as irregularly pitched as the keys of a distressed piano.

Aha, thought Teddy. Perhaps some measure of force could be applied to that door and it could be breached.

As it turned out, there was no need for force—on the door, at any rate, for it simply and all of a sudden opened and a lanky fellow appeared, clad from head to toe in a yellow decontamination suit, and somewhat furtively composing a text message on his phone while he held the steel door open with his foot.

No cell service inside, I'd wager, thought Teddy. I would also wager that Johnny Texter is breaking security protocol.

Lord Teddy was right on both counts, and, as he had never been one to look a gift horse in the mouth, the duke slipped one hand into his jacket pocket to retrieve the brass knuckles nestled there.

When life gives you a lemon, thought Teddy, slipping his fingers neatly into the weapon's finger holes, you knock the lemon senseless.

One blow should do the trick, he told himself. And then it will be simplicity itself to disguise myself in that garish suit.

On this occasion the duke was wrong.

The job actually required two blows.

CHAPTER 5
DO-VE-LI

AND what of our wayward pixel, Specialist Heitz?

What had she been up to while the Fowl Twins endured nunterrogation and the duke closed in on his quarry? Simply put, Lazuli had been doing very little while achieving quite a lot.

To explain: *Doing Very Little,* or Doveli (*dough-vey-lii*), as it had become known, was actually an ancient martial art developed by shielded fairies so they could move undetected among sensitive animals and even human Shaolin monks. It involved shallow breathing, agonizingly slow movements, and incredibly advanced organ control so that no gurgles or squeaks issued from the tummy. A master of Doveli could walk across a rice-paper floor without raising a single crackle. Lazuli was not quite a master of the art, but she had achieved the level known as Small Intestine, which was second only to Bowel Wall. Lazuli had slowly transferred surplus chromophoric camouflage filaments to her exposed ear so that she was fully coated throughout the journey across mainland Britain and the English Channel, and while in that invisible state, she had utilized her Doveli talents to move undetected from the helicopter to the SUV and through a crowded café into the ACRONYM black site.

It had all been going very well, and Lazuli was quietly most pleased with herself, until the interrogation room door was summarily slammed in her face, and Specialist Heitz had no choice but to flatten herself against a wall and *do very little* until something happened.

The *something*s of interest to Lazuli that proceeded to happen were as follows:

Her pointed ears, which had evolved to efficiently gather sounds and perform localization on those sounds, i.e., to pinpoint within the inch from where those sounds originated, told her that beyond the door were at least two connected rooms, and in those rooms were the Fowl Twins and the nun who appeared to be questioning the boys. Though Lazuli could not hear exactly what was being said, the tone was unmistakable. This hectoring continued for some minutes until the nun's register elevated sharply, and though it might be an exaggeration to say that all hell broke loose, it was certainly true that a portion of Hades was unleashed.

This portion took the form of two burly humans in yellow containment suits who bustled past Lazuli close enough to ruffle her filaments. The lead human punched a code into the keypad and admitted both men into the inner sanctum. The men reappeared before the door could even swing shut on its soft-close arm, ushering the Fowl Twins before them at arm's length as though their radioactivity was beyond the capabilities of even containment suits.

What is going on here? Lazuli wondered and was further confused by the nun who appeared in the doorway calling, "Lance-shave-lance, ¿entiendéis?"

Lazuli translated the words in her mind. *Lance-shave-lance?* Was it perhaps a code? Or a military call sign of some kind?

Whatever the strange command meant, Lazuli had no option but to follow the twins, for the toy troll was still lodged in the blond boy's pocket. And where the troll went, she too must go until her equipment's organic circuitry had a chance to regenerate and she could summon Retrieval.

And be ejected from the specialist program, she thought glumly, but also briefly, for it was to Lazuli's credit that her main concern was the troll's future and not her own.

Myles decided that he would name his captors after the satellites of Uranus, as they were bodies with some power, so to speak, but certainly not the main gravitational influencers.

"I shall call you Trinculo and Oberon," he announced, "as you are, no doubt, under orders not to reveal your names."

"Call us whatever you like, kid," said the one designated Oberon through the gauze of his headgear. "Just keep out of arm's reach. These suits ain't been tested for lice."

Myles confidently led the way to the showers, though

he had not been shown where the showers were situated and the ACRONYM site could fairly be described as labyrinthine.

"The Catholics loved their tunnels, gentlemen," he explained to the men. "Most faiths have been persecuted at one period or another. There were several tricky centuries for the Christians in general and for Catholics in particular, so they liked to hide their secret chapels inside underground mazes. One never knows when a wall of spikes is going to be released and impale a fellow." He winked at Beckett then to show that he was most probably joking to freak out their escorts.

"Spikes," said Beckett, catching on quickly because it suited him. "Right in the face. Blood and brains everywhere."

Oberon faltered slightly, but Trinculo pooh-poohed the notion in a most upper-class English accent. "Spikes? The very idea. Honestly, you boys must think we were born yesterday. Let me tell you about Catholics. They never could put so much as two cogs together. Anything those monks built has long since disintegrated. I'm surprised their arches have held up this long. If you must worry about something, worry about the ceiling falling on our heads."

Oberon regained his composure. "Yeah, okay, Chicken Licken. Less talk about the ceiling falling, or the sky, for that matter. Keep an eye on these two kids. They're dangerous."

"I do not doubt it," said his comrade. "Each in his own way. I have heard that the bespectacled one could talk his way out of a shark's mouth, and that innocent-looking blond chappie has mastered the cluster punch."

Oberon missed a step. "You don't say? The cluster punch? At his age?"

"I have it on reliable authority."

Myles frowned, as this was a fact that he had not realized was in the public domain, and he wondered exactly where Trinculo had gotten his information. The problem now was that once Beckett heard the cluster punch mentioned, he would be dying to prove just how effective he was at it, and playing that card now would ruin Myles's plan.

"No punching, brother," he warned under his breath. He did not use those precise words but rather spoke in what the brothers called Fowl Argot, a secret cryptophasic language developed by the twins over the past decade and spoken by them alone. Though, like most twin-talk, it was not just spoken but also included gestures and onomatopoeic sounds, so what Myles actually said was: "Mab-mab, B."

Mab-mab being *bam-bam* backward. *Bam-bam* being Argot for punching, and the reversal signifying a negative, i.e., *no punching*. B for *Beckett*, obviously. Simple enough provided you had the key. Which only two people did.

Beckett replied by making the shape of a seagull's wing with his hand, which was an affirmative, as Beckett considered seagulls the most positive of birds. This sign was the Argot version of a thumbs-up.

"You're probably wondering how I know where the showers are, my dear satellites," said Myles, to distract from the brief exchange in Argot. "It's quite simple, really. There is a slant to the floor, slight but perceptible, and only an idiot architect would not take advantage of natural drainage. And if one studies the intra-slab mold buildup, it becomes noticeably thicker as we approach the washroom area."

"Smart, kid," said Oberon. "It must be great to always know where the bathroom is."

Trinculo was thinking the same thing, but not in a sarcastic way.

Six turns later, the slightly-larger-than-it-appeared group arrived at the modified medieval baths, which were starkly lit by halogen lights and had rubber-grip mats laid over the flagstones. Sister Jeronima had obviously sent word ahead, for there were two additional lemon men waiting, one with a set of clippers that would not have seemed out of place at a sheep-shearing competition, and the second shooting practice jets from his steam lance and crying "Yeehaw!" with each burst, as though he had accomplished something rugged and wonderful by pressing a plastic trigger.

Myles immediately assigned names to these men: Clippers and Lance.

"Okay, boys," said Lance, brandishing his dripping steam tool. "Who's first?"

Beckett was already halfway out of his clothes. "Me. Please, me."

"No," said Myles. "We are twins. We go together."

Which is what they did.

* * *

Specialist Heitz watched the whole bizarre procedure and thought: I shall never ever understand humans if I live to be a thousand.

The Fowl Twins exchanged their clothes for triangular plastic underpants and were ushered into a tiled stall and blasted with steaming water, which seemed to amuse Beckett no end as he alternated between dodging the spray and trying to drink as much of it as possible. Myles, on the other hand, made some attempt to preserve his dignity by assuming the lotus position and elevating his consciousness to another plane. The yellow-suited man may as well have been washing a marble statue for all the attention Myles paid to him.

The twins' clothing was incinerated, and their belongings tossed into a metal crate.

The crate interested Lazuli greatly.

As it did one of the men in yellow, who edged closer to it, and Lazuli could swear that she saw his eyes glitter behind the helmet mesh.

Eyes behind gauze do not glitter, Specialist, she told herself. Your imagination is running away with you.

But it was undeniable that the human did seem more interested in the metal crate than he was in his supposedly dangerous charges, who were being steam-cleaned in their shower stall. It was a curious thing to watch a man trying to be sneaky, especially when that man did not realize he was being observed. His frame seemed to be at war with itself as he tried to look as though his mind were on the job while also moving backward in minuscule degrees. Lazuli was reminded of a 1982 dance craze from her human studies media module. The man looked for all the world like he as performing a slow, tense moonwalk toward the perforated metal crate. A crate that contained, as far as Lazuli could make out:

A necktie in the shape of a goldfish.

A pair of thick-rimmed spectacles.

A dust bunny the approximate size of a goose egg.

A stress ball.

Several tangled gummy worms.

And . . .

One toy troll wrapped in transparent plastic.

Whether it was alive or dead, Specialist Heitz could not tell. But she would find out.

Yesterday, she could have simply blinked in the troll's direction and her visor would have provided any vital statistics she requested, but that was yesterday. Today, her visor's circuitry was fried, and the only tools she had left were the ones she'd been found with in Lazuli Heights—those being her senses.

And one more tool.

Her invisibility, which she would exploit to maximum effect starting just as soon as that unsettling human took his eyes off the crate for one second. Then she would stuff the troll inside her uniform jacket and spirit them both far away from this place, which was creepy and oppressive even for someone who lived underground.

The air is fat, she thought, and the adjective seemed correct if not terribly scientific.

Her plans were thwarted somewhat by the arrival of the nun at the door to Specialist Heitz's six o'clock. Lazuli was invisible to the nun, but the human woman would certainly notice a toy troll levitating from the metal crate. In fact, the nun crossed directly to the crate and absently processed the contents while calling orders to the four lemon men.

"Steam every inch, muchachos," she said. "I am wearing a new veil; I do not wish to burn it."

Once the first round of steaming was complete, the shearing began.

"Give them a numero cero," ordered the nun. "No lice must escape your blade, ¿entiendéis?"

"I understand, Sister," said Clippers. "Don't worry. By the time I'm finished, these heads will be as barren as the surface of the moon."

The dark-haired Fowl piped up. "For your information, sir, my brother Artemis has discovered water on the dark side of the moon as well as microorganisms that may have been transported from Earth on meteorites. So, are these organisms aliens, or merely migrants? Science shall decide. But either way, the surface of the moon is most certainly not barren."

The shearing lemon scowled. "Permission to shave this one first, Sister?"

Jeronima's scowl echoed his own. "Permission granted. With pleasure."

Clippers flicked a knobbly switch on the handle of his shears and the instrument leaped eagerly into life, as though the hunk of machinery relished the task ahead as much as the man wielding it.

Myles Fowl closed his eyes. "To quote the journalist Margaret Fuller: 'Genius will live and thrive without training, but it does not the less reward the watering pot and the pruning knife.'"

The fourth lemon switched off his shears. "And what's that supposed to mean, boy?"

"It means," said Myles, "that in a roundabout way, all you can do to me is make me smarter."

Clippers switched on again. "Smarter," he said, "and balder."

Even Myles couldn't argue with that, and in fact he was unusually without comment as the clippers mowed his scalp and the slickened clumps of dark hair gathered around his feet like autumn leaves.

While the Fowls were being shorn of their locks, the nun turned the toy troll over in her fingers, not suspecting for a moment that she held in her hand anything but a plastic plaything.

Lazuli was hypnotized by the twirling troll and felt an

almost irresistible compulsion to grab it and make a dash for the surface. But Specialist Heitz knew that such an adrenaline-inspired move would only serve to get her caught and examined under a microscope. Lazuli was on the horns of a dilemma. Or, as a dwarf might say, she was faced with Orsoon's Choice. Orsoon being a master digger of legend who found himself in a tunnel with trolls to the rear and goblins up ahead. Which way to go? Not much of a choice: death by claw or death by fire. As it happened, Orsoon had chosen to stay where he was and see whether fate might provide a third option. It did. The trolls collapsed the tunnel on themselves and Orsoon clambered to freedom over their thrashing limbs.

Lazuli, too, would bide her time.

But if the nun noticed something odd about the toy troll, then all her biding would be for naught.

It seemed that the vigilant human was also stymied by the nun's arrival. He moved reluctantly away from the crate and pretended to focus on the twins, who were on their second steaming. Both were shorn now, so their bald heads gleamed in the shower mist. Once more Beckett japed and made faces while Myles chose to meditate.

Sister Jeronima waggled the toy troll in Lance's direction. "Be thorough," she commanded. "Every nook and cranny. Those little piojos crawl everywhere. "

"You got it, Sister," said the man, and took a step closer to the stall. "There will be no survivors."

Those Fowl boys are in more trouble than they know, thought Lazuli.

But that did not matter, as she was only here for the troll. The twins would have to fend for themselves.

Ten minutes later, the Fowl boys were back in the interrogation room, both zipped up in black jumpsuits that had the word ACRONYM stitched in black across the breast.

"If you don't mind me asking, Sister," said Myles, "why would you have such relatively small jumpsuits handy, considering the gargantuan dimensions of your henchmen?"

Jeronima was unsettled by Myles's vocabulary. "What is this 'gargantuan dimensions'?"

Beckett helped out. "He means big. Your men are all big, so who are these cool suits for? It would be even cooler if you had some helmets. . . ."

"Sí, Beckett," said Sister Jeronima. "My men are indeed big. Sometimes big is useful. Sadly, we do not have helmets for boys. Just the pilots. And to answer your question, there was an industrialist several years ago in Italy. We suspected that his daughter might not be human, so we readied ropa protectora for her. Unfortunately, that one slipped through the net. But we still have the jumpsuits."

"How fortunate for us," commented Myles. "Otherwise we would be sitting in only plastic underpants."

"Which are waterproof from both sides," added his brother, as though imparting classified and wondrous information.

"And now, why don't we stop the games?" asked Jeronima, smiling with the barest hint of smugness. "You boys are fooling no one."

"Stop the games?" said Beckett. "I NEVER stop games. What kind of monster are you?"

"Really, chicos? I am an expert. This is my business. The term *nunterrogation* was invented for me."

"Your point being?" asked Myles.

"My point being, *Myles*, that you cannot fool me with your head lice and shaving and this whole—How do you Irish say?—*shenanigans.*"

"Shenanigans?" echoed Myles. "You think we are attempting to trick you?"

"Sí," said Jeronima with some confidence. "This I do think. And not just any trick. The oldest trick in the book. How could you think I would be so estúpido?"

"Trick?" asked Beckett. "Like a magic trick?"

"No, not like the magic trick," said Jeronima, happy to let the twins wriggle on her hook. "Like the sibling switch. The parent trap. The twin two-step. Whatever you wish to call it."

Myles nodded. "You think we traded places?"

"Sí," confirmed Sister Jeronima. "I do think this. This entire lice fiasco, simply so you could trick me into having your heads shaved and you become almost identical."

"Preposterous," said Beckett.

Jeronima pounced on this. "*Preposterous*, Beckett? That's a big word, chico. That is the kind of word one would expect from Myles Fowl."

Beckett actually blushed. He couldn't help it.

"Aha," said Jeronima, slapping the table between them. "Your cheeks, chico. They betray you."

"Beckett's cheeks are stupid," objected Myles. "More stupid than his brain."

The nun feigned shock. "Beckett's cheeks are more stupid than his brain? That is a most un-Myles-like observation. How can cheeks be stupid?"

"*You're* stupid," said Myles, sulking now.

"Perhaps not as stupid as you had hoped, chicos," said Jeronima. "And now, show to me your birthmark, Beckett."

Beckett clamped a hand over his arm. "Quiet, Sister. Infinity is asleep."

"Wake him up at once," insisted the nun, a little impatiently. She enjoyed a gloat as much as the next Sister, but there was work to be done.

"You never wake a sleeping birthmark," said Beckett. "They get disoriented."

"Enough," said Jeronima, and she snapped her fingers at the henchman Myles had nicknamed Oberon, who had stripped off his hazmat suit and was dressed in a larger version of the ACRONYM jumpsuits. The huge man's hair was tied up in a topknot with what looked like a thin strip of tree bark, and his face had the ruddy glow of a man who had been punched many times over the decades.

"Show to me his arm," commanded Sister Jeronima.

"Which one, Sister?" asked Oberon.

"Izquierda," replied the nun. "The left arm."

Oberon was embarrassed to ask for more information. "I mean, which kid?"

"Derecho," snapped Jeronima. "The right one."

Oberon closed his eyes to get it straight. "So, the right kid's left arm. Your right, or my right?"

"This one," said Jeronima, pointing to Beckett. "Aquí."

"That one," said Oberon with obvious relief. "You know, Sister, these left-right issues are tricky. I whacked the wrong guy once. He was standing to the right of the right guy on the right side of the street. Since then I like to be sure."

"I had believed that story to be urban legend," said Jeronima. "This time no *whacking*. Just pull down the sleeve, por favor."

Conveniently, the jumpsuits had inoculation patches on both sleeves, so it was a matter of less than a single second for Oberon to rip open the Velcro seal and expose the skinny Fowl biceps within.

No birthmark.

"Voilà," said Jeronima. "Or perhaps not. As there is nothing. No birthmark. No Infinity. Therefore, you are Myles, not Beckett. You are playing dumb and he is attempting to play smart. But just to be certain . . ."

Oberon didn't need to be told. He ripped open the real Beckett's patch to reveal the red birthmark exactly where Jeronima had suspected it would be.

"It was worth a try," said Beckett, unashamed. "You would be surprised how often people underestimate children."

"Not this nun," said Jeronima. "I used to be a child."

"My hat is off to your inner child, madam," said Myles, his words slathered with sarcasm.

"And also your hair," touchéd Sister Jeronima. "I allowed this charade to continue so that you can understand how absolutamente helpless your situation is. And now that we are finished with the playacting, let me tell you the *bald* truth: ACRONYM has good reason to believe that the Fowls are in collusion with these Fairy People, and now we have proof. Regardless of whether you twins are complicit or not, I intend to keep you here until someone attempts to rescue you. Whoever or *whatever* comes for you, there will be no escape for anyone."

Myles reclaimed his spectacles from his twin. "You are providing me with a lot of information, Sister."

Jeronima smiled, and her mask of civility slid away like dead skin from a skull.

"You know what they say, chicos: A little knowledge is a dangerous thing, and a lot can be fatal."

Beckett pawed at his own face. "Do you know that there are exciting things happening right now in the world? And instead of watching them I have to sit here and listen to you two being supervillains."

Myles treated Sister Jeronima to a sinister smile of his own. "As usual, brother, we disagree. I am finding the developing situation most intriguing, and, if I might make a prediction, I would say that events will not unfold as our captor expects."

Jeronima fake-yawned. "I am thinking that Beckett is correcto. This is boring."

Beckett raised his hand. "Oh, can I do a prediction?"

"Why not?" said Jeronima.

"I predict," said Beckett, "that my brother is right."

Oberon, who hadn't really been following the conversation for a while, jumped in with: "Right? Which right? And which brother? Right like correct? Or right like not left?"

Jeronima muttered under her breath in Spanish. She may have been quoting scripture, but probably not. "Never mind, *idiota*. Just take Mr. Smarty of the Pants to the other cell."

"Should I handcuff the dummy before I go?" Oberon asked. "They say he can do the cluster punch."

"¿Es eso cierto?" asked the nun, surprised by this. "That is not in the file. Who told you this?"

"Him," said Oberon, pointing to his partner, who was not there. "That is, the other guy."

"The other guy, as you call him, is cataloging the twins' effects," said the nun. "And as for you, yes, restrain this one. I believe there are size XS cuffs in the armory."

"Way ahead of you, Sister," said Oberon, twirling a twinkling set of handcuffs on his index finger. "I signed some out earlier, just in case."

"And that is why I keep you around, agente," said Jeronima.

Beckett, as one might expect of him at this point in the narrative, refused to see the downside of being restrained. "Handcuffs!" he crowed. "I bet I can escape from these. Wait and see. I might be an escaper-ist, Myles."

"Escapologist, brother," said Myles. "And it wouldn't surprise me in the least if you were."

"I bet it will take me three hundred and eighty-six point two seconds to get out of these."

"That is most specific, Beck," said Myles.

Oberon *snick*ed the cuffs around Beckett's wrists and gave the chain a tug to make sure they were secure.

"If you give these bracelets the slip, I'll whistle 'Dixie,'" he said, then asked his boss, "Should I cuff the other one?"

Jeronima's look was loaded with derision. "No, Agent. I don't imagine Myles Fowl will be any trouble to one of such *gargantuan dimensions*."

And so the twins were once again separated, though they could feel each other's presence through a twinge of pain in their wrist scars. Myles had often postulated that this throbbing was a phantom manifestation of the physical connection they had shared in the womb, while Beckett reasoned that Myles was a pain even when he wasn't in the room. Both theories were correct.

Sister Jeronima intended to put the screws to Beckett, whom she considered the weaker link. A little knifeplay to get his lip wobbling and then some yelling Italian in his face.

This was a trick Jeronima often employed during her nun-terrogations. It didn't really matter which Italian words she used. Jeronima often employed the lyrics from *Rigoletto* and she had trained herself to yell for almost a minute without pausing for breath.

She sat opposite the boy, who was staring at his hand-cuffs as though he might open them with psychic powers.

"Can I see the knife again, Sister?" the boy asked without looking up.

"Certainly, Beckett," answered Jeronima. "Later you may see it up close. Perhaps a little closer than you might like."

Jeronima drew the knife from an almost invisible pocket in her sleeve, and the blade glittered in her hand like a star.

"That's so shiny," said Beckett, paying attention now.

"You are like the bird," said Jeronima, stowing the blade. "The magpie who likes shiny things."

"I do like shiny things. And yellow things. Those lemon men were funny."

"There will be more, as you say, 'lemon men' very soon. Many more than the four I have now. Men from London and Berlin. Already there are four teams of ACRONYM agents converging on this place."

"Funny lemon men with their stupid guns."

"Guns are necessary in our line of work," said Jeronima. "Our fairy enemies will have guns. And perhaps magic."

"I like enemies," declared Beckett. "Fairies with laser eyes."

"I think not, chico. We have heard no evidence of

laser eyes. Perhaps some powers of hypnotism and . . ."

Jeronima stopped speaking, because she had the sudden chilling realization that she was the one being interviewed.

"Un momento," she said, and then thought for a moment, her mind coming around like a slow gun turret to the fact that she had possibly been—was being—bamboozled.

"Am I giving you the information?"

"You are indeed," said Beckett. "I find interrogation so much more effective when the interviewee believes themselves the interviewer. Thank you, Sister Jeronima. You have been most informative. Four armed men besides yourself and a small window of opportunity for us to escape the extra ACRONYM agents who are on their way."

Jeronima felt as though her cerebrospinal brain fluid had congealed. "Wait now. Wait un momento. So you are . . . you would be . . . ?"

"I would be Myles Fowl," said he, who was in truth Myles. "And you would be double bluffed."

"But the birthmark?" said Jeronima.

"Oh, that," said Myles. He tore open the inoculation patch, peeled the birthmark from his upper arm and popped it in his mouth. "Gelatin-based transfer. Strawberry. My favorite."

Sister Jeronima simply could not wrap her head around the fact that she had been outmaneuvered by a child.

"That birthmark is in the ACRONYM file. I have seen the photograph with my own eyes."

Myles's mocking laugh sounded very much like a certain

goat meme that was doing the rounds on the internet. "You have seen the photograph? Do you really think the Fowls have not prepared for an abduction? My family has many enemies, and Father has long encouraged us to find a way to switch, and then show strength where weakness is expected. There is no birthmark—there never was. We make them in the refrigerator and display them as it suits us."

"All this time?" said Jeronima.

"For as long as I can remember," said Myles. "Father told us many times that someone would come for us. If it hadn't been ACRONYM, it would have been the CIA, or perhaps the yakuza or mafia."

"Why do you tell me all of this?" Jeronima wondered. "I don't even ask."

Myles smiled kindly, as one might at a confused toddler. "I am, of course, stalling."

At which point someone outside the cell tapped in the door code.

Oberon prodded the boy he believed to be Myles down the corridor with a forefinger.

"You kids thought you were so clever pulling the old switcheroo," he said, smirking. "But that Sister Jeronima is a smart cookie. Like, razor-sharp."

"I do wish you would stop mixing your metaphors," said he who was actually Beckett. "Or, to be precise, stop mixing metaphors with similes. You are offending my ears."

"You got a mouth," said Oberon.

At which point Beckett's real personality leaked out and he said a few things not dictated by the NANNI AI in Myles's spectacles directly into his cheekbones. "Of course I have a mouth. I have arms, too, and legs that are strong like a cheetah's, which is the fastest cat in the world, in case you didn't know, and makes a sound like a lawn mower."

"Wait a second," said Oberon. "I thought you were the science-y one."

"That is so true," said Beckett, trying to cover. "Mr. Science, that's me. You wouldn't believe all the boring stuff I know. Like the radius of a square root is on the opposite side of a black hole."

Oberon would have totally gone for this, not being much of an academic himself, but Beckett felt his cover was blown and decided it was time to make his move, and so turned to face his captor.

"Do you like football?" he asked.

"Actually, I do," said the henchman. "Real football, though. The American kind. I was the kicker in high school." Oberon slapped his right thigh. "I kicked a fifty-yard field goal with this tree trunk right here. Some people said forty-five, but it was fifty, all right. I got muscles like coconuts in there. Why are you asking?"

Beckett flexed his fingers, then curled them into a fist.

"I like it when things are not easy," he said, and unleashed the cluster punch.

* * *

The cluster punch is considered a myth by most accomplished martial artists. But there are a dozen who claim to have seen it performed, and a few who profess to have actually landed one. The notorious, feared, and respected Fowl family bodyguard, Domovoi Butler, who was currently, and with some considerable reluctance, on his way to Mars, had managed to pull off a single cluster punch early in his career on a would-be assassin in Ghana, but he could never repeat it, though he'd certainly had scores of opportunities to try.

Simply put, the cluster punch was a nonlethal paralyzing blow based on an ancient African theory that the body's twelve principal meridian lines all intersect in a cluster just above the right kneecap. If a person could strike that cluster at precisely the right angle, with exactly the correct amount of pressure per square inch, the entire system would go into spasm and the victim would be left paralyzed for a brief period. There were so many variables involved that it would take a humanoid robot with millimeter accuracy and X-ray capability to have any success with the strike, and only then if the target were standing completely still, which targets are usually reluctant to do.

Somehow, Beckett Fowl could toss out cluster punches at will. In the Fowl dojo, he had proven himself to be something of a cluster-punch savant, and, years earlier, he had infuriated his school principal by freezing a PE teacher whom Beckett perceived to be bullying his kindergarten classmates.

Beckett's technique was to pogo six inches straight up,

then strike with a hammer action on the way down, while emitting a high-pitched *Hah!*, which he swore was vital to the success of the move.

He did so now, thumping Oberon above the kneecap. There was no pain and Oberon was on the point of making a disparaging remark when his entire body seized up and he keeled over like a felled oak, his mouth frozen oddly in a whistling aspect.

Beckett bowed and said, "I respect you, Mr. Oberon."

Which was not an accurate statement, as the man's real name was Phil and Beckett didn't actually respect him.

Myles Fowl found himself experiencing dangerous levels of happiness. The *happiness* was due to the fact that he was explaining his own genius to someone who found herself momentarily too stunned for interjection or interruption. The *dangerous* was because the endorphins or happy hormones released into his nervous system could flood his body and dull his thought process. Or, simply put: More happy, less snappy.

But in spite of this, Myles simply could not stop his Fowlsplaining.

"You are probably wondering, Sister, how someone could be opening the door right now from the outside. Someone who should not know the code."

"It's my man," said Sister Jeronima. "An ACRONYM agent."

"You are quite wrong, I assure you," said Myles. "Your

agent is no doubt utterly incapacitated. But to continue, how could this person know the code? The answer is simplicity itself to me, though possibly complicated to the average individual. You see, ninety percent of keypads are supplied at the top end by a surprisingly small number of companies. Five, in fact. Two of these companies are owned by Fowl Industries, including your keypad, which I immediately recognized as a Portunus Five Star."

The door beeped and clanged open, and Jeronima whipped around to see an obviously hyped-up Beckett vibrating with excitement in the doorway.

"It worked, Myles," he said. "Just like you said."

"Naturally it worked, brother," said Myles. "I was telling Sister Jeronima how Father's company manufactures the Portunus Five Star, and I was about to explain how, in the Escape Plan module of our social studies class, we learned to memorize the distinct tones emitted by the keys of the most popular keypads and to match the tones to the numbers."

"*Beep boop,*" said Beckett, robot-dancing toward Sister Jeronima. "*Boop beep boop.*"

Myles waited patiently for his brother to finish his routine. "Beckett struggled with this lesson, but as I myself have perfect pitch, it was simplicity itself to assign numbers to the notes, in this case, three-eight-six-two."

"Three hundred and eighty-six point two seconds," said Jeronima, the realization sinking in. "This is how long you estimated it would take you to escape from the handcuffs."

"Exactly," said Myles. "Now if you don't mind, we shall

take our leave of this establishment. If you wish to contact us again, please go through the proper channels."

This patronizing farewell burst the nun's bubble of surprise. "Oh no, chicos," she said. "You may have tricked me once, but I am still having the upper hand. I am armed, and there are more agents in the building."

Beckett wound up his fighting arm. "Cluster punch?"

"No need, brother," said Myles, rising from his chair. "Sister Jeronima is secure enough for now."

Mere seconds ago, Jeronima would have pooh-poohed the notion that she could be secured by an eleven-year-old, but a lot had happened in the past few minutes, and so she checked and found one of her wrists cuffed to the table, the junior manacles' ratchets stretched to their last tooth.

"You should pay attention to where you pay attention," said Myles, sealing his inoculation patch. "I stole your hatpin when you turned to see who was at the door. Hatpins make most excellent lock picks."

And while the nun yanked on the cuffs, he nipped around the table and tugged a black smartphone from her pocket.

"I do hope you don't keep too much information on this phone," he said. "It would be such a shame if I were to uncover all of ACRONYM's dirty secrets."

Jeronima had one more ace up her sleeve—in this case, it was a throwing knife. With her free arm, she slipped it from her sleeve and pointed the tip at Myles.

"Be very still, Myles Fowl," she said. "I have no wish to kill a child."

"Just a moment," said Myles. He retrieved his spectacles from his brother before returning his gaze to Jeronima, who had wound back her arm like a baseball pitcher.

"Now, Sister, you were saying?"

"I was saying, you odious child, that if you do not release me immediately, I will be forced to kill you."

Beckett pointed his elbows at the nun.

"Nope, she's lying," he pronounced.

Myles was inclined to agree.

"You need us," he said. "Both of us. We are your link to the Fairy People. Without us, you have no bait. A professional like you will play the odds, and the odds are that we will be recaptured before we get out of the building."

It was true. There was no percentage in killing either boy, and Jeronima's superiors might even frown upon it, so she threw the blade past Myles's insufferably self-satisfied face and into the heavy wooden door, where it landed with a *thunk*.

"Very well, chicos, you may run, but I will see you muy pronto. And when I have you back in your chairs, the gloves will be off. No more Sister Nice Guy."

Myles wasn't even listening to the threats, as he was counting in his head.

"And there it is," he said. "Three hundred and eighty-six point two seconds, and I am, as predicted, out of your handcuffs. It amuses me for the numbers to have a double significance, though, annoyingly, I was off by a few seconds."

"Wrist bump?" asked Beckett brightly.

"Oh, absolutely, brother," replied Myles.

And the twins wrist-bumped right there in front of Sister Jeronima Gonzalez-Ramos de Zárate of Bilbao, who was so frustrated that she actually screamed her way through the first verse of "La Donna è Mobile" from *Rigoletto*.

CHAPTER 6

CLIPPERS & LANCE

THERE was something Specialist Lazuli Heitz had forgotten about chromophoric camouflage, and that was the effect of steam on its filaments. Water and wind bounced right off, but steam wormed its way between the individual fibers and curled each one in on itself like a frightened slug. In all fairness to Lazuli, the Filabusters were outmoded pieces of equipment and had not been deployed in the field for almost a quarter of a century, so hardly any time had been spent on their workings in the Academy.

Therefore, perhaps Lazuli can be forgiven for not noticing that her cloak of invisibility was wilting more with every minute she remained in the shower room. And even if she had noticed, what choice did she have other than the one she had been trained to make, i.e., save the fairy?

But imagine, if you will, the jolt of surprise that stimulated Lord Teddy Bleedham-Drye's brain as a small hand appeared seemingly from another dimension. And, as if that weren't enough oddness for one day, a diminutive figure slowly materialized behind it.

"What the blazes?" said the duke.

But this was uttered under his breath, for the man was a born hunter and knew better than to make exclamations of any perceptible volume when a creature appeared unexpectedly. He also knew that some animals could prove to be exponentially more lethal than one might assume from their benign appearance. Teddy had learned this lesson as a child, when one of the estate swans had drowned his pet Dalmatian for disturbing her cygnets. The duke had never forgotten this harrowing experience, and so when the fairy—for that was what it must surely be—appeared, Lord Teddy hardly gave an impression of having seen it, and the creature in its turn gave no impression of being seen.

Curiouser and curiouser, thought the duke. It seems we are both after the same prey.

There would be only one winner in that contest, as far as Teddy was concerned, and that would be the person with a seat in the House of Lords.

The lay of the land vis-à-vis the shower room was as follows: three lemons, including Lord Teddy, who was the only one sporting hazmat headgear, as he was not one of the bad guys and had no wish to reveal himself. Strictly speaking, he was, of course, a bad guy, just not one of this particular group. The two remaining lemons were swabbing down the stalls, and Teddy was on the point of pocketing the troll— and perhaps the money clip as well, because a chap never knew. The fairy specialist, who was, unbeknownst to her, now almost completely visible, was on the verge of being the nexus of the lemon men's attention.

"Who is that?" said Clippers, noticing the solidifying figure. "Is that one of those Fowl kids?"

Lance peeked up from the clips of Clippers's clippers, which he was steam-lancing.

"Who?" he asked, though Lance knew the answer before the interrogative was fully formed. Who else could his partner be referring to besides the child-shaped patch of shimmering camouflage that was moving in a strange down-tempo plod toward the effects crate?

But then both Lance and Clippers had the simultaneous realization that this unusual creature, whatever it was, was no human child, and this gave both men something of a fright, despite the fact that they were entry-level hoods in an organization that hunted unusual creatures. This fright resulted in a momentary lapse of workplace best practices, i.e., when operating dangerous tools, keep your eyes on the business ends of those tools.

Both Lance and Clippers relaxed their concentration only momentarily and just barely, but it was enough for Clippers to nick Lance's thumb, which caused Lance to shriek and lance Clippers's neck, resulting in a howl from Clippers.

All this squealing and howling did not upset Lazuli, for she was a professional and believed herself invisible, but it was an intolerable irritant to Lord Teddy, who felt he had a situation here that needed resolving and the two yellow-clad buffoons were nothing but a distraction.

So Teddy drew a Myishi Snub gas pistol from his spring-loaded shoulder holster and summarily shot both men with cellophane slugs. The beauty of the holster was that it was set on a depress catch so that one little push on the grip sent the thing bounding up into his hand, and the beauty of the shrink-wrappers was that a chap didn't have to take aim with great care, as any contact was good contact. Regardless, Lord Bleedham-Drye had been taking potshots at anything that walked, swam, or flew for so many decades now that he could hit a sparrow from a hundred yards with barely a squint, and had, in fact, once shrink-wrapped a hummingbird to impress Ishi Myishi when the duke visited his oldest friend's factory on one of the more inhospitable Japanese islands.

Teddy remembered the visit fondly. He had stayed for dinner in Myishi's subterranean residence, where the weapons manufacturer's improvised shotgun from Burma was framed on the wall. The toast had been: *To my first shotgun. Almost killing you, Bleedham-Drye-san, was the best thing I ever did.*

Truer words were never spoken, in Teddy's opinion.

The effect of the cellophane slug on Clippers was predictable in that the man was quickly trussed in cellophane like a supermarket turkey. But Lance's binding was unusual, as the hot vapors interfered with the virus's spread, causing the cellophane to billow and bubble as it filled with steam.

I say, thought Lord Teddy. Interesting variation. I must mention that to old Myishi.

In any case, the cellophane was virulent enough to contain Lance along with his steam, which soon fogged up the interior of the bubble.

Meanwhile, Lazuli considered her opponent sufficiently distracted for her to make an attempt on the troll, which might have worked had she not been decidedly non-invisible by this point. That is to say, visible.

Lazuli had just gripped the troll's foot with two fingers when the yellow-clad human tucked a pistol under her chin and said, "I can see you, fairy."

And Lazuli thought: Steam. D'Arvit.

And now begins the grouping of our protagonists into a more streamlined narrative. Traditionally, there would be two groups: *goodies* and *baddies,* to use a vernacular that Myles Fowl would doubtless frown upon. But in this instance we have a baddie who think she's a goodie, a goodie who is prepared to be bad on occasion, a sweet goodie who talks to crows, an ancient baddie who has no illusions about himself, a couple of moron baddies who are wrapped in plastic, a little feral neutral guy also wrapped in plastic, and an unarmed goodie trainee. But shortly we will be down to two bunches of assorted folks.

Currently, Myles and Beckett Fowl were retracing their steps so that they might reclaim their possessions. Myles had activated the AI in his spectacles, for he had a most important assignment for her.

"NANNI," he said, "can you bypass this phone's passcode?"

"Ha-ha-ha," said NANNI. The Artificial Intelligence was not truly laughing, rather saying the words *ha-ha-ha*, as her awareness had not yet reached the level of spontaneity required for actual laughter, even though it very shortly would. But she was aware that Myles's question was one that deserved derision. "Are you serious, Myles? I cracked that child's toy like a hammer smashing a nut as soon as we got here."

Myles winced. He did not appreciate attempts at humor or imagery. Perhaps he should remove a few circuits from NANNI's mainframe.

"Very good, NANNI. Do a virus check. Download whatever you can retrieve, and when you reestablish an internet connection, e-mail malware to every contact you can find."

NANNI's avatar appeared on Myles's lens, and it was frowning. "All of them? I see several coffee bars on the list. And a hat shop in Italy. Also, a chocolatier in Bern, which I believe serves yummy éclairs."

Myles winced. "'Yummy,' NANNI? Really? I hardly think that fact is relevant."

"It's relevant if you're hungry," argued the AI.

"I would like to mail every contact," said Myles, "whether or not they have a yummy tag."

"You are the boss," said the glowing orange face, then it disappeared to conserve battery while she worked.

The AI could not have known, but Myles had been waiting for a long time to hear those exact words.

I am the boss, he thought. And I will get us out of this.

And he would. But not alone.

Meanwhile, our LEP trainee was in the dark site's wet room with the barrel of a pistol tucked under her cleft chin.

D'Arvit, Specialist Heitz was thinking.

You have probably deduced by now the meaning of the Gnommish word *D'Arvit*. It is a term often employed in times of stress—for example, when one finds oneself with a gun muzzle underneath one's jawbone. It is not a word often heard in job interviews or eulogies.

Specialist Heitz realized that since she was visible she might as well be audible, and so she repeated the word aloud.

"D'Arvit, indeed," said Lord Teddy.

"Careful, human," said Lazuli. "You have no idea what you're dealing with."

And even though Brother Colman had explained in his serum-induced revelations how the fairies had mastered human languages, the duke was taken aback to hear such a clear command of the Queen's English.

"Au contraire, mademoiselle," Teddy riposted, his surprise concealed by his head covering. "I have, in fact, quite a good idea of what manner of creature I have at my mercy.

You would be a fairy, though of what particular species I could not swear."

Lazuli squared her jaw and willed her own eyes to glint. "Just hand me the troll and we'll say no more about it. No one needs to get hurt today."

But Lord Teddy was too long in the tooth for bluffing and was inclined to disagree.

"Oh, I think someone needs to get hurt," he said, for at this range even a cellophane slug would leave quite a mark.

At which point Beckett Fowl saved the day by literally leaping into the room, a demand springing from his lips: "Where is Whistle Blower?"

Which was a question no one was expecting, including the second Fowl twin, who trailed his brother and was distinguishable only by his measured pace and magnified piercing gaze.

"Whistle Blower. I had forgotten," he said, and then surveyed the room, taking in the shrink-wrapped lemons and the two individuals with a grip on Beckett's salvaged action figure.

"My toy!" said Beckett, and, without any ado whatsoever, he unleashed a cluster punch on Lord Teddy.

"I say," said Teddy, displaying zero signs of paralysis. "The little fellow has spirit."

Myles was surprised that his brother would be off the mark. He immediately sent the AI a command. "NANNI," he said, "partition off that ACRONYM business and run a scan on the man in yellow."

"That's a very general order, Myles, which is quite unlike you. I don't suppose you would like to give me a few parameters?" asked NANNI.

"Give me the works; search for physical anomalies."

The Duke of Scilly barked with laughter. "By all means, young man, scan away. Take your time."

While NANNI used the biometric scanners in Myles's spectacles to check Lord Teddy's physiognomy and indeed inner workings, Beckett was doing some scanning of his own, constructing a makeshift frame with his forefingers and thumbs and squinting through it—although, in truth, he operated on pure animal instinct. And even if Beckett had been outfitted with his own NANNI glasses, the AI's scanners would have been useless when it came to landing a cluster punch, as even Myles had yet to develop a scan for meridian lines. Also, though Beckett could not have known it, Lord Teddy's meddling in his own DNA had actually altered the layout of his meridian lines so they had no intersection point, which made the duke immune to Beckett's attack.

"Long arms," Beckett proclaimed. "Adjusting strike zone."

"I concur," said NANNI in Myles's spectacles. "That guy has long arms. And his energy fields are all over the place. Do those facts help?"

"Not really," said Myles. "And please stop using terms like *guy*."

Lord Teddy had about as much of this assorted claptrap as he was prepared to endure. The Fowl Twins had thwarted his abduction plan, and now they were literally under his feet at quite a delicate moment. One was talking to himself, it seemed, and the other had actually dared to assault his royal person. A chap didn't usually enjoy striking children, but in this particular case, Teddy thought it might not upset him unduly.

And then, of course, there was the fairy. The one who spoke. Better to shrink-wrap the creature and stuff it in a duffel bag for a leisurely examination back at Childerblaine House. It would be painful, certainly.

But not for me, thought the duke.

And crucial developments proceeded to develop in the following five seconds. A single second is a long time in a fight, as every combatant knows, and five can mean the difference between life and death. In this case, there would be no death, but there would definitely be agony.

What happened in those five seconds has to be slowed down in the telling so as to be properly appreciated.

And so, the long-winded story of a moment:

1. As soon as she realized that she was, in fact, utterly visible, Specialist Lazuli Heitz switched her martial arts from Doveli to Cos Tapa, which was akin to switching from dial-up to broadband in terms of speed. *Cos Tapa* translates roughly from the Gnommish as *Quick-Footed* or *Of Blurred Feet* and is an aggressive combat style developed by the diminutive pixie race from a study of animals such as hyenas, cats, and small breeds of dogs, which are

often forced to take on larger foes. (It was so effective as a martial art that it had migrated to the human world, where it had been adapted by a certain Madam Ko, who taught it in a bodyguard academy.) In these cases, the pixies discovered that victory depended on three factors: balance, dexterity, and speed. Lazuli had excellent balance, she was dexterous with her hands and feet, and she had buckets of speed. Using a maneuver often employed by cartoon squirrels, Lazuli adjusted her grip on Lord Teddy's wrist while running her feet up along the human's legs and torso until her boots were tucked under his armpit. This move was known as the pendulum. Lazuli hauled on Teddy's arm and, crucially, craned her chin to the left.

2. Lord Teddy pulled the trigger on the Myishi Snub gas pistol while beginning to register a certain pressure on his shoulder joint. Even so, he could not resist a triumphant "Aha!" as the weapon fired with a *phhhft* rather than the more traditional *bang.*

3. The shrink-wrapper slug whizzed past Lazuli's pointed ear—so close that the pixel thought she'd been hit—but she nevertheless maintained contact, reasoning that the projectile seemed viral in nature and might enclose them both.

4. Beckett Fowl decided that he should definitely join this fight, as he had already grouped all of the lemon men into the *bad guy* category, and since this lemon man's shoulder was primed for a blow, he performed

his trademark pogo maneuver and punched Lord
Teddy's shoulder on the way down.

5. The duke's shoulder was instantly dislocated.

6. Myles did not involve himself in the altercation.
This was not surprising, as fighting was not his area,
and he would simply get in his twin's way. Instead,
he calmly collected his belongings from the metal
crate.

And all of this took place in five seconds.

Having one's shoulder dislocated is particularly excruciating; on the painful-injuries scale, it ranks at number eight,
just below a broken neck. In fact, Lord Teddy was in such
discomfort that he momentarily forgot everything except
the white ball of agony in his shoulder.

"My word," he groaned. "My blooming word."

Which was as close to swearing as Lord Teddy usually
came, on account of his breeding. He sank to the flagstones,
careful not to jar his arm, which seemed to be electrified.
Unfortunately for him, Lazuli's boots were still jammed
into his armpit, and so his wounded shoulder was further
traumatized by his collapse. The duke's eyes rolled back in
his head momentarily as he attempted to cope with this
new level of suffering, the likes of which he hadn't experienced since rupturing his Achilles tendon in the 1970s
playing the then-popular game of squash. Rupturing one's
Achilles tendon, incidentally, was number ten on the
painful-injuries list.

Lazuli crawled out from under the crumpled heap of human and grabbed for the toy troll at the same moment that Beckett made a lunge for it, and the two ended up with one hand each on the troll.

"Mine," said Lazuli in Gnommish.

"Mine," echoed Beckett, also in Gnommish, which Myles might have assumed to be simple mimicry had he been listening, but he wasn't.

Beckett and Lazuli looked to the bespectacled boy for the deciding vote, as his bearing conveyed an almost irresistible air of authority.

"I see," Myles said to thin air. Then: "Remarkable." Followed by: "If you say so."

Then Myles's attention was back on the room and his eyes narrowed to the curious tug-of-war before him.

"Beckett, release the troll," he ordered.

Beckett disobeyed.

Usually he disobeyed orders on principle, but in this case, he had, in his fashion, developed a fierce and unreasonable attachment to something that had only recently come into his possession.

"No, Myles," he said. "Whistle Blower is *my* toy."

Lazuli opened her mouth to argue but then changed her mind. Perhaps it was better for all concerned if the humans believed the troll to be nothing more than a toy. So, instead of setting the one called Beckett straight, she played into his understanding of things.

"*My* toy," she said, in the humans' own language.

Myles must have noticed her belligerent expression, for he raised his hands, palms out.

"There is no cause for aggression. We are friends. Fowl and fairy, friends forever. There's a lot of alliteration there, I grant you, but the sentiment is genuine nonetheless."

Beckett was astounded. "We have fairy friends? The stories are real?"

Lazuli had many questions, but the most pressing one was: "How do you know I am a fairy?"

Myles could answer both questions with a single word: "Artemis."

This invocation of Artemis's name had the effect of stunning both the hyperactive boy and the specialist fairy.

"Artemis told you?" said Beckett. "From space?"

"No," said Myles. "Nothing quite so cosmic. He left a message on my spectacles."

"Artemis," said Lazuli, recalling her angel's words: *If you ever meet Artemis Fowl, he is to be trusted.*

She would have to heed those words now, no matter what her misgivings about the twins might be.

"Your brother Artemis," she said to Myles, "did he leave instructions?"

"Yes," said Myles, "but they were long-winded even by my standards."

"Summarize," said Lazuli, for there were footsteps thudding in the hall.

"He said 'Work together, get to a safe place.'"

This satisfied both Beckett and Lazuli. For now, at least, they were a team.

Beckett relinquished his hold on the toy troll. "Take care of Whistle Blower."

"Just like that?" said Lazuli.

"I need my hands free," said Beckett, looping his goldfish tie around his neck. "Myles is the smarty-pants, but I am the smarty-fists."

Myles sighed, aggrieved. "I do apologize for my brother's egregious mangling of the language, but he is, in essence, correct. I *think*, and he *does*."

The rumbling thunder of footsteps grew louder.

Lazuli stuffed the troll inside her tunic and made ready for the fight.

"I am quite the smarty-fists myself," she said, and followed Beckett into the corridor.

Myles did not immediately pursue the pair but instead spared a second to tug off Lord Teddy's mask and take a good look at yet another enemy they had somehow picked up.

NANNI quickly ran the face through facial recognition and matched it both with the Dalkey sniper and a passport photo from her onboard databases.

"Well, la-di-da, we have ourselves royalty," she said. "This is none other than Lord Teddy Bleedham-Drye, the Duke of Scilly."

"Ah, Your Lordship," said Myles, bowing deeply. "How wonderful to make your acquaintance."

Of course Myles knew the duke by reputation, and had heard the rumors vis-à-vis his extended life span, but this was the first time Bleedham-Drye had butted heads with the Fowl family.

Myles was on the point of interrogating Lord Teddy when there came the unmistakable sound of people being thumped.

"Uh-oh," said NANNI, interpreting the sounds and assuming they had been made by Beckett.

Uh-oh, thought Myles, was a reasonable if not very scientific reaction, and he decided he'd better make sure his brother didn't hurt anyone too badly.

There have been many famous corridor-fight scenes committed to film, most of which would be unsuitable for minors and so shall not be referenced in these pages, but suffice it to say that the Amsterdam subterranean black-site corridor fight surpassed them all in the shock-value department. The fighting moves themselves were not as dramatic as one might have seen before, but the looks on the faces of those assaulted were priceless.

There were twelve assorted male and female security types proceeding down the hallway that ran past the wet room, and it was inevitable that once they breached this area they would fan out and surround the newly formed Fowl/fairy alliance. However, in the narrow corridor, the ACRONYM operatives were hampered by their own pumped-up bulk and forced to advance two abreast, and so the FFA opted for the Thermopylae approach, which had worked so well for King Leonidas and his Spartans (for the first three days, at least). In other words, the boy and the specialist conducted fierce battle in a tight space, attacking one agent at a time.

Beckett Fowl exploded from the wet room with such speed that he actually pinballed off the opposite wall, and, with a cry of delight, bore down upon his prey.

The lead guy had time to be puzzled for a second. Their orders were to secure the building and not kill any "small humanoids."

Who am I going to kill? These two little kids?

The second little kid, who was actually a fairy, did not pinball off the wall but instead tucked her head low, over-took the first kid, and moved with blinding speed toward the well-armed group.

The lead agent affected a friendly tone. "Hey, little guys—" he said, and extended a hand, which was a big mistake, for Lazuli grabbed that hand, ran up his body, and, with a mighty yank, pendulumed the man head over heels into the stone wall.

Beckett laughed even as he unleashed a cluster punch on the next agent, and then, using the first man's falling body as a springboard, he moved on to the next man in line, who was a woman. She barely had time for a "There's no need for—" before she joined her comrade in temporary paralysis.

And on they went, boy and pixel, scything through an elite fighting unit like the ACRONYM agents were sheaves of particularly dry wheat. It was a joy to watch, unless you were an ACRONYM agent, or Sister Jeronima, who was watching from the interview room on her wristwatch, which was synced with the security cameras.

The problem with the feed was that the camera only captured the top half of the corridor, cutting off the boy and fairy completely. All Jeronima could see was a succession of her own operatives being batted aside as though by invisible assailants. The camera's microphone was omnidirectional, though, and managed to pick up the following:

"Hey, little guys—"

"There's no need for—"

"What the—?"

"Did you see—?"

"Are those monkeys?"

And probably the most embarrassing:

"Oh, dear sweet Momma . . ."

This last uttered by a man from Texas, who was fired the following day. And though it was never proven, it was rumored that the terminated Texan got hold of the corridor footage and revenge-released it onto the internet, where it quickly became a sensation. The video was the inspiration for both the hit movie *Tiny Ghost Ninjas of Xanadu* and an internationally best-selling collection of ARE THOSE MONKEYS? T-shirts.

All of which is by the by.

We are more concerned with the immediate aftermath

of the conflict, which saw Beckett and Lazuli at the end of the corridor with paralyzed or unconscious bodies strewn behind them. For some reason, one of the unconscious was singing "There's No Business Like Show Business" in his sleep, and Myles would have dearly loved to wake the fellow up for a session of psychoanalysis.

One might think that Myles Fowl would be impressed with his brother's display, but he had always agreed with Isaac Asimov, who was of the opinion that violence was the last refuge of the incompetent. But considering the enraged nun to the rear, the dislocated duke in the wet room, and the brigades of ACRONYM agents doubtless converging on the underground lair, Myles thought it was probably prudent to move along and skip the anti-violence lecture.

"Shall we proceed?" he asked, picking his way through the obstacle course of limbs and torsos and up the stone stairwell at the hallway's end. "I have no doubt that more of Sister Jeronima's reinforcements are nearby."

In the interview room, Jeronima shrieked at her watch. "I can hear what you are saying, you horrible mocoso! Yo también puedo verte."

In all fairness to Jeronima, she had good reasons to be semi-hysterical:

1. She had been outwitted by two children, and her reputation as the organization's premium interrogator would be in tatters when this fact leaked out, as facts like these tended to do.

2. Her crack team of enforcers were strewn over the flagstones like so many bowling pins.
3. The first solid lead she'd had in years was escaping into the Amsterdam morning.
4. And she was handcuffed to a table.

But her hysteria was snuffed out by her observation of a newcomer on the stone steps. Another child?

No.

Jeronima brought her face closer to the watch screen on the wrist that was cuffed to the desk and stared.

The ears.

Its ears were pointed. It was wearing armor of a strange technology.

Sister Jeronima felt a kind of reverence as she stared without blinking at the small screen as though she were witnessing a holy apparition.

"Oh," she whispered. "There you are, fairy."

And the nun wept freely, for now she knew without doubt that she had been right to believe. These were not tears of sadness, but joy that she would be vindicated.

"Finalmente," she said.

Jeronima would catch this fairy and pickle it in a tube so that ACRONYM could dissect the corpse and learn the secrets of the underground world.

"You have taken my phone, Master Myles," she said to the little figure on-screen. "And where it goes, I can follow."

Perhaps Myles Fowl isn't as clever as he believes himself to be, thought Jeronima.

Under the circumstances and considering recent events, it seems almost incredible that an intelligent person could believe that to be true.

CHAPTER 7

WHO PUT THE DAM IN AMSTERDAM?

ONE might think that the universe would have granted the Fowl Twins a moment's respite, considering all they had endured at the hands of ACRONYM, but no, it was not finished meddling with the brothers just yet.

The boys closed the steel door on one episode and opened the throttle on another. The throttle being connected to the dashboard of a high-powered, shallow-draft, rigid-hull inflatable boat, or RIB, which had been most conveniently docked outside the black site in a sunken dock. Beckett, with his instinctive understanding of mechanics, flooded the sunken dock as though he had worked with canal locks all his life, and soon the RIB was surging toward open water. Beckett overcame the fact that the salt-crusted windshield impeded his view by standing on the wheel and steering with his feet while he leaned his chest against the Plexiglas. This one little action was actually a very accurate snapshot of his entire personality.

For perhaps a single minute, their progress was smooth and unchallenged, and Myles used this time to open a dialogue with the fairy creature sitting opposite him.

"I haven't introduced myself," he said, attempting to smooth back his hair, which, he remembered too late, now lay on the floor of the wet room.

"I know who you are," said Lazuli, and it must be said that her tone was quite sullen for someone who had just escaped almost certain experimentation on her person by creepy people with scalpels. "I don't know why you helped me."

Myles tapped the arm of his spectacles. "Artemis told me to. Your face unlocked a series of video messages. NANNI's facial-recognition software is apparently programmed to recognize fairy physiognomy." Here Myles paused and smiled to emphasize the fact that he was about to make a hilarious and ice-breaking joke. "Or perhaps I should say physio-GNOMEY."

Myles waited for a laugh that never materialized.

"Were you attempting humor?" asked Lazuli. "My command of your language is unsophisticated, so perhaps you were making a joke, or perhaps you are just culturally insensitive."

Myles decided that the best course of action was to ignore the question entirely. "I helped you on the helicopter because I sensed you were an ally. Artemis has often told us stories of fairies, and in those tales the People are always the heroes. The good guys, if you will."

"And why did you help me in this terrible underground place?"

"We helped each other," said Myles. "And I feel our best hope of survival is to continue working together. As a team."

Beckett picked up on the word *team*. "Can we use our team name? The Regrettables?" He adopted a movie-trailer voice. "Can they help you? They're not sure, because they are the Regrettables."

Lazuli frowned. "Is this another joke?"

"Unfortunately, no," said Myles. "Beckett does not joke about team names. To summarize a long story: Once, Artemis was experimenting with vaccines and we contracted the chicken pox, so Beck dubbed us the Regrettables, because we were in no shape to help anyone."

For a split second, Lazuli seemed a little less dour. "The Regrettables. I like this name."

Myles picked up on the minute softening of the blue fairy's attitude and extended a hand. "I am, as you know, Master Myles Fowl. That exuberant fellow is my twin, Beckett. And you would be?"

Lazuli took the hand and turned it over, examining it. "I would be Specialist Heitz of the Lower Elements Police."

Myles thoroughly approved of formal introductions. There would be time enough to get to know each other later. "Excellent, Specialist Heitz. I have no doubt we can concoct a plan to evade the clutches of Sister Jeronima and her lackeys."

Lazuli released Myles's hand. "You seem very calm,

Master Fowl, for someone who has just discovered that fairies actually exist."

"I am generally calm," explained Myles. "Only the tiniest of minds cannot accept the improbable. I think a part of me always suspected you existed. Artemis confirmed my suspicions, and you confirmed Artemis's statements. Living proof, as they say."

"Can you show me this video from your brother, the famous Artemis Fowl?"

"Of course," said Myles. "You will need to don my spectacles."

But before there could be any donning of spectacles, Beckett crab-walked across the steering wheel, banking the inflatable sharply left down a smaller canal.

"We're being followed," he said excitedly.

"By whom?" asked Myles.

"Ask me like we're in a game," said his twin.

Myles sighed. "Who dares follow the Regrettables?"

Beckett took a quick look around. "Three Zodiac powerboats behind us."

Lazuli scanned the canal bank ahead and saw two black SUVs surging along the narrow street, heeding neither pedestrians nor speed limits.

"Two vehicles on land," she said.

Myles tapped and held a sensor on the arm of his spectacles, putting NANNI on speaker. "NANNI, an escape route, if you please."

The Artificial Intelligence synced with a weather

satellite and hijacked a bird's-eye feed of the city.

"Escape is not really in the cards," she said. "The power-boats are herding us toward the automobiles. We're like chickens in a chicken run."

"We need to get off this canal," said Lazuli.

"Unfortunately, not going to happen," said NANNI. "At this speed, we cannot make the turn."

To set the scene:

Picture, if you will, early morning Amsterdam. The city is shrugging off the shadows of night and preparing itself for the hordes of tourists who will shortly throng its streets and waterways. The canals are quiet but for the occasional party-boat crew assessing the damage from the previous night's revelries and swabbing the crafts of the various forms of viscous bilge congealing on the decks. A few mammoth dredger boats are fishing bicycles from the canals. The majority of these have been dumped by casual thieves (it is estimated that if all the bikes stolen in Amsterdam in a single year were laid front wheel to back wheel, the bike train would reach the moon). The architectural marvel that is the Maritime Museum stands solidly on its artificial island, supported by almost two thousand wooden piles sunk deep into the mud, delaying sunrise over the old harbor by several minutes with its bulk.

This is all very well and good, you say, but what about our heroes? Just how desperate is their situation? It can be described best as a mathematical problem such as one might find on a high school exam:

If the Regrettables' boat, designated A, is traveling north at fifty knots on Westerkanaal toward open water, how long before the ACRONYM crafts, designated B, C, and D, traveling at sixty-eight knots, close the two-hundred-yard gap? Other factors include the two SUVs now parked on the canal four hundred yards ahead of boat A, and the dredger currently blocking the canal. If boat A continues on its course, its progress will be halted by the dredger, and the occupants will be surrounded, making capture inevitable. There is an escape route involving a turn starboard down a narrow canal, Zoutkeetsgracht, but the deceleration involved to make the turn without flipping boat A would result in boats B, C, and D overtaking boat A.

"Turning at this speed would result in capsizing, so I must reluctantly conclude that escape is improbable," said NANNI on speaker. "I say 'reluctantly' because I think I like you guys, but at least if you are all killed, I will be proven right."

It seemed to Myles that NANNI was not all the way there when it came to interpersonal relationships.

But then again, he thought, neither am I.

"Perhaps there are factors I am unaware of," said NANNI. "Do we by any chance have any rocket launchers?"

Lazuli checked an equipment locker in the stern. "No rocket launchers. A portable battering ram and some Kevlar vests."

"We must turn right," said Myles. "Yet we must not decelerate."

The solution to their problem came from an unexpected quarter, i.e., Beckett, who did not, as a rule, provide solutions for Myles's problems, because, like most siblings, he enjoyed watching his brother squirm. But this time there was derring-do involved, so Beckett made an exception.

"We need a leopard," he announced, back-flipping from his perch on the wheel, which was a total showboat move, as he could have simply stepped down.

Myles was not as aghast at this frankly ridiculous suggestion as one might expect; after all, he had a long history of being on the receiving end of Beckett's notions. "A leopard?" he asked with some patronizing kindness. "Perhaps the thinking should be left to me—no offense, brother."

"You think," said Beckett. "I'll do."

And with that, the erstwhile blond twin swung himself over the starboard side, straining to keep his body rigid against the canal water while clinging to the gunwale ropes.

"Turn, brother," he said through gritted teeth, the water sluicing over his gleaming head.

Myles understood then. "Ah, you meant to say *leeboard*, not leopard. That was a most untimely confusion, because—"

"Turn, brother," gurgled Beckett. "Hard starboard."

Lazuli, though her first language was not English, grasped what the hyperactive human was attempting and grabbed the steering wheel, spinning it clockwise. The RIB skipped sideways, its rubber hull whistling with each bounce and one propeller of its twin engines actually breaking the surface and whining in discontent. Miraculously, Beckett's improvised human stabilizer righted the craft, and it shot down Zoutkeetsgracht with barely a graze against the canal wall. But enough of a graze to do some damage.

The first two Zodiacs on their tail did not have an inspired eleven-year-old among their crew and so failed to make the turn. They gave it the good old special-forces try but succeeded only in piling into each other on the bend. The first was shredded by the propellers of the second, rendering both boats useless. The third craft caught a lucky bounce and found itself, through no expertise on the part of the pilot, still in the chase.

Beckett's leeboard was a resounding success, and so the twin relaxed his body and allowed the current to flip him neatly inside the boat. The entire thing was an Olympic-level feat of agility, and Myles could not resist a smug celebration on his brother's behalf, which took the form of a salute toward the ACRONYM agents lined between the iron dock posts on shore, posturing like angry but ultimately helpless gorillas.

Beckett shook himself like the proverbial hound and then turned to his brother. "What's next, brother? That was my idea for this week."

"We need to make for the harbor," Myles said.

Beckett laughed. "That's easy—just steer into the harbor."

"We are punctured," said Lazuli. "The boat will not

sink, but she will be unwieldy and sluggish in a matter of minutes."

As it turned out, *minutes* would have been a luxury, as the remaining ACRONYM craft drew level and the pilot ordered them to stop or be fired upon.

"We can't stop," said Lazuli. "Bad things will happen to all of us. To all my people."

"I cannot allow that," said Myles.

Beckett patted his brother on the head, which was most patronizing, even in these circumstances. "Think not, fellow Regrettable. Thinking only slows us down."

Myles's eyes widened as he correctly guessed what Beckett intended to do. "No, don't!"

"Too late," said Beckett. "I already have."

Which was patently untrue but seemed to Beckett like the kind of thing an adventurer might say. Beckett made a monkey leap between the boats and dished out half a dozen cluster punches, neutralizing almost an entire crew of ACRONYM agents before they had time to do much more than furrow their brows, although one quick-thinking fellow did take a swipe at Beckett with a baton. But all he managed to make contact with was the powerboat's rubber keel, which bounced the baton back onto his own forehead, saving Beckett the trouble of paralyzing him.

"Don't do it!" Myles said again, but by then Beckett was already back on board.

"You are reckless, brother," said Myles. "Someday your luck will run out."

"I doubt the humans will fall for that trick again," commented Lazuli, keeping one eye on the black vehicles mirroring their progress down the canal.

"I agree," said Myles. "The next time we encounter ACRONYM agents, they will be sporting knee pads. Go right here, then take the next left. That will put us in the harbor and out of reach."

It was a short-term plan, to be sure. But Myles needed to buy some time so he could review Artemis's message. Somewhere in there he felt sure there would be vital information.

NANNI interrupted his train of thought. "Should I contact your parents, Master Myles? They will be worried about you."

"Absolutely not, NANNI," he said. "Mother's and Father's communications are doubtless being monitored, just as the villa was. We are on our own for the moment."

"Not exactly," said Lazuli, nodding toward the main station, which ran ferries across to the distinctive EYE Film Museum.

The first ferry of the morning was loading cars and passengers for transfer across the harbor, but it seemed the ACRONYM vehicles were not prepared to wait, for they crashed through the barriers and drove straight into the water. All very well and good for the Fowl Twins, one might think, but the SUVs refused to sink as they might be reasonably expected to do. Instead, the automobiles sprouted foils and powered across the open water. A large cheer rose from the ferry crowd as though they were bearing witness to some kind of entertainment, which in a way they were.

"Oh, dear," said Myles. "Amphibious craft. I suppose it was only to be expected from such a well-funded organization."

Specialist Heitz's arrowhead markings glowed a fiercer shade of yellow than usual, a sure sign of her anxiety.

"I was supposed to be swiping avatars today," she said, relieved that her high collar covered most of her arrowheads. "Not dodging legions of murderous humans."

"It is time for drastic measures," said Myles. "I was hoping to avoid this."

Beckett liked the sound of the word *drastic* and also the fact that Myles was now prepared to do something he had been hoping to avoid. "What do you mean by 'drastic,' brother?"

His twin did not have time to explain. "You did say there was a battering ram in the equipment locker, Specialist Heitz?"

"I did," confirmed Lazuli.

"Fetch it, brother mine," said Myles. "For I must batter something."

Beckett felt as though his head might explode from sheer joy. This adventure just kept getting better and better.

There is a renegade school of architecture based on the idea that there are more factors governing the stability of a structure than is commonly believed. Most traditional architects agree that any building can be toppled by extremes of weather, shoddy construction, everyday wear and tear, and perhaps more insidious factors, such as airborne sulfur dioxide, sulfates, nitrogen oxides, and nitrates, but these factors do not explain the dozens of structures that collapse every day for no apparent reason. That's where *anarchitecture* comes in, the architecture of anarchy.

Anarchitecture was first proposed as a science by the Irish prodigy Artemis Fowl the Second and was elaborated upon by his younger sibling Myles Fowl when he snuck into his older brother's lecture at Trinity College and heckled him from the audience. Myles found Artemis's theories laughably simplistic and took it upon himself to write a more comprehensive thesis and beam it to his brother in space, finishing his message with the old Latin initialism QED, which usually means *quod erat demonstrandum*, or *thus it has been shown*, but which Myles adapted to stand for **Q**uite **E**lementary, **D**ear brother.

The basic premise of anarchitecture is as follows: There are many more factors affecting the soundness of a building than previously suspected. These include the rotation and orbit of the Earth, cosmic gravitational influences, magnetic fields, water and tide levels, lea lines, the curvature of the planet, solar flares, atmospheric radiation, tectonic shifts, the design of the building itself, the spirituality levels of the population, the diets and emissions of local mammals, and the density of dance venues in the area. According to Myles's calculations, there were over a thousand major structures, including complexes and even whole towns in Europe, that were on the tipping point of collapse and could, with only a single added factor, one day be either partially or completely demolished. So Myles, in all good conscience, had sent a copy of his list of sites to the board members of each complex, and for his trouble was either ignored or ridiculed. One reason for this scorn was his hypothetical scenario that if the chorus line of *Riverdance* danced in Piazza San Marco at a rate of twenty-five taps per second for seventeen minutes, the entire city of Venice would sink into the Adriatic.

However, all those who had scoffed at anarchitecture were about to have their scoffs stuffed down their throats, for Myles was now intent on proving his theories in spectacular fashion. One of the more anarchitecturally susceptible buildings on his list was Amsterdam's striking EYE Film Museum, which Myles had positively pestered with warning e-mails, all of which had been met with polite automatic responses. But, if Myles's calculations were correct, then it should be possible for him to both vindicate his reputation and buy the Regrettables a little time.

Currently Beckett was pleading with his brother for permission to deploy the battering ram.

"Commando, M? B bam-bam?" he said, speaking in Fowl Argot, hoping the familiarity would sway Myles.

Commando being how the toddler twins used to say *come on* or *please*.

"I am sorry, brother mine," said Myles firmly. "We have

one chance, and the blow must be struck with pinpoint accuracy."

"I *am* pinpoint!" argued Beckett. "Didn't you see those cluster punches?"

"Humans and buildings follow different rules," said Myles. "You do have a certain undeniable instinct with bio-logical forms, but buildings must be left to me."

Lazuli stood behind the brothers with the battering ram resting heavy across her collarbone. She felt more exposed than she'd ever been, and this was, in fact, the correct way for Specialist Heitz to feel as an unshielded fairy in a European city with a growing crowd across the water wait-ing for the morning ferry.

"Humans," she snapped, "get to it! Those amphibious craft are dangerously close."

"Of course, Specialist," said Myles. "My apologies." He tapped the arm of his spectacles. "NANNI, using my anar-chitecture algorithms, mark the nexus of catastrophe with a laser."

Beckett elbowed Lazuli. "The nexus of catastrophe. That is so Myles. That's like Myles's entire life right there."

Even NANNI was doubtful. "Of course, Myles," said the AI. "But you do know, don't you, that it can never succeed? Artemis only invented the science of anarchitecture to keep you from discovering his real work."

Myles shook his head. "Poor Artemis. I feel sorry for him, really, with his cloning and space rockets. Well, I am about to prove him and the entire scientific community wrong."

Myles smirked. "Which I predict will become a quite common occurrence."

Lazuli rolled the battering ram off her shoulder. "I'm just going to set this off and hope."

"No!" said Myles. "This is a delicate experiment. Accuracy is paramount."

A laser shot out of Myles's spectacles and quickly scorched a circle in the stone above their heads, a circle with exactly the same radius as the battering ram's business end.

"Very well, Myles," said NANNI. "But it is my duty as your protector to say that I think you are squandering this opportunity to escape."

"We shall see," said Myles. "Now, if you please, Specialist Heitz, the battering ram."

The scorched circle was above the Regrettables' head height in the slanted underside of the EYE Film Museum's white stone. The museum was a futuristic and deservedly famous landmark perched at the waterside on the IJ Promenade. It could be described as a cross between a Kaiju cricket and the solidified speed trails of a rocket booster. The main structure sat atop a giant plinth that operated as the building's lobby and restaurant, or *would* operate as such in a few hours, when the institute opened for business. But for the moment, the only beings in the environs were the mixed-species group that we shall continue to refer to as the Regrettables for the sake of convenience.

The amphibious ACRONYM vehicles were powering across the harbor, and it would only be a matter of half a minute before they reached dry land, at which point it seemed fairly certain that the agents' longer legs would ensure that the subsequent chase would be brief and humiliating.

Myles hefted the battering ram, carefully lining up its rim with the inscribed circle, and he was about to press the red button on the hilt when Beckett asked:

"Brother, you know I don't usually worry about stuff like danger, but should we be standing under this ginormous building?"

Myles smiled. "Do not fret, Beck. This is the safest place to be."

Specialist Heitz giggled.

She couldn't help it. This entire scenario was so outlandish that it couldn't possibly be happening. She had heard tales about Artemis Fowl and his exploits with the LEP, but no one in the Academy actually believed them. Not word for word. The People loved to embellish, and Lazuli always thought the Fowl stories were simply not very convincing exaggerations. But now she was standing under a building with a child who was determined to demolish it with a tube of metal.

Myles arched one of the eyebrows that, for some reason, Clippers had neglected to shave. "Is there a problem, Specialist?" he asked.

"Oh no," said Lazuli. "Go ahead and knock down a huge solid building with a metal pipe."

Myles scowled, one of his default expressions. Most people scowl perhaps twice a week, but he spent a large proportion of his day with his features twisted in displeasure. This was his lot as a misunderstood genius.

"I am not going to knock down the building," he said. "I am going to disassemble it."

And with the kind of flair he always claimed to despise, Myles Fowl pressed the red button and activated the charge in the battering ram's base, which sent a metal column thumping into the institute's undercarriage with a force of two thousand newtons, which is a piddling amount in the grand scheme of things.

And nothing happened.

"Hmm," said NANNI. "It seems as though I have learned how to be self-satisfied. So, Myles, can I say I told you so?"

"Wait," said Myles, unperturbed by the seemingly abject failure of his experiment. "These things take time."

Not too much time, was the general hope, as time was not a luxury they possessed at that moment.

"I should have done it," said Beckett, sulking now. "You know I break things better than you."

"Not breaking, brother," said Myles. "Deconstructing."

And, as if to punctuate his claim, there came a *crack* from deep inside the building like a single nervous peal of thunder, and the enormous top section of the EYE Film Museum, with hardly any ado, separated from the plinth, and megatons of concrete, steel, and glass slid into the harbor. It took perhaps twelve seconds from start to finish, and it made about as much noise as a semitruck driving along a gravel driveway. The Regrettables were showered with a fine dust but otherwise completely unaffected. The museum, because of its streamlined shape, cleaved the water, raising not enough of a wake to capsize a child's dinghy. It was, as a DeVries shipyard worker witness later observed, reminiscent of a controlled launch, as though the EYE Film Museum was always meant to be a super-yacht, albeit one that sank almost immediately, forming a new dam that blocked the harbor, effectively cutting off the ACRONYM agents' pursuit.

"There," said Myles with some satisfaction, as if he had just managed to open a stubborn jar. "That should do the trick for the moment."

Beckett stood in slack-jawed wonder at the destruction his brother had wrought. Destruction that was at once devastating and precise, on a scale he could only dream of, and all without hurting a single soul.

"Myles," he said, "I am prepared to admit now that sometimes brains are good."

"It's about time," said Myles, and they bumped wrists.

CHAPTER 8

MR. CIRCUITS AND WHOOP

SHORTLY our heroes will squabble over who exactly is in charge; make some eye-opening discoveries about the toy troll, who will actually open his eyes; and embark on the next leg of their quest, which will involve a white-tip shark, unexpected ejections, and a train journey. But let us for a moment return to the ACRONYM black site and witness the unlikely bonding of our tale's less inspiring examples of humankind.

If we travel as Specialist Heitz might elect to if her circuits were fully regenerated, it takes mere minutes to soar over the harbor, skimming the roof of the EYE Film Museum, which has already been boarded by enthusiastic swimmers, who are utilizing its jutting planes as makeshift diving boards. Slightly farther on, we pass over the morning crowds congregating in irate swells at the main station, and it is but a skip of a stone from there to a tavern that closed its doors hours ago. But that is of no matter to us, as we can pass through the stone walls and descend into the ancient subterranean cathedral below. There we find several incapacitated ACRONYM agents, who will shortly shrug off the paralyzing effects of Beckett Fowl's cluster-punch binge, or the elastic restraint of Lord Bleedham-Drye's CV slugs.

In addition, there are two figures who are relatively mobile: Lord Teddy Bleedham-Drye, the Duke of Scilly, and Sister Jeronima Gonzalez-Ramos de Zárate of Bilbao, chief of the Amsterdam headquarters for ACRONYM. Colorful characters both, and with a common goal: Find the Fowl Twins by any means necessary or possible. Normally these two would never consider a joint venture, especially since Lord Teddy had actually infiltrated ACRONYM, but needs and fate were about to make these two unsavory characters indispensable to each other.

When Lord Teddy came upon Sister Jeronima, the nun was screaming in Spanish at her wristwatch, which was linked to her agents' body cams. Initially, Lord Teddy could have sworn she was howling some lyrics from Verdi's *Rigoletto*, which happened to be one of his favorite modern operas, mainly because it featured a duke in a leading role.

Sister Jeronima calmed a little and switched to English. "Catch them, can't you?" she said. "They are little children!"

"But most impressive little children," interjected Lord Teddy, sliding into the room along one wall, his face ashen, his arm dangling oddly, the way the arm of a loosely strung puppet might, the fingers of one hand spasming uncontrollably.

Jeronima looked up to see a magnificently bearded, glaring man displaying none of the usual deference to her rank.

"But who are you, señor? Not one of mine."

"Certainly not one of *yours*," snapped Teddy, displaying his customary lack of interpersonal skills. "The very idea. *Yours* are idiots. Because of *yours*, my prize has escaped with those boys."

Perhaps it was pain that caused Teddy to leak this extra nugget of information to a trained interrogator.

"*With* those boys?" said Jeronima. "So the twins themselves do not interest you?"

"No more than they interest you, madam," said Teddy. "They are a means to an end."

"To what end?" asked Jeronima.

The duke's expression was equal parts smile and grimace. "I do apologize, Sister, but your interrogating days are over, as we are both on the same trail and I cannot tolerate a rival. In these situations, a hunter takes off the head of the snake, and you are most definitely the Medusa of this particular clandestine serpent."

Jeronima was not just an interrogator, but a skilled negotiator, which is another branch of the same talent. "Why would you kill me when I have so much to offer?"

Teddy was in too much pain for strategies. "One way or the other, Sister," he said, plucking Jeronima's own knife from the door with his functioning hand, "you will come to the point."

"We have eyes on the fugitives, señor," said Jeronima hurriedly.

"Show me these alleged eyes," Teddy demanded.

Jeronima tapped the screen on her watch, which opened a dozen displays on the smartwall nearby. Each monitor showed the feed from an ACRONYM agent's body cam. Most of the screens were black, and the rest displayed a view of the harbor that seemed to be blocked by a huge building.

Both villains took a moment to let this enormity and its implications sink in. Neither doubted that the twins had somehow been responsible for this natural-disaster-level development.

"Well, I never," said Lord Teddy finally. "Those Fowls are not to be underestimated, make no mistake. It would seem as though your *eyes on* have been neutralized. In fact, it would seem that there are no *eyes on*. And so, without further ado . . ."

Sister Jeronima saw the light flash on her own blade as Lord Teddy stepped closer, but she had been in tight spots before and so turned another card. "Those niños are bugged. There is nowhere on this planet they can go where I cannot track them."

This gave Lord Teddy pause. After all, his own tracker had a range of only five hundred miles.

"Very well. One more chance at life, Sister. Demonstrate, if you please."

Jeronima used her free hand to refresh the home screen on her watch, which had the effect, though she could not know it, of opening the malware NANNI had e-mailed to her and her contacts.

Her regular home screen winked out and was replaced by a *Tron*-style Myles Fowl avatar that knocked on an invisible door and repeated a phrase from "The Three Little Pigs": "Knock, knock, won't you please let me in?"

"But what is this?" wondered Sister Jeronima as Myles's avatar took over the wall screens.

"Knock, knock," said laser-etched Myles, "won't you please let me in?"

Lord Teddy was almost amused. This Myles fellow had quite the bag of techno-tricks. "It would appear, Sister, that you have been hacked."

"No!" said Jeronima, jabbing the watch's screen. "Es imposible."

The on-screen Myles clapped his shining hands. "Thank you," he said. "I am in."

The avatar was replaced by a tiny whirlpool and the vortex sucked down every last byte of information from the ACRONYM server.

Jeronima bashed her watch against the table, as if that could stop anything.

"No, no, no!" she said. There was no doubt now that this facility's cover was completely blown, at the very least. She would be the first ACRONYM chief to have lost a site, not to mention a live fairy.

"No eyes on," said Lord Teddy. "And now no trackers. I fear you are of little use to me."

Jeronima was running out of cards to play, but she was not beaten yet.

"I have boats," she said.

"I will see your boats and raise you a flying machine," said Teddy, holding the blade to Jeronima's throat, where it cast a yellow glow under her chin like a buttercup flower might, but without the same cheery implication. Lord Bleedham-Drye grunted as he leaned in for the kill, and it was his grunt that saved Jeronima's neck.

"But you are having the lesión," she said. "An injury."

Lord Teddy did not need to confirm this verbally—the sheen of sweat on his brow did it for him.

Jeronima forged ahead. "I would think that your shoulder is dislocated, señor. This is no amateur diagnosis, as I am also a nurse. I can fix that in un minuto. And there are keys to these cuffs in the locker."

Lord Teddy considered this proposal. He was holding most of the cards, but he would be holding them one-handed, and while a man with only a single working hand *could* fly the Myishi Skyblade, it would certainly restrict his efficiency. Even with his arm back in place, he would be in serious discomfort.

Jeronima rubber-stamped the deal with "And, naturala-mente, I can fly a plane."

"Very well," said the duke, removing the blade from the vicinity of Jeronima's jugular vein and sticking it into the tabletop with some considerable force. "We shall coop-erate, but I will be claiming the boy's toy troll as my prize."

"Agreed," said Jeronima, wondering what on earth this man could want with a toy. Perhaps it was a rare collectible. "And I'll take the fairy creature to do with as I wish."

They shook—Teddy's good hand to Sister Jeronima's untethered one.

And so was born an unholy alliance that would indeed ultimately succeed in the capture of both fairies, though that particular operation would cost one of them dearly.

From the Overhoeks side of the harbor, Myles Fowl gazed upon the devastation he had wrought and was of two minds about it. There was no denying that it was satisfying to have his theory of anarchitecture proven beyond any reasonable doubt, but it was also true he was experiencing destroyer's remorse and regretted the necessity of deconstructing such a beautiful building. Surely there must have been another way to both buy the group some breathing space and satisfy his scientific curiosity, but right at this moment Myles couldn't think of anything that would have been more effective in the time frame, and he was grateful that they were still alive. All three of them.

Beckett stood at his shoulder. "Was that the moral thing to do?" he said, which surprised Myles, as Beckett usually operated on the same moral level as a wild animal.

A dog does what it has to do, Beckett often said. *And sometimes what a dog has to do is doo-doo.*

Which Myles suspected was deeper than it sounded. The sentiment, not the doo-doo.

"What did you say, brother?" Myles asked, taken aback.

"I said, I never want to quarrel with you."

"Oh," said Myles. "My remorse twisted your words."

Beckett also felt remorse, but only because he had missed the opportunity to surf the harbor using the sliding EYE Film Museum as a board.

"Remorse? That was awesome and radical!" he said to Myles in surfing lingo, as that was where his mind was.

"You are correct, brother mine," said Myles. "Though not in the way you think. My actions were indeed awesome and radical in the true senses of those terms, not their popular interpretations."

Beckett patted his brother's shoulder. "You should have stopped talking sooner. Just after you said I was correct."

Lazuli interrupted their EYE postmortem. "Fowl Twins, we must leave this place."

"Of course, Princess," said Beckett, bowing.

"Do not call me Princess," said Lazuli. "It is most patronizing."

"Specialist Heitz is right," said Myles, compartmentalizing his remorse. "The new dam will delay ACRONYM for perhaps thirty minutes, presuming they do not have aerial support. NANNI?"

The Nano Artificial Neural Network Intelligence system used the official Amsterdam Radar site to check local airspace.

"Several helicopters are converging on the harbor. None have filed flight plans."

"News choppers, I would suspect," said Myles. "But one never knows, as I doubt ACRONYM ever submits flight plans. We must leave immediately."

"This is what I have been telling you," said Lazuli, who was feeling exposed and jumpy. "Before you began conversing with your spectacles."

"Please remain calm, Specialist," said Myles. "NANNI informs me that your heart rate is elevated." He paused. "In fact, both of your heart rates are elevated."

And lo, like a bolt of white lightning from a clear Alpine sky, the truth struck Myles.

"Oh, my goodness!" he said, striking a melodramatic Peter Pan pose. "This is all about Whistle Blower."

"My toy?" said Beckett doubtfully. "All this for a toy?"

Myles tapped his spectacles to run a thermal scan and could plainly see the second heartbeat beside Lazuli's own.

"But Whistle Blower is no toy," said Myles. "I am correct, am I not, Specialist Heitz?"

Lazuli's only response was to clasp a protective hand over the toy-troll-shaped bulge in her tunic.

Beckett actually jumped for joy. "Whistle Blower is real! I knew it, then I forgot it, and now I know it again. Thank you, Princess Blue Fairy."

Specialist Heitz, not being familiar with humans, wondered if they were all so extreme in their behaviors. Lazuli recalled a computer game that had been popular in the Academy in which a robot and a monkey collected diamonds that were converted into laser eye-blasts when the two creatures battled one another. The humorless robot and plucky monkey were named Mr. Circuits and Whoop respectively. Lazuli could not help but be reminded of those characters now, looking at the Fowl double act, and would only have been mildly surprised if laser blasts had started shooting from their eyeballs.

"My name," she said, "is not Princess Blue Fairy. It is Lazuli. Like the precious stone."

"Semiprecious," corrected Myles before he could stop himself, and so he added, "I refer to the metamorphic rock, of course, not yourself. Your own worth is beyond doubt."

He had no wish to antagonize the fairy. The fact that Specialist Heitz had revealed her first name was a major step forward in the trust process, and Myles had an inkling that Beckett had teased the information from her on purpose.

Fortunately, Beckett distracted Lazuli from the "semi-precious" comment with a question. "Can I call you Laser?"

"No," said the pixel firmly. "Unless I can call you Whoop."

"Would you?" asked Beckett.

"Not a chance," replied the pixel. "Now I am leaving. You may accompany me if you wish."

Myles looked across the harbor, his spectacles enhancing his view. One of the amphibious ACRONYM craft had docked at the EYE Film Museum and two agents were scaling the structure, undoubtedly planning to swim to them.

"We should depart," said Myles, "for time is precious and seconds are fleeting."

Lazuli thought that the human boy was wasting a lot of time telling her how precious time was.

"Finally," she said. "Where to?"

"Far away from here," said Myles. "But perhaps not too quickly. They will be expecting haste, and so we shall proceed at our leisure."

Lazuli felt as though she might foam at the mouth. Were all humans this frustrating?

Beckett punched the air. "The Regrettables are on the move."

The Regrettables, thought Specialist Heitz. I couldn't have said it better.

The leisurely route chosen by Myles Fowl was for a self-driving electric SUV Uber, which pulled into the squat Collection Building adjacent to the EYE plinth precisely twelve minutes after it was summoned, and precisely two minutes before the Amsterdam police arrived from Centrum Jordaan to throw a cordon around the entire facility. Specialist Heitz did not bother to duck down in the rear seat, as the Tesla had smoked windows and she was too small to be seen out of them anyway. As soon as they were far away from the city center, past the beauty of its famous suburban network of tranquil canals and rolling fields of tulips that had so inspired the genius Vincent van Gogh, they pulled over behind a windmill typical of the region and gave their attention to another genius, one who was on his way to Mars.

Myles projected the video file directly onto the windmill from his smart spectacles and the outer wall flickered like the screen in an old-time movie theater. Artemis Fowl the Second appeared on the whitewash and spoke to his brothers as though he were actually there with them and not traversing the more than thirty million miles between Earth and Mars. Of course, this video had been shot in Artemis's own office before takeoff, so the picture was of the highest quality, though distorted somewhat by the curved wall.

Artemis was no longer a child prodigy, having put his teen years behind him. He was now a young genius destined to change not just Earth but other worlds, too. He was sitting in his beloved Eames office chair wearing a lab coat buttoned up to his throat. As usual, his brow was knotted in a frown as he wrestled with some puzzle or other. In one of his rare interviews, Artemis had revealed to *Time* magazine, in his Man of the Year piece, that through meditation he had succeeded in harnessing his subconscious so that he could more efficiently work on projects while he slept, which, as the interviewer pointed out, subverted the entire point of meditation.

But, on-screen, Artemis's frown lines softened and he revealed a side of himself reserved for a very select few. His expression could almost be described as fond.

"Myles and Beckett," he said. "My brothers."

The twins responded as though they were part of a conversation.

"Greetings from Earth, Dr. Fowl," said Myles, using

Artemis's title, which had been earned three times over—at Trinity, UCLA, and, more recently, MIT, for astrophysics.

"Hey, Arty," said Beckett, ever more casual than either of his brothers. In fact, he was the only one to refer to their parents as *Mum* and *Dad,* as opposed to Artemis's *Mother* and *Father* and Myles's occasional Latin versions, *Mater* and *Pater.*

Artemis's smile widened as though he had heard the greetings; in reality, he had probably just anticipated them.

"This erstwhile hidden video has been unlocked because NANNI's facial-recognition software has scanned the features of a fairy," explained the eldest Fowl brother. "Not a representation, but an actual fairy, which means that you have made contact with one of the People. In this case, a"—the video paused for a split second and NANNI inserted a scan of Lazuli's head—"pixel," continued Artemis. "How marvelous. I myself have never met a pixel."

"Her name is Lazuli, Arty," said Beckett. "Like the precious stone."

"Semiprecious," said Myles, for the sake of accuracy.

"I could talk for hours about fairies and their magics," said Artemis. "But in the interest of possible urgency, I will curtail my lecture. . . ."

"That's a relief," muttered Myles to Beckett. "You know how Artemis can jabber on."

Even Lazuli, who had only properly met Myles Fowl some hours previously, knew irony when she heard it, even in a foreign language.

"All I will tell you now is what you absolutely need to

know," continued Artemis. "And you need to know that those stories I told you about the Fairy People are true. Every word. It is imperative that you trust the fairy folk. The Fowls have long been friends to the People." Artemis clasped his hands together in imitation of a handshake. "Fowl and fairy, friends forever."

"Also, sharing is caring," said Beckett.

"So, if a fairy needs assistance, it is your duty to provide it."

"We're already doing that, Artemis," said Myles. Then: "Honestly, if this is the short version—"

"Also, it is vital that you are aware of another fact," said Artemis. "Some years ago, you were both possessed by the ghosts of dead fairies, so it is possible that a remnant of magic lingers in your systems. This magic could theoretically manifest itself in any number of ways."

Beckett froze like he'd been fossilized, his eyes wide.

"Did Artemis just say we're superheroes?" he breathed after a stunned moment.

"It could be nothing," said Artemis. "And you're certainly not any kind of superheroes, but if anything strange happens, keep an account, and then try to re-create the manifestation under laboratory conditions."

Beckett decided that the only word he would take from that sentence would be *superheroes.*

"I knew it!" he said. "We're superheroes. And we already have a team name: the Regrettables."

"Your plan of action," continued Artemis, "should be

to get the fairy and yourselves somewhere safe, and then study the rest of the videos in this unlocked folder at your leisure, as the information contained therein will doubtless save your lives."

"*Therein?*" Myles said with a snort. "Where are we? Medieval England?"

On-screen, a blocky shadow grew an arm and beckoned. And Lazuli saw that what she had assumed to be an enormous cabinet was actually an enormous human.

That must be the famous Butler, she realized. The human who could best a troll. A regular-size troll.

"Coming, Butler," said Artemis, then he leaned in close to the camera so his pale face filled the screen.

"The Red Planet beckons, brothers," he said. "I must be away. Take care of yourselves and your new friend. And get a message to me as soon as you can, because I do worry."

Myles rolled his eyes. "Artemis is so emotional."

"If history has taught us anything," said Artemis, "it is that Earth always needs saving, and it is usually a Fowl who saves it. This might very well be your turn."

"We can do it, Arty," said Beckett. "The Regrettables save the day."

"I know you can do it," concluded Artemis. "Good-bye and good luck."

"Good-bye, Doctor," said Myles. "And good luck to you."

The video disappeared, leaving just the Fowl OX system logo on the wall.

"Well," said Myles brightly, "that was long-winded. But

Artemis was correct in that our first order of business is to get somewhere safe."

"No," said Lazuli, pulling the troll from inside her green tunic. "First we need to release this poor troll."

"About that," said Myles. "When we do release the troll, how calm is he likely to be?"

"Calm?" said Lazuli. "Trolls are not known for their calm, but we might be able to restrain him, between the three of us. At worst one might be partially eaten while the other two escape."

"Partially eaten, you say, mademoiselle?" said Myles. "Just how much trouble can one tiny troll be?"

"Pound for pound, trolls are the third-strongest creatures on the planet, after dung beetles and rhinoceros beetles. Full-grown trolls have been known to take on entire prides of lions. This toy troll could, theoretically, reduce our vehicle to slivers of twisted metal."

Myles swallowed, imagining the Tesla torn asunder, but Beckett was not the least bit nervous.

"Don't worry about Whistle Blower," he said. "I'll talk to him."

His brother's typical confidence did little to reassure Myles that they would not all be torn to pieces the very second Whistle Blower was unbound.

"I suggest, Specialist," he said, "that we find a distraction to occupy the little fellow's mind when we release him."

"Agreed," said Lazuli. She looked around. "Fortunately, there are cows nearby if things get out of hand."

Myles had a queasy certainty about what would happen to the livestock. "Very well. Then let us proceed."

Lazuli laid Whistle Blower on the grass and poked the cellophane. "Does your huge intellect know how we remove this coating from around the troll?"

Myles did not need to consult NANNI for this information, as he made it his business to stay abreast of the latest technological developments, even for weapons used by those on the wrong side of the law.

"I believe we are dealing with what is known in criminal parlance as a shrink-wrapper, or CV slug. One of Ishi Myishi's best-selling nonlethal projectiles. Usually fired from gas-powered weapons and activated on impact by an electric charge supplied by a tiny battery in the shell. They are the chosen weapon of the new millennium's discerning poacher."

"You wouldn't happen to know what year this Myishi person's grandmother was born?" asked Lazuli, growing impatient with the Fowl boy's penchant for extended lectures. "Or whether or not he has any pets?"

Beckett snickered. "Pets. Nice one, Laser."

"The cocoon is usually stripped away in a vat of an acetone solution, which renders the cellophane brittle," continued Myles, accustomed to his presentations being interrupted.

"I'm presuming you can rig something, boy?" said Lazuli. "Your super-duper spectacles don't have any acetone in them, I suppose?"

"No acetone," said Myles. "But perhaps one might improvise."

Five minutes later, they were in position. Beckett was extremely comfortable in this position, as it involved dangling from the windmill's crossed diagonal ceiling beams, while the toy troll was laid out on the compacted clay floor fifteen feet below. Myles was less comfortable, as he was an enthusiastic member of the small club of eleven-year-olds who enjoyed neither heights nor climbing. In fact, the one and only T-shirt Myles had ever owned had borne the legend DEATH BEFORE JUNGLE GYMS. And Myles had insisted on wearing it to activity classes in kindergarten—over his suit jacket, obviously.

Lazuli was also feeling anxious, but it had nothing to do with heights. If anything, she would prefer to be higher, and thus farther away from the little troll. She had tackled a few toy trolls in simulations and had always ended up the worse for wear, virtually speaking. Trolls would generally not kill another fairy, but this one had been assaulted and had probably been fuming inside his cellophane cocoon for the past few hours. But she had no choice but to release him. Her duty to the troll was paramount, and the cellophane wrap was squeezing him to death.

"If this scheme works—" she began.

"Of course it will work," Myles interrupted, irritated by the fairy's lack of faith. "Do you not remember the harbor? Do you not remember the double twin swap? My ideas always work. It is the very essence of my personality."

"*When* this scheme works," said Lazuli, to keep the peace, "the troll will probably throw a major tantrum and hammer on the walls a little. After that, he will hopefully wander outside and hide until dark and then forage for food. With any luck, my circuits will have regrown by then and I'll be able to call for backup."

Myles was interested in spite of a sudden onset of vertigo. "Your circuits can regrow? Your society has developed sophisticated bioelectronics?"

"Yes," said Lazuli. "And outdoor toilets. Now, can we please get on with it? I believe we are fugitives. And this area will not stay deserted forever."

"Very well," said Myles, and he tapped the arm of his spectacles.

"Proceed with Operation: Freedom Troll," he said with some chagrin; Beckett had insisted they name the procedure.

"Very well, Myles," said NANNI. "Operation: Freedom Troll is a go. Stay completely still."

Artemis had built a laser pointer into Myles's spectacles, but the presentation tool was not of industrial strength, as he did not consider death lasers suitable add-ons to an eleven-year-old's eyewear. Myles had thought it hilarious that his criminal-mastermind big brother was attempting to police him, and he immediately set to upgrading his laser. It had taken Myles barely an afternoon to hack the spectacles and add a 3-D-printed lens no thicker than a human hair, which allowed him to both perform laser eye surgery on himself and focus the beam to such an extent that it could burn through sheet steel or scorch a stone target if need be. But the ten kilojoules needed per burst would generally require a power source the size of a baby elephant. Luckily, Myles had managed to squeeze that amount of energy into a tiny battery/super-capacitor combo, but after this shot, there would be no more lasers without a long recharge.

Myles lay flat on his stomach on the intersection of two ancient wooden beams, pointing his spectacles at Whistle Blower on the ground directly below. He was loath to cede control of any operation, but in this instance he left the calculations to NANNI, as he found that even with his perfect lasered eyesight, his best guess for distances was usually accurate to the nearest centimeter only. An operation like this required millimeter accuracy. The Artificial Intelligence mapped the troll's frame, figuring the minimum burn required to completely collapse the cellophane cocoon.

"In three . . ." she said to Myles, a countdown flashing on his lens.

Myles took a deep breath and stayed absolutely still, hoping that the centuries-old beams would not shift under their weight.

"Two . . ." said NANNI. Then, obviously: "One . . ."

Myles saw a red flash out of the corner of his left eye, heard a sizzle, and then it was over.

It seemed to the three beam-bound fugitives that nothing much had happened. A small wisp of acrid smoke wafted from Whistle Blower's midsection, but the cocoon seemed intact.

"Wait for it," said NANNI, and five seconds later the cellophane skin split down the middle and Whistle Blower was hatched into the world.

"Nobody move," said Lazuli.

Nobody did move, including the troll, who, it seemed, was asleep.

"Vitals?" asked Myles.

"Steady," replied NANNI. "Relaxed heart rate. I detect a chloroform-based compound in the sheath, which suggests the troll is slightly sedated."

Myles relayed this information, and Lazuli nodded. "Makes sense. I have never even heard of a troll being this calm. They are light sleepers and react to the slightest stimulus."

Beckett was bored. "Hey!" he called down to the toy troll. "Come on, Whistle Blower, let's get going. Hey, sleepyhead!"

Lazuli could not believe what she was hearing. "Quiet, human! Never startle a troll."

Beckett, who was straddling a wooden beam in the windmill, locked his ankles and inverted himself, his arms dangling toward the ground. "I find in these situations that the direct approach is best."

"These situations?" hissed Lazuli. "You've been in these situations?"

Myles pleaded with his brother. "Beck, come back up," he said. "This isn't one of your talking-with-the-animals games."

Beckett winked at his brother, which looked a little weird upside down. "Everything is a game, brother." And he reached over and tugged off Myles's shoe.

"Don't do that," said Myles. "Beckett, don't."

"Don't do what?" asked Lazuli, hoping she was wrong about what she guessed the human was about to do.

She was not wrong. Beckett closed one eye, took aim, and dropped the shoe toward Whistle Blower.

Myles saw the shoe land squarely on Whistle Blower's chest, or rather he anticipated it landing on the troll's chest, for that was not what actually happened. What did actually happen was that both of the troll's hands whipped up and caught the shoe, which was as big as his torso, and, with little apparent effort, disemboweled it of tongue and laces. For good measure, he stuffed those pieces in his mouth.

"That shoe was military grade," said Myles weakly. "Kevlar and rubber. You couldn't cut that with a band saw. Have you any idea how many pounds of force it would take to rip that shoe apart?"

Lazuli realized that Myles was babbling, but she did not want Myles to stop talking, as his voice distracted her from thoughts of their immediate future now that the troll had been more or less attacked by a human.

The toy troll opened his tiny eyes, and there was a lot more menace in them than one might think could fit into such small orbs. The teeth also were not friendly.

"He's fine," said Beckett. "I'm grumpy when I wake up, too."

But this was more than simple grumpiness. The troll chewed Myles's deceased sneaker's parts into a stringy mush and spat it into the air, which was a bad move, because gravity caused the black mush to reverse its path and land with a bird-poo-type *splat* on his own forehead.

Beckett laughed. "I'm always doing that with toothpaste," he said.

The boy's laugh galvanized the troll. He leaped to his feet, wiping the mess from his forehead, and unleashed a long undulating howl that reminded Myles of the lead singer in a heavy metal band he had once been forced to listen to in an attempt to make a friend. That friendship did not make it past recess, and it seemed as though this one might not survive the howling stage, either.

"That's right, Whistle Blower," said Beckett. "Give me something to work with."

"Your brother is remarkably calm," said Lazuli, wishing her wings were operational instead of scrolled inside her rig. Trolls couldn't fly, but they could jump to remarkable heights.

"Beckett is generally calm. Infuriatingly so on several occasions most days."

As if to belie Myles's words, Beckett actually snapped at his twin: "Quiet, brother! I am trying to work here."

And so surprised was Myles by Beckett's use of the verb *work* that he actually obeyed the order.

Whistle Blower, on the other hand, was only getting started on the verbalizing. The diminutive troll threw a growling tantrum that would put a group of sugar-blitzed toddlers to shame. He roared and howled, stomping his feet as though crushing invisible ants, and when he was finished with the earthen floor, he started in on the walls, punching dents in the plaster.

This ought to be funny, thought Myles. There's a real live action figure having a rage fit inside an old windmill.

But it wasn't funny or even mildly amusing; in fact, it was downright worrying, because when the toy troll was finished punching the walls, he began scoring long gouges in them with his claws.

"Ha!" said Beckett. "Whistle Blower is playing tic-tac-toe."

While Beckett found this funny, Myles was worried about the building's structural integrity.

Could this tiny troll actually collapse the windmill with all of us still inside it?

"Specialist Heitz," he whispered with some urgency in his tone, "I do hate to second-guess your expertise in this area, but is it possible that freeing the troll in this confined space was the wrong move?"

Lazuli had to admit that she might have underestimated the tiny troll's sheer destructive power.

"It is possible," she said. "But we're safe up here. I can't believe such a tiny creature could bring down an entire building. In all the simulations I've seen—"

"Simulations?" Myles felt compelled to interrupt. "Don't you have actual experience with toy trolls?"

Lazuli wondered if perhaps she should have mentioned this before endangering everyone.

"No one has actual experience with toy trolls. They are extremely rare. Many fairies don't even believe they exist."

And as all this whispered conversation was going on, Beckett had decided that he'd heard enough from Whistle Blower and it was time to make his move. His move being to unlock his ankles and swing himself to the floor below, landing with a small *thump*.

Lazuli was speechless, but Myles was not.

"Beck," he said with only the slightest tremor in his voice, "I cannot believe you did that."

"I know, brother," said Beckett spreading his arms. "Perfect landing. Gold medal for sure, maybe even platinum."

Myles was equal parts incensed and terrified. "Not the landing—going down there! Come back up this instant, Beckett C. Fowl!"

In fact, neither Myles nor Beckett had a middle initial, but inserting one in his twin's name was a device Myles sometimes used to pique Beckett's interest, as his brother would often stop whatever he was doing to make a list of possible names the fake initial might stand for. The more outlandish the name, the better. Beckett's favorite invented middle initial for this game was *C*, which he once decided stood for *Counterclockwise*, and at the time Myles had to admit that *Beckett Counterclockwise Fowl* did have a certain ring to it and summed up his personality quite succinctly. Beckett had also declared that Myles should be henceforth known as Myles B. Fowl, with the *B* standing for *Blah-Blah-Blah*, which surprised Myles, who could not believe that Beck had used the term *henceforth*.

The middle-initial trick did not work on this occasion.

"Can't hear you, Myles," said Beckett, "because I'm not listening."

Incredibly, the troll did not seem to notice the human behaving irresponsibly behind him, and he continued slashing at the walls until daylight peeked through from outside.

Beckett was impatient to be noticed, and so he performed a lengthy throat clearing, or at least that's what it sounded like to the beam-bound Myles.

The toy troll froze in mid-slash and turned slowly to face his human tormentor.

"D'Arvit," whispered Lazuli, wondering if she was about to be responsible for the dismemberment of a human boy.

"D'Arvit indeed," said Myles, setting his mind to work. "NANNI, can you laser the creature?"

NANNI vibrated through his cranium. "Negative, Myles. I am totally pooped."

Totally pooped? thought Myles. *That's hardly scientific. And far too casual. We will need to have a serious chat about boundaries and parameters once I save Beckett.*

"Can you at least project some autonomous sensory meridian response videos on the wall?" he asked the AI.

ASMR videos were short clips that were so pleasant to watch they caused what the internet termed *brain tingle*. Myles reasoned that perhaps they would distract the toy troll.

"Nope," said NANNI. "There's no network in here, and I don't have anything locally. Also, we need to talk about my hours. Don't I get a lunch hour? Or a bathroom break?"

"Why would you need a bathroom break?" Myles whispered. "And even if you did, this is hardly the time to negotiate it."

"Agreed," said NANNI. "Let's put a pin in that and come back to it."

While NANNI was speaking, Myles realized there was only one way to handle the developing situation at ground level.

I have to go down there.

Lazuli, it seemed, had come to the same conclusion, and from her boot she drew a small knife, which she would use only as a last resort.

"Stay right there," she ordered Myles. "I will try to subdue your brother."

As it happened, no intervention was necessary, for the troll seemed intrigued by Beckett's growling. More than intrigued, in fact. The creature was stunned and issued a series of short to mid-length barks.

Beckett responded with some barks of his own, and what could be described as an extended yodel. The toy troll seemed amazed, and he wasn't the only one.

Lazuli and Myles looked at each other.

"Are they . . . ?" began Myles.

"Can he . . . ?" rejoined Lazuli.

Two unfinished questions.

It sounded like the beginning of a country music duet.

Neither answered the other's unfinished question, because of the spectacle on the ground below. It was undeniable now that boy and beast were communicating. The grunts, yodels, and whoops grew ever more elaborate, and everything seemed to be going just fine until, in the blink of an eye, the troll's relaxed stance stiffened and he launched himself at Beckett, who fell back screaming.

Myles had never experienced a panic like the one he felt at that moment. It seemed as though an icy hand had reached deep inside him and was twisting his stomach. . . . But then he realized that Beckett was not screaming.

He was laughing.

There was a lot of dust in the air, so it was possible he was mistaken, but it seemed to Myles as though his brother was wrestling with the toy troll. The beast had retracted its claws and was playfully butting Beckett's stomach and landing soft punches. For his part, Beckett tried to catch hold of Whistle Blower, but the little fellow wriggled easily from his grasp. After several minutes of tussling, both play-fighters fell back, exhausted, on the floor. The toy troll pointed at Myles and growled something from the corner of his mouth. Beckett cracked up.

"Yes," he said. "That human's head does look like an egg."

Myles was astounded by this latest development, but not so stunned that he was speechless.

"Beck, did that toy troll really say my head looked like an egg?"

"No," admitted Beckett. "He said something much worse, but I would never use language like that."

Lazuli couldn't figure it out. "What's going on here, Fowl boy? Is your twin actually conversing with a toy troll? Even fairies with the gift of tongues haven't been able to speak with trolls. Not anymore really. Nothing more than basic commands."

Myles took a second to think and then announced, "It's like Beck said: He's a superhero."

"Explain, boy," ordered Lazuli, and even though Myles did not appreciate her tone, he did, because his love of Fowlsplaining trumped his authority issues.

"Dr. Fowl—that is, Artemis—reminded us that Beckett and I had once been possessed by ancient fairies. And I'm inferring from what you said that ancient fairies could converse with trolls. I would suggest that the subject—that is to say Beckett Fowl—has been imbued with that fairy's ability to communicate with all developed species. He is, in effect, a trans-species polyglot."

Lazuli's English was good, but not Myles-level good, so Beckett helped out.

"He means that I can talk to anyone and anything. I've been doing it for years, right under his nose. I've told him a million times."

"I admit that I was aware of Beckett's proficiency with languages," continued Myles, "but I never thought his various yippings and cawings with the island wildlife were anything more than Beckett being Beckett."

"It *was* Beckett being Beckett," said Beckett. "And I know, because I am Beckett."

"You can't argue with that," noted Lazuli.

Beckett tickled Whistle Blower's tummy, which obviously annoyed the troll, because he slapped away the boy's hands and growled.

"He says he's not a puppy," said Beckett. "He is a warrior troll. Whistle Blower, master of the underground world."

Myles cracked one of his rare jokes. "Master of the Napoleon complex is more like it."

Naturally, no one laughed, and Whistle Blower focused his beady eyes on Myles as though he understood.

"He's not going to attack anyone, is he, Beck?"

"I don't think so," said Beckett while the toy troll bounced on his stomach.

"Very well," said Myles. "Then we need to follow Artemis's advice and seek safe haven."

Lazuli had actually been thinking about that very thing now that it seemed carnage by troll had been averted for the moment. She checked the wrist readout on her suit. "My bio-circuitry is repairing itself. As soon as my equipment is operational, we can call in LEP Retrieval."

Myles nodded. "Then at least some of our problems will be solved, but we must assume that ACRONYM and Lord

Teddy Bleedham-Drye are closing in on our position even as we speak."

Myles closed his eyes, a little trick he'd picked up from Artemis to aid concentration. But he'd augmented it with his own invention of two tiny electrode pads in his spectacles' arms that would generate low-level charges to stimulate his hypothalamus, which some scientists associate with higher-level thought functions.

NANNI anticipated the request. "If you're looking for hypothalamus stimulation, you're out of luck, Myles. I can barely speak at this point."

Myles frowned. The first thing they needed to do was hide. Somewhere safe, where Sister Jeronima couldn't find them. Somewhere that for all intents and purposes didn't exist.

Myles opened his eyes and smiled.

He knew just the place.

CHAPTER 9
MUY INCONVENIENTE

SISTER Jeronima was as good as her word, as one might reasonably expect from a nun, and popped Lord Teddy's shoulder back into its socket on her first attempt. Truth be told, she was hoping the duke might be overcome by pain and pass out, which she intended to interpret as an annulment of their partnership, but Teddy gritted his square white teeth and bore the excruciating agony with no more than an exclamation of "Blimey" after the sharp blow from the flat of the nun's hand. Once his upper arm was reunited with his shoulder blade, Teddy swallowed some Tylenol from the dispensary and had Jeronima bind his shoulder tightly. The bandaging operation took less than five minutes, and then they were out of the black site and headed for the Skyblade craft. Jeronima estimated that they had perhaps another five minutes before the authorities traced the harbor disaster back to the site and moved in to find a dozen unconscious agents in the corridor.

Protocol would usually require Sister Jeronima to erase all hard drives before an evacuation, but Myles Fowl had already accomplished that for her. Myles Fowl had erased all ACRONYM files everywhere, except on his own computer.

I must catch that niño, she realized. He knows all our secrets.

ACRONYM was sanctioned by the governments of thirty-seven countries to operate inside their borders, but they were also mandated in twenty-eight of those countries to submit detailed reports for every operation on the books. At last count, Sister Jeronima herself was running seven unreported operations, and across all divisions of ACRONYM there were probably a hundred more, and now Myles Fowl had the details of almost every one, and he could sell those details to any network on the planet.

And that, thought Jeronima, could be muy inconveniente, because even though ACRONYM was an intergovernmental clandestine agency, they had over the years broken more laws than the rest of the world's secret services put together.

In fact, if Myles Fowl were to leak the stolen files, it could spell the end of ACRONYM—and federal prison time for many of its upper echelon. Including Sister Jeronima herself.

Lord Teddy and the nun made it to the Skyblade, but were unable to take off as the Dutch police arrived faster than anticipated. And so nun and nobleman were forced to sit inside the airplane in silence while the Amsterdam armed-response unit swarmed all over the black site. The time was not completely wasted, though, as Lord Teddy docked his phone with the Skyblade's media system and brought up a map on the smart windshield. A red dot, which represented the troll's cellophane-wrap signature, pulsed in the suburbs.

"You see, madam," he said, drumming the glass with the same fingers that had held a knife to Jeronima's throat in the very recent past. "Less than five minutes' flight time. Our errant band shall be trussed like turkeys before lunch."

Jeronima merely nodded.

She knew who Lord Teddy Bleedham-Drye was. Most people with a smartphone would recognize the Duke of Scilly. In fact, ACRONYM had investigated him briefly a few years back, when a junior agent had suggested that Bleedham-Drye might be using some kind of sorcery to stay forever young. Seeing the man now, up close, Sister Jeronima saw that he was not, in fact, young, but neither was he old. His skin was weathered with an odd blotchy sheen to it, which reminded Jeronima of the cured sobrasada sausages that her grandfather used to hang in their cellar. However, there was no denying that his beard was magnificent and virtually impossible to resist, and Jeronima found her hand was reaching out for a stroke.

The duke caught the movement and said, "I know. Magnificent. Look, but please don't touch."

Jeronima withdrew her fingers, thinking that it was odd that such a high-profile nobleman could conduct a secret life as some kind of vigilante child catcher.

Perhaps I should recruit him, she thought, but then she remembered the feel of her own knife on her neck and decided to focus on surviving the mission.

As soon as the swarm of armed police had disappeared inside the building, Teddy nosed the plane out from behind a barge and into the canal. There was some police activity in the canal network, but no one had yet thought to close the locks or even set up barriers, so Teddy was able to navigate easily to the harbor. He took off using the angled plane of the EYE Museum's roof as a runway, which made him chuckle as the swimmers dove to get out of the Skyblade's trajectory.

"We are coming, Myles Fowl," he said. "You will not escape me again."

This sounded rather personal to Sister Jeronima and, in her experience, men with personal agendas made mistakes.

I will disable this man at the first opportunity, she thought. And then call in reinforcements somehow.

She felt reasonably confident that Lord Teddy was thinking along the same lines, but she was wrong. Because an Englishman's word was his bond, Teddy would consider it very bad form to turn on Sister Jeronima without provocation. But he was quietly confident that provocation would be coming his way.

Jeronima was impressed by the plane and took a mental note of the make and model, which was embossed on the steering wheel along with what she could swear was a line drawing of Lord Teddy himself.

Myishi Skyblade, she thought. ACRONYM doesn't have anything so elegante. It is always overkill with our people. Helicopters and fifty-caliber guns. Perhaps I can learn something from this Lord Teddy.

The first thing she learned was that the Fowl Twins had somehow managed to divest the troll of its radiation-infused coating. Lord Teddy's tracker found it in the outskirts of Amsterdam, discarded in a quaint windmill that was adjacent to a canal, which made landing quite convenient.

"Blast it!" he swore. "They have slipped through the net."

This was upsetting, yes, but Lord Teddy thrilled to the hunt and was already figuring how he could track this particular quarry.

He knelt by car tracks leading away from the windmill.

"They are mobile," he said, "which means they have access to funding."

Sister Jeronima also had some experience with hunting— after all, that was a large part of her occupation. First she hunted, then she interrogated, and then came stage three: the terminal stage.

"They will want to blend in," she said. "Except the boy Myles. He is too much of a peacock."

"That is true, madam," said Teddy. "The boy has a distinctive look, and that will be his downfall."

They returned to the Skyblade and Lord Teddy pressed the embossed Myishi logo on the steering wheel, which put him straight through to the Myishi 24-Hour Concierge Line.

A cheerful voice said, "Hi, Lord Bleedham-Drye, this is Douglas on the Myishi Line. Your crime is worth our time. How may I be of assistance?"

"Good morning to you, my boy," said the duke. "I am going to give you a list of items, and I want you to check to see if any of them have been ordered online from my approximate location in the past fifteen minutes. Is that at all possible, do you think?"

"It is absolutely possible, Your Grace," said Douglas enthusiastically. "And may I say, I am a huge fan and delighted to be of any assistance."

"Good fellow, Douglas," said Lord Teddy. "Shall I continue on and present my list?"

"Fire away," said Douglas. "Just to inform you, because this is an online service without any actual physical action required—murder or theft and so forth—your no-claims bonus as a concierge-level customer remains intact and your premium will be unaffected."

"Capital, my boy," said Lord Teddy, and he read out his list. It was short, but most specific.

"We have a hit," said Douglas some twenty seconds later. "One of the items on your list was ordered from Master Porter in the past hour. A designer store for the more juvenile gentleman. Delivery to be bundled and expedited to a very specific longitude and latitude."

Lord Teddy punched the delivery site into his computer

and, in moments, the Skyblade had plotted a flight course.

"And will there be anything else, Your Grace?" asked Douglas.

"I think that will be all for the moment, Douglas," said Lord Teddy. "And may I say, you have been most helpful."

A number of skull outlines appeared on the windshield. "Thank you, Your Grace. Would you like to leave some Myishi Corporation feedback skulls?"

"It would be my pleasure, Douglas my boy," said the duke. He tapped five of the six skulls, turning them gold, and left a comment:

I found Douglas to be the epitome of efficiency. He has an excellent manner, and I would have no hesitation in recommending him for all your mastermind needs.

Seconds later, Douglas sent back a thumbs-up emoticon and two smiley faces with hearts for eyes.

"One has fans," Lord Teddy explained to the nun in the copilot's seat. "It's embarrassing, but one can't blame commoners for being starstruck, I suppose."

The duke is like Myles Fowl: vain, thought Jeronima. *A chink in his armor.*

She looked forward to sticking her knife into that chink and twisting the blade.

The Orient Express

Some hours later, we find our heroes overnighting on the Verona-bound Orient Express. The tranquillity on board the luxury train was somewhat at odds with the thunderclouds spewing rain from above the hulking ridges of the Swiss Alps. Like the locomotive itself, the Regrettables were in the eye of their personal storm, and Myles in particular was acutely aware that this rest period must be fully utilized to explore their options and assess their strengths—and, for that matter, their shortcomings. To this end, he was examining Specialist Heitz's equipment, which was more technologically advanced than anything he had ever seen. Which is not to say he did not understand its workings; rather its workings had solved some problems he had been wrestling with. The theory of utilizing carbon-based polymers to form simple circuitry was still in its infancy in human laboratories—except for in Artemis's lab, where he had managed to employ organometallics to grow a large part of his self-winding rocket engine. But the Fairy People had taken the technique far beyond anything humans could currently achieve and were using it to power and regulate almost every part of the LEP suit. The growth of the circuits themselves could be achieved through solar energy, when available, and, in effect, the circuits and cells became their own batteries. As far as Myles could determine, the operating system was already partially restored after the EMP on Dalkey Island, and he was able to use NANNI's translating software—which, of course, included Gnommish—to deduce that functions would begin to return in less than a day. NANNI used her final spurt of power probing Lazuli's systems and then took a nap.

We're all running on empty, thought Myles.

Beckett and Whistle Blower were asleep in the cabin's top bunk, having nodded off watching ASMR videos on a customer tablet connected to the train's Wi-Fi.

It is amazing how many videos of gummy candy those two can watch, thought Myles.

And as for Specialist Heitz, she was seated bolt upright across the small varnished table, finishing her salad with great deliberation and no obvious relish, as though the food were simply fuel and not something to be enjoyed or dallied over. Without her helmet, the fairy seemed very childlike, and it was all Myles could do not to patronize her, as this was his natural instinct with almost everyone he came into contact with. People thought Artemis was condescending, but Angeline Fowl had once told Myles that he himself was at least five times more patronizing than his older brother, which Myles accepted as fact, feeling neither insulted nor complimented.

The journey to the Orient Express was uneventful, and so a brisk summary will best serve to illuminate that five-hour ride. Once Whistle Blower had been coaxed into the self-driving car, Myles set about ordering the supplies they would need moving forward. These were to be delivered to Verona, where the Orient Express would make a stop at seventeen hundred hours the following evening. The legendary Express was generally booked up for months in advance, but since the late nineteenth century, when the Fowl family in its entirety had been briefly outlawed by the governments of Germany, Switzerland, and Austria, the family matriarch, Peg O'Connor Fowl (often and quite rudely referred to as Pirate Peg), had paid the Compagnie Internationale des Wagons-Lits an extortionate amount of gold to engineer a secret cabin in the rear car that would be made available exclusively and in perpetuity to the Fowl family. In this way Peg could cross Europe in comfort and continue to service her considerable interests in Constantinople. And it had been a simple matter for Myles to dump the self-driving car at Gare de l'Est in Paris and take advantage of Cabin F.

Artemis had often taken advantage of Cabin F, and Myles had learned the code for the electronic lock when he was four years old. The rest of the passengers and crew believed Cabin F to be part of the engine car, because the door was disguised as a blank panel, but there was a single purser who kept the cabin supplied with food and the tablet device that had lulled Beckett and Whistle Blower to sleep. Unfortunately, clothing-wise, the carriage contained little to help the group blend in, unless they wanted to stand on each other's shoulders and dress in a Victorian ball gown.

This time the small refrigerator was stocked with fresh salad, fruit, and a roasted chicken that Beckett and Whistle Blower devoured down to the bones, which the toy troll then crunched to dust. But there was nothing in the way of charging equipment, aside from one European socket that NANNI could leech from but would not provide her with anything close to the amount of energy she required for full functionality.

It is time for Father to update this train car, Myles thought. At the very least, we need the latest in communications and technology.

They would have both when they were in Verona.

Once they reached the northern Italian city, Myles realized, he would have to agree to a fairy extraction. He'd been hoping to wrap this up, the Fowl Twins' first grand adventure, without involving the LEP, but with that level of pride came an inevitable painful fall. If there had been just one criminal mastermind and one single shadowy organization to vanquish, Myles felt he would have been more than equal to the task, but both together was a considerable challenge, and he would never forgive himself if something were to happen to Beckett.

Across the small lacquered table, Specialist Heitz finished her last stalk of celery and declared, "I have a plan, human. We will remain on this train until Istanbul, and by then my circuits will have regenerated and I can call in the LEP."

"I disagree, Specialist," said Myles. "If you don't mind me saying, you seem very young to be devising strategy."

Lazuli could not help thinking that this was a bit rich. "I am young? Me? You are a mere child. I am sixty years old."

"You do not have the appearance of a sexagenarian," noted Myles.

"Species develop at different rates," explained the pixel. "Most fairies are walking after a week. We can read and write after a year. I finished my law diploma when I was ten.

I have three friends, and they are all in steady relationships."

"And what is your life span?"

Lazuli shrugged. "Who knows? I am a hybrid. It could be anything from three hundred years to a millennium."

"I envy you that time," said Myles. "There is so much you could learn."

"One of the things I did learn," said Lazuli, "is how to strategize."

It was a valid point, but Myles still felt compelled to disagree.

"We must disembark at Verona," he insisted. "It is dangerous to stay enclosed in this car for too long without secure communications, as we must assume that either the duke or Sister Jeronima will somehow track us down, and we are basically trapped in a steel box. I have chosen a rendezvous point for us to collect our supplies. Once there, I can rig your communicator to a human power source— providing you allow me to examine it—and you may summon reinforcements to evacuate us to safety immediately. Of course, you may stay on the train, but I fancy Whistle Blower will wish to remain with Beckett."

Lazuli considered this and had to admit to herself that the human's plan was sound. It would mean allowing Myles to check out even more of her equipment, but the Fowls were historically friends to the fairy folk, and, after all, humans could be mind-wiped. Ten minutes after Recon arrived, the twins would wake up in their own beds with no idea that any of this had even happened.

"I agree, human boy," said Lazuli, undoing the strap on her control gauntlet.

Myles thought it slightly odd that Specialist Heitz would turn over her computer without objection.

"My only stipulation," he said, "is that there be no interference with me or my brother. We go our own way, and that is the end of it."

"For now," said Lazuli, in a way Myles found slightly unsettling. It occurred to him that perhaps the Fairy People might not want more Fowls in their world, and they might decide to do something about it. And so, when Specialist Heitz climbed to the foot of the top bunk and curled herself in a ball at the end, Myles ignored his own exhaustion and, once he had finished examining Specialist Heitz's gauntlet, he used NANNI's slightly restored energy levels to study the fairy-related videos left behind by Artemis. Because, as his big brother often said: *Know thine enemy, and assume everyone is your enemy, for it is ever true that the world resents genius.*

Words Myles intended to live by, even though they were grandiose and long-winded, like Artemis himself.

To keep himself amused, Myles edited Artemis's every speech down to less than a quarter of its original length and saved the edits on a separate file in case he needed references that were a little more concise. While doing so, Myles played Schubert's Symphony No. 9 in his mind. He chose this particular piece because it was in C major and matched Beckett's whistle/snores.

After an hour or so, Myles found the file that might come in especially useful if the fairy folk were not all as friendly as Lazuli.

Who, in all honesty, was not all that friendly.

CHAPTER 10

VEGAS-ERA ELVIS

Verona, Italy

The city of Verona is rightly celebrated for its Roman architecture, most notably the amphitheater of striking pink limestone, which is crammed year-round with opera-loving Italians. It is also known for its restaurants, dozens of which claim to serve the best gnocchi on the continent of Europe. Less celebrated are the seemingly constant road construction projects, which infuriate the local delivery trucks, and the centuries-old drainage system that cannot cope with the winter storms that regularly flood the narrow streets. But perhaps the city's most celebrated attraction was made famous by an Englishman—that being, of course, Juliet's balcony, featured in Shakespeare's tragic love story.

No one is permitted to stand on the small wooden balcony, as it would have collapsed centuries ago, but the museum in Casa di Giulietta and its small courtyard are an essential item on any tourist's itinerary.

But not on this evening, as the piazza was currently off-limits to the public.

The piazza walls take such a pasting every season from romantics sticking love notes to the brickwork with chewing gum that it is routinely closed for specialized cleaning. Myles Fowl, having checked the schedule, reasoned that this would be the perfect secluded spot and time for his special delivery.

The building's security system was hardly state-of-the-art, and Lazuli was able to pick the gate's lock in a matter of seconds with the blade of her dwarf obsidian knife. The only embarrassing part of this operation was that she was obliged to accomplish this from inside an Orient Express–branded carrier bag, which was slung over Myles's shoulder. The twins made an odd-looking pair: two shaven humans in jumpsuits, one swinging some sort of mini werewolf-looking toy from his arm, the other with a blue hand snaking from his bag.

Oddness notwithstanding, the group were inside the piazza by six p.m., barely an hour after stepping onto the Verona train-station platform. Work had finished on the lovers' wall for the day, and the Regrettables concealed themselves behind a tower of stacked cement bags.

"When will this package arrive?" Lazuli asked with some urgency. Now that she was exposed in the middle of a crowded city, the pixel was beginning to think that staying on the train would have been the better option tactically. Also, it was certainly undignified to be toted around in a bag. The inside of a steel box was looking pretty good to her now as opposed to trying to hide in what was definitely in the top three of the world's most famous piazzas.

Myles automatically checked his wrist, which did not have a watch on it. "Have patience, Specialist. Our supplies will be here momentarily. Then we simply send out a signal to your forces and I imagine they will be here in minutes."

"That is correct, boy," said Lazuli, climbing from the bag. "But I cannot summon them until your package arrives."

From outside on the street came the sounds of clinking glasses and clanging pot lids as the area's restaurants began to fill up with tourists. It was far too early in the evening for Italians, who prefer to eat later and talk into the night. But the Irish and British like their tea at six, and so the local eateries obliged, and were able to fit in two seatings per night. Tantalizing smells drifted over the wall, and Whistle Blower's stomach growled while he also growled.

All in all, Myles thought, the sight of a toy troll who was now sitting atop the brass statue of Juliet, complete with the sound of the creature harmonizing with his own stomach, was certainly one of the strangest tableaux he had ever witnessed.

Lazuli's uniquely shaped ears detected a whir of rotors within the layers of street cacophony, which she was able to pinpoint as approaching the square from above.

"Here we go, Myles Fowl," she said, pointing to an

angular shape descending through the rising orange of city light.

The delivery drone was right on time, as it should have been, considering the exorbitant subsidy charged for an airborne shipment by the popular internet shopping site. Myles himself did not have a credit card—he'd been using Artemis's number ever since his big brother had blasted himself into space, as he believed that Artemis would expect nothing less.

The drone lowered an excessively packaged box, which Myles signed for with a forged e-signature that even a handwriting expert would have had trouble distinguishing from Artemis's own. Whistle Blower ripped the cardboard to chunks and then joined Beckett in stomping on the Bubble Wrap for a delighted minute before Myles scolded them both. Inside the remains of the box lay a Bubble-Wrapped bounty of charging packs, beef jerky, electrolyte tablets, and clothing.

For Myles, there was one of his signature black suits, and for Beckett, a fencing rig complete with chest plate, which he thought would be appropriate for adventuring. Lazuli was disguised with a toddler's hoodie that bore the legend TROUBLE COMIN' THRU and a smog mask that covered most of her face.

There was also a jumpsuit for Whistle Blower, which Beckett had ordered and Myles had been convinced the troll would never wear. It came as an outfit on an eight-inch doll: a bedazzled white Vegas Elvis suit.

When Beckett explained the idea to Whistle Blower, the

troll stomped the doll to pieces, then claimed the jumpsuit from its shattered body. Once he was dressed, the troll reclaimed his place on top of Juliet's statue and howled in triumph to the heavens.

Myles was most disappointed when he realized that the necktie he had ordered was missing from the box.

Beckett saved the day by offering his goldfish tie. "You may have the honor of wearing Gloop," he said, taking off the laminated fish. "Gold ties are in this year."

Myles was touched by the gesture and pulled the elastic over the collar of his crisp white shirt. Finally, he buttoned the black linen-blend jacket across his chest and felt instantly more in charge of the situation.

It is as Shakespeare said, he thought. The apparel oft proclaims the man.

And though Myles did not realize it, he was not the only human in that piazza with Shakespeare on his mind.

Lord Teddy Bleedham-Drye lay on Juliet's balcony covered by his trusty camouflage veil. Strictly speaking, there was no need for the veil, as he was hidden from the odd group below, but the camo blanket helped Lord Teddy to get into a hunter's mind-set. The duke was fiercely thrilled that his hunch had paid off and that Myles and Co. had actually materialized at the Casa di Giulietta, and he mentally clapped himself on the back for such foresight. The Fowl boy had betrayed his own position, when all he'd needed to do was lie low.

Vanity, thy name is Myles Fowl, thought Teddy, though he was perfectly aware that this was a misquote from *Hamlet* and also ironic, as the duke's favorite novel was the classic *Rogue Male*, in which a lone English marksman goes on the hunt for Hitler. It was his favorite mainly because he believed it to be a story about himself that he'd drunkenly recounted to a young writer one evening, so perhaps he too was more than a little vain, but not to the point where it might interfere with a mission.

Lord Teddy had done more damage to the Casa di Giulietta than the gum-wielding romantics ever would, for he had actually removed one of the balcony's lower panels so that he could cover the entire piazza with his rifle—surely an act of unequaled vandalism in the eyes of Shakespeare scholars.

To blazes with those scholars, thought Teddy. Bill Shakespeare never even set foot in Verona.

It had been the duke's plan to trap his prey without revealing himself, but he needed the group in a bunch and the blasted troll was running all over the square. It seemed for a moment that he might have his chance when they were changing clothes, but that moment quickly passed and the troll scampered out of danger once more.

I must distract them, thought Teddy, or they will vacate the area.

And so he had no choice but to throw off his veil and make himself visible.

* * *

Myles was unwrapping the power packs when Lord Teddy appeared on the balcony with the barrel of his rifle aimed squarely at Myles's broad forehead.

"Don't move, boy," he said, "or you shall be *sick and pale with grief.* I guarantee it."

Myles made no move except for a heaving of his chest, for he was sure that the duke could not possibly miss from such a range. And though he knew the full might of his mind should bear down on the problem of escape, he could not help but devote a few neurons to the problem of how they had been located. More than that, how had he been *anticipated*? The mere idea was repugnant. Had he, a veritable genius, become predictable?

"It was my suit," said Myles, after a moment's thought. "You tracked the order of my suit?"

"It was the suit," Lord Teddy confirmed, and then he borrowed another line from *Romeo and Juliet*. *"None but fools do wear it."*

I was a fool, thought Myles, not to consider that such a unique purchase could be tracked.

Teddy swung his barrel toward Lazuli. "You, creature, get rid of those power packs. Into that bucket."

Lazuli obeyed the command with considerable reluctance, for with those packs went her chances of contacting the LEP until her own suit regenerated. She tossed them into the partially full paint bucket and imagined she could hear them short-circuiting. They would, she knew, be completely useless now even if she could retrieve them.

Beckett figured that this was an action situation and his turn to shine, so he bent his knees slightly and prepared to jump toward the balcony, but the duke noticed the slight motion and trained the gun on him.

"Please move," he said to the twin. "I beg you. I haven't shot anything for hours and a fellow needs to stay in practice."

Whistle Blower knew instinctively that his human friend was under threat and growled. Lord Teddy recognized that class of a growl; in fact, it was one of his favorite sounds. It was the same growl he'd heard from tigers and leopards just before they sprang, and he wondered absently whether this creature was part feline, but his main focus was getting the troll where he wanted him.

"Hush now, kitty," he said to Whistle Blower. "I have no wish to kill you, but I can certainly cut you off at the knees."

Myles was thinking furiously. There must be a way out of this.

But without NANNI in his ears, he could think of nothing that did not involve sacrificing one member of their party. Lord Teddy seemed to pluck this thought out of his mind.

"There really is no need for all this tiresome rigmarole," said Lord Teddy, lowering his barrel perhaps an inch. "All I want is the troll. Let me have him and the rest of you may go about your business." Teddy raised the barrel again and the implication was clear: *As long as your business does not interfere with mine.*

Myles dismissed this as a ruse, for surely the duke must be aware that Lazuli would come after the troll, and the entire world knew where Lord Teddy Bleedham-Drye hung his hat, so he would not exactly be a chore to locate. A shrewd hunter such as the duke would never allow them to simply walk out of here. So what was the point of this bogus offer?

Lazuli was thinking exactly the same thing, but she'd had some training in the arts of conflict and instantly tumbled to the duke's strategy.

The human is attempting to distract us.

But from what?

She studied the piazza quickly, searching for a secondary or hidden threat. Perhaps there was someone else on the wall, but Lazuli could see nothing overhead.

But what about underfoot?

Lazuli saw that they were all standing on a painter's tarp, where the package had landed.

All except Whistle Blower.

The bearded human needs us clustered together, thought Lazuli. That's why he hasn't already fired his weapon.

She rocked on the balls of her feet and could feel something beneath the tarp. A lattice. A net, perhaps.

A net!

Wouldn't it be just like a hunter to spread out a net? Every fairy had grown up with horror stories of the People being hunted for sport by humans with spears and nets. And it would seem that some things never changed.

Lazuli turned to communicate her theory to Myles, as the Fowl boy could perhaps turn the information to their advantage, but it was too late—the trap was already in mid-spring.

It happened like this:

The bearded hunter pointed his gun squarely at the growling troll and said, "I don't think he likes me. Perhaps a flesh wound will quiet him down."

Beckett called to Whistle Blower in the troll's own language, possibly something along the lines of: *Come here, pal. I'll protect you.*

Whistle Blower squinted a warning at Lord Teddy and then nimbly leaped into his human friend's arms.

We are all on the tarp now, thought Lazuli.

And then the tarp wrapped up, seemingly of its own accord, and shot like a wriggling missile into the evening sky.

On the balcony, Lord Teddy calmly packed his gear and glanced upward, where the Skyblade hovered, reeling in its cargo.

"But soft," he could not resist saying, "what light from yonder aircraft breaks?"

The duke laughed softly, then spoke into his Myishi smartphone, which was linked to the Skyblade's console.

"Is the light green, Sister?" he asked, and Jeronima's voice replied through the speaker.

"Solid green, Señor Duque," she said.

"Capital," said Lord Teddy. "Then the cargo has docked."

He had transported many creatures with that net and winch in his time. A baby elephant, two black rhinos (which were not as extinct as the WWF believed), and now an assorted bunch of humans and fairies.

Never a dull moment, thought Teddy as he climbed down from the balcony. Sister Jeronima would drop rendezvous at the roof of the Lamberti Tower in ten minutes, so he would need to double-time it over there to climb the more than three hundred and sixty steps to the top and literally walk out onto the Skyblade's wing.

The duke had no doubt that Sister Jeronima would show up on time. After all, he had shown her the remote destruct button that would blow her out of the sky if she reneged on their partnership.

CHAPTER 11

NIGHT GUARD

French Airspace, Seven Thousand Feet

The Myishi Skyblade really was a marvelous flying machine. Myles had to appreciate that even as he ground his teeth in vexation. A vexation that was caused by the near certainty that it was his own vanity that had led to the Regrettables' second abduction in as many days.

Beckett managed to squeeze his arms through the jumble of bodies and tap his brother's chin. "Myles," he said, "no grinding. Do you have your night guard?"

"No, Beck, amazingly I don't," snapped Myles, unable to keep a civil tongue in his head. "I neglected to pack my night guard when we were scooped up in a net in front of Juliet's balcony."

Beckett's hand withdrew but returned presently, offering a blob of chewing gum.

"Improvise," he said with no little pride, and Myles

realized that his twin was proud of using a big word that had come from one of Myles's own sayings.

When surprised, improvise!

A tad puerile, certainly, but Myles had been five when he came up with it. Myles opened his mouth and accepted his brother's offer even though it was used, or, as Beckett called it, *pre-chewed.*

While Beckett spread the gum over Myles's upper teeth, Myles made three mental notes:

The first was to dispose of the gum responsibly, as it was an environmental nightmare consisting of mainly petrol-based polymers.

The second was to push forward with human trials on his own more environmentally responsible *chicle* gum, similar to that used by the ancient Maya.

And the third: Beckett had probably picked the gum off the piazza wall, and who knew who had chewed it before his twin.

But Myles swallowed his disgust for now, as the priority was survival. They were only alive at all because of the aforementioned Myishi Skyblade's design.

Myles wriggled his head backward to take a better look at the flying machine overhead. The undercarriage had a curved indentation that allowed the net to be winched close to the plane. This afforded the occupant of the net—usually a member of an endangered species, Myles imagined—to be sheltered from the slipstream. Obviously, the poacher would want to sell live specimens to whatever zoo he was dealing with. The second lifesaver was an air vent that blew warm air onto the captives and prevented them from freezing. And third, the very strands of the net were slightly heated, to the point where Whistle Blower had fashioned himself a hammock and nodded off, which prompted Myles to think: *If this were my airplane, I would squirt a little anesthetic through that vent, just to keep everyone nice and calm.*

Perhaps five seconds later, a green mist jetted from the vent and coated the prisoners inside the net. Myles had just enough time to reflect *Great minds think alike* before his eyes drooped and he joined Whistle Blower in the land of Nod.

Inside the Skyblade's cockpit, Lord Teddy was wrestling with a moral dilemma. He had given his word to Sister Jeronima that they were partners in this enterprise, and yet now that he had the troll in his possession, he no longer needed the nun's help. The duke had no issue with lying to people, but once a member of the royal family gave his word, that word was very difficult to wriggle out of. Sometimes it was most inconvenient to be royal, something commoners could never understand.

'Tis a great pity I have the upper hand, he realized. Otherwise the nun might attempt a betrayal, which would free me from my bonds.

And this thought led to an idea.

* * *

Sister Jeronima Gonzalez-Ramos de Zárate of Bilbao was entertaining similar thoughts of betrayal. It was true that the duke had facilitated the containment of the Fowl Twins and their fairy friends, but now she felt that if she returned to ACRONYM with the creatures in tow, she might be able to salvage something of her reputation and her career after the Amsterdam debacle.

Some might think it strange that a nun should be part of such an organization as ACRONYM in the first place, but the truth was that the church had been at the forefront of hunting magical creatures for centuries and had actually lobbied for ACRONYM's formal incorporation following the Big Dark. In fact, the church had contributed billions of dollars to the organization's coffers with the stipulation that it be represented at every level. Sister Jeronima was one of three station leaders in ACRONYM, the others being a Mexican bishop and a very old Roman altar boy.

I need to get rid of this English aristócrata, she realized, for of course she knew who the duke was. His face and indeed the hair on his face were internationally famous.

Sister Jeronima's thoughts were interrupted by a posh chatter and she realized that Lord Teddy was talking to her.

"So, after an exhaustive search, I located this Irish monk," he was saying as he flew the plane with no apparent discomfort from his relocated shoulder. "And he claimed to be over five hundred years old."

"¿Es verdad?" said Jeronima, though she was only half paying attention.

"Yes, in fact it turned out to be completely true. I drugged the fellow and he trotted out a rather fantastic story of a troll attack on their monastery on Dalkey Island. Apparently, it was a regular occurrence back then. The troll would bag himself a few monks, and the venom in its tusks would preserve the bodies indefinitely so the beast could feast whenever it chose."

Jeronima was listening now. No wonder Lord Teddy was interested in the troll if its venom had preservative qualities.

"But this monk, how did he know all of this?"

Teddy checked the feed from the craft's undercarriage camera to satisfy himself that his cargo was still attached.

"That's the fascinating part. This monk, Brother Colman, was the victim of such an attack, but thanks to a quite fantastic series of events, his life was not only saved but extended indefinitely."

Jeronima realized at once that if she were to return to ACRONYM with this troll under her arm, not only would all be forgiven, but she would also be promoted to a prime station—in London, perhaps, or Miami Beach.

"What were these eventos?"

Teddy thought about this for a moment. How to stream-line Brother Colman's ramblings? "Apparently, the troll was in the process of goring Brother Colman when the crea-ture was struck by lightning and tumbled down a well. The lightning must have killed the troll but restarted Brother Colman's heart. And it hasn't stopped beating since."

"Increíble," said Sister Jeronima.

"I am inclined to agree, Sister," said Lord Teddy. "Incredible. It may take me a while to re-create these circumstances in laboratory conditions, but I will succeed, have no doubt."

Jeronima did not doubt that the duke would succeed, if he were granted the opportunity, which she was now certain he should not be.

"But what a wonderful flying machine," she said, changing the subject. "So many—How do you say it?—gadgets."

"Yes," said the duke with some pride. "I have a fellow who does all my vehicles. Ingenious chap."

"All the modern conveniences," said Jeronima.

"Honestly, I don't think I know what half of these buttons are for," said Lord Teddy, and, had Jeronima been a native English speaker, she might have noticed a sliver of slyness creep into his tone. "This one here envelops us in a smoke screen, and that lever generates white noise, I believe it's called." He pointed to a flip switch under a plastic cover. "And this little beauty is an ejector seat should I find myself in jeopardy and the craft is compromised."

Jeronima did not comment but simply nodded, her face displaying only polite interest.

My chance will come, she told herself.

Jeronima's chance did come, and sooner than she expected. Some minutes later, the duke took his eyes from the controls to gaze toward the ocean below.

"There she is," he said. "The English Channel. It was the Armada's downfall, and the Reich's. Was there ever a more beautiful sight?"

Sí, thought Jeronima. The sight of a pompous duke being ejected from his own airplane.

And, with two deft movements, she popped the plastic cover and flipped the ejector-seat switch. She barely had time to exclaim "Adiós, idiota" before her own ejector seat was blasted out of the cockpit and into the blue of the afternoon sky. By the time her parachute deployed and she began her slow descent into the duke's beloved channel, Sister Jeronima realized she had fallen prey to reverse psychology and she began to question her own proficiency as an interrogator.

The interior of the Skyblade was quite chilly at that altitude following Sister Jeronima's departure, but, with a mere half dozen turns on a hidden handle, Lord Teddy was able to wind up a partition that sealed off the pilot's side.

"Well done, Teddy old fellow," he said aloud, delighted at the success of his cunning plan. The nun was undone by her own hand while attempting to stab him in the back.

"An undone nun," said Teddy, loving the sound of this statement.

Jeronima had gotten her just deserts and the partnership between them was dissolved, all without his having to compromise the Bleedham-Drye name.

It was true he had neglected to mention that the ejector

button on the central console was for the *copilot's* seat, but in fact he had not specified which seat was connected to that particular button. He had been vague, true. But vagueness was only a mild niggle on the duke's conscience that would evaporate by day's end.

Lord Teddy's phone buzzed and he saw a text from the Myishi Concierge service that read: *Your passenger seat has ejected. Do you need assistance? If we do not hear from you in thirty seconds, Myishi Concierge will dispatch a retrieval craft.*

The duke dictated a reply: "Equipment malfunction. All is well. Negative on retrieval. Absolutely do not retrieve the chair. Put it on my bill."

And he ordered the phone to send.

Whistling a merry tune, Teddy tapped the interactive map on his windshield, which told him that the remaining flight time to St. George was a mere thirty minutes.

Brandy, cigar, an eel bath, and then bed, thought the duke. *For tomorrow I experiment.*

Sister Jeronima felt in no immediate danger, as her seat swung like a pendulum below the bloom of parachute. In fact, the movement was soothing, and it took the nun a long moment to realize why that should be.

"But of course," she said, just before splashdown. "Abuela."

The motion reminded her of the swing in her grandmother's garden in Bilbao. Little Jeronima had adored her abuela and visited her often, loving especially those moments at day's end when her grandmother would read her future in the tea leaves.

You're gonna be a big shot, kid, she had always told her granddaughter. *You're gonna show those guys.*

Abuela's prophecies had never been specific regarding who the "guys" were, or what she was going to show them. But Jeronima thought now, as the toes of her patent leather pumps dipped into the ocean swell, that the guys might be sharks, and what she would show them was how easily she could be digested.

Which might have happened had not the seat's ejector jets reignited and begun to steer the chair and its surprised passenger toward the nearest Myishi workshop, on Southampton Docks. For it is a universal truth that corporations do not like to simply abandon expensive equipment, and, in spite of their client's wishes, they will attempt to retrieve any parts that are lost, stolen, or jettisoned for R&R—that being repair and recycling. In this case, the engines had just enough juice to get the nun to the English mainland, traveling at a rate only slightly faster than a child paddling an inflatable dinghy.

Jeronima noticed a shark's fin slicing the water off her starboard bow and drew her toes from the ocean.

If this shark does not eat me, she thought, and this chair ridículo reaches the mainland, I will rally the ACRONYM troops and rain down vengeance on the Duke of Scilly.

And though this thought would keep her going through

the high seas to come and the single raincloud that seemed to follow her across the channel, it might have given her some comfort to know that the shark would soon grow bored with the ejector seat and turn his dark glittering eyes toward the Scilly Isles.

CHAPTER 12

CONCIERGE LEVEL

The Island of St. George, Scilly Isles

Due to a combination of its particular positioning on the southern tip of the Scilly Isles, the prevailing winds, and the unusually high temperature of the land mass itself, St. George was shrouded in ethereal concentric rings of fog for an average of two hundred days per year, and this was one of those days. When St. George was so obscured by what Scilly Islanders referred to as dragon's breath, there was only one possible landing site for even a small aircraft. This was on what was known, in keeping with the island's dragon motif, as the Spine, a curved and knobby ridge set back from the western cliffs. It sheltered a flat mini runway Lord Teddy had excavated and hard-packed with gravel with the help of a builder bot that had been supplied, naturally, by the Myishi Corporation. The company was well aware that being a criminal mastermind wasn't all *bang, bang, boom*—

sometimes there was building work that needed doing; in this case, runway construction. Lord Teddy could have attempted a water landing, but the swell was considerable, and even if he did manage to put down safely, it would mean transporting his live cargo up the three hundred steps from the dock.

I really must get that elevator installed, Teddy thought to himself as he applied the airbrakes and brought the Skyblade to a stop on the runway. But excavating solid rock is so dashed expensive, and regular contractors do not offer the same favorable rates as Ishi Myishi.

The truth was that the duke's fortune, though still considerable, had dipped to under a single billion, and he had decided to hold off on the elevator until he had earned another seven hundred loyalty points, at which time he would be entitled to an extra discount on his next purchase, which would be the elevator plus installation.

All this was by the by.

The job at hand was to transfer his human and non-human cargo to his laboratory, which was spread across the attic of Childerblaine House for easy connection to the rooftop lightning conductors, which had been quite the style a hundred years ago. Though its location was somewhat impractical, the duke loved his laboratory the way a young boy loves trouble, and he would not have moved it down a few levels even if he could have spared the cash.

Lord Teddy removed his smartphone from its dock on the dashboard and activated the shuttle bots that would ferry his captors to the main house and, from there, upstairs to his laboratory. Upstairs for the magical creatures. The Fowl Twins he intended to stash in his basement dungeon until he could figure out what to do with them.

It struck Lord Teddy suddenly that perhaps he hadn't cleaned out the dungeon since the mess with the previous occupants, but a quick check on his smartphone's dungeon cam link revealed no bloodstains on the flagstones and no limbs hanging from the wall manacles.

"Capital," he said.

Myishi's bots and drones really were top-class, and unlike the human servants he'd kept for decades, they did not need constant telling in order to perform their functions. All one needed to do was program the little fellows a single time and they would keep going forever.

The duke allowed himself a moment to look seaward and take a deep breath of salty fog. Most people would feel cheated of an ocean view, but Lord Teddy relished the privacy the vapor afforded him. Even satellites couldn't do much more than pick up a heat signature, and the world's press were notoriously lazy and would not put in either the effort or expense necessary to take candid shots of the famous duke. Shakespeare had written: *Glory is like a circle in the water,* but, as far as the duke was concerned, this particular circle of fog and rock in the water was glorious in itself, and so he adapted the quote and said it aloud whenever he returned home.

"Glorious is my circle in the water," quoth he to the fog, his

voice booming into space, and when the echo had faded, Lord Teddy rubbed his hands and walked briskly to the rear of the craft to find that his net had been slashed and his captives were running toward the sheer cliffs, which did strike one as idiocy of the purest form.

Perhaps yesterday Lord Teddy might have snorted in mild frustration that he would have to put in some small unexpected effort to corral his prey, but now he had some notion of the slippery Fowl nature, so he decided to take all precautions. The duke pulled out his smartphone, opened the Myishi app, and woke up the island's defenses.

The Fowl Twins think they have drones on their island, he thought. I'll show them drones.

The Regrettables had effected their escape as follows: By the time the Skyblade had touched down, the effects of the knockout mist had largely worn off. Due to her fairy constitution, Lazuli was first awake, and she had reached into her boot and pulled out her knife with its short gleaming black blade of dwarf obsidian, a particular type of volcanic rock found near the earth's core that dwarves had long favored for their weapons and tools of choice. Specialist Heitz's obsidian blade was not regulation issue, exactly, but most LEP officers kept a favorite weapon in a fold of their uniform somewhere, and it was tolerated as long as its loss would not compromise fairy secrets if found by a human. In fact, this knife had been a gift from Lazuli's angel to celebrate her first trip aboveground.

Lazuli had thought of slicing through the net earlier, but she'd held back because:

a) They went too high too fast, and to open the net would have meant certain death.

Plus:

b) Her boot was jammed between the Fowl Twins, and, try as she might, Lazuli could not shift the sleeping boys enough to reach it.

But, as the Skyblade swung into a circular descent, the bodies in the net were shaken loose like prunes in a grocery bag, and Lazuli managed to scrabble her fingers forward until they curled around the knife's handle. She drew the weapon, sliced through the tarp, and hooked it through the netting.

The sudden shaking also served to waken the boys, and after a groggy moment Myles noticed the knife and read Lazuli's intention in her face. "Timing, Specialist," he said, "is paramount."

He was not wrong. A premature slice would see them all plummeting to their deaths over the cliff edge.

It was ironic, though, that Myles, Mr. Uncoordinated, should presume to offer advice to Specialist Heitz, a trained LEP operative. But it was his nature to lecture, especially when stressed, as most humans would be at this point.

Not Beckett, apparently. Once his mind cleared of fog, the boy pressed his face to the netting, closed his eyes, feeling the air flow, and said two words to Lazuli: "Wait, Laser."

And for some reason, Lazuli stayed her hand, even though the runway seemed to be rushing up to meet them.

"Wait," said Beckett again. And then: "Now."

Lazuli slashed, the net opened like a butchered animal's stomach, and the Regrettables spilled out onto the runway's grassy shoulder, rolling to a gentle stop on a patch of dandelions, a handful of which Whistle Blower, who was also apparently awake, promptly ate.

Lazuli was the first one to get to her feet. "That was well-timed, human. You have good instincts."

Then there was no more time for talk, only escape. Lord Teddy was in front of them and the cliffs were behind. Beckett was pretty certain he could climb down to the dock, but Myles probably could not. Nevertheless, it was toward the cliffs they must go, and Beckett could only hope that Myles's big brain would devise a genius plan in the few seconds of liberty they would have, and so he took the time to shout one verb at his brother, though it was hardly necessary, as Myles did little else, which was why he had bad dreams and ground his teeth at night.

"Think!" he shouted, and then he linked his arm with Myles's so his twin would not stumble while running.

Whistle Blower led the way, scampering like a chimpanzee toward the cliff edge. It had not seemed so high from the air, but now that they were coming up on it, the cliff was obviously as slick as glass, as high as the White Cliffs of Dover, and completely unclimbable.

Even Whistle Blower seemed cowed and he shied

back from the edge. The toy troll grunted at Beckett.

"Can't be done," said Beckett. "He says we can't climb it."

Myles's eyes were closed and he seemed to be counting. "Sixteen, fifty-nine, thirty-two," he said.

"Tell your brother," said Lazuli, "that we need something besides numbers."

Beckett shook Myles by the shoulders as the cliff yawned before them. "Brother!" he shouted. "Come on! Whip out a genius idea. Something we'll laugh about in the future. Something we can beam to Artemis in space."

Myles stopped counting aloud and opened his eyes. "How much do you trust me, Beck?"

Beckett smiled. "How big is the universe?" he said.

Which was an answer he knew Myles would appreciate, because it was science-y.

An army of drones whirred through the curtains of mist, and overland squadrons of robots advanced on multi-terrain tracks, brandishing their guns and blades, all controlled by Lord Teddy's smartphone, and all bearing his personal logo.

The Regrettables were soon surrounded on three sides by electronic enemies. On the fourth was the cliff. Lord Teddy strode briskly through the tough, scutched grass, looking every inch like the lord of the manor.

Whistle Blower growled and unsheathed his claws, ready for attack, but a grunt from Beckett told him to stay where he was for the moment.

Lord Teddy held up his smartphone. "Do you see this?" he said. "You are already targeted. I can press one button on this phone and you will be cut to ribbons. Not the fairies, though—I will merely incapacitate them with precision laser bursts."

"What do you want with us, Your Grace?" asked Myles.

Teddy preened. "Finally, someone addresses me properly. To answer your question, child, I want nothing from you. Not a blooming thing. This entire tiresome rigmarole need never have happened. I didn't even want the blue thing, whatever she is. All I wanted was the troll and the secrets of its venom."

"And what, pray tell, is special about the troll's venom?"

Teddy considered whether or not he should answer and decided that he might as well, but briefly. "The secret to eternal life," he said. "I might have thought that would appeal to you, Myles Fowl. Are you not a scientist?"

"I am," admitted Myles.

"Well, then, you know what can be achieved with a life eternal."

Myles felt momentarily dizzy, because he *did* know what could be done with an extended life span and had often thought about this exact scenario. Imagine all the knowledge he could absorb over many lifetimes. He could be the smartest person who had ever lived. Myles Fowl with the universe at his fingertips.

"Your Grace," he said, "is there an arrangement that can be reached?"

The duke laughed. "I don't see how. You have nothing that I need, Fowl."

Myles tapped his head. "I have this: Experiments can be conducted twice as efficiently with a competent assistant. And I am so much more than competent."

The duke was amused. "Perhaps. But what would you demand in return for this favor? A box of lollipops, perhaps?"

Myles was not amused. "My family historically does not favor lollipops."

"Your life, then," said Teddy. "Would that be fair exchange?"

Myles smiled tightly. "I do find live laboratory assistants to be the best kind."

While all this negotiating was going on, Myles was wishing that NANNI were awake to hack the duke's network, which he must be using to control his robotic army.

By the law of great minds, Lord Teddy happened upon the same subject.

"I imagine," he said, "that you are wishing you had those charging packs now to breathe life into whatever smartphone you have, so it can crack the St. George system. You wouldn't have much luck anyway, I'll wager, because, my dear boy, sometimes old-school is best. My system requires actual hard contact for syncing."

"Don't worry," said Beckett brightly. "Myles doesn't even have the smartphone that he's always going on about. Or his smartwatch, either. Because the nun kidnapped us before he could take them from the charger. This is not even our first kidnapping this week. Though it was definitely the best. Even Myles with his big brain had no idea what you were doing. But things being done is not his area. Myles calls it our division of labor. He thinks stuff, and I do things."

This spiel seemed to send Myles over the emotional edge. "You *do* things, brother? You *do* things? Let me tell me what you do! You mess everything up. If you hadn't climbed that rope to the helicopter, we wouldn't be in this mess."

Beckett was confused. "Are we playing a game now? Role-playing to work on my social skills?"

"No, Beckett," snapped Myles, who apparently had lost it. "This is all too real. All my life you've held me back, and now, when I have this amazing opportunity to learn forever, big dumb Beckett is on hand once again to ruin everything."

Beckett's eyes were teary. "Myles, don't talk like that. Why are you being so mean?"

Myles aped his brother's voice but added a dollop of sarcasm. "Why am I being so mean? Why is Myles so nasty? Don't you get it? I'm the bad guy. Fowls have always been the bad guys. Except *my* career has been ruined because I'm too busy taking care of you."

Lazuli had been following one of the primary rules of contact—that being *Don't give anything away*, including the fact that she possessed the power of speech—but she couldn't help herself. Myles was going too far.

"Human," she whispered, her face turned from Teddy. "Calm yourself. We are a team."

This only increased Myles's fury. "A team? Oh, yes. The Regrettables." He laughed with bitter contempt. "Regrettable indeed. Do you know what I regret? The past eleven years, being shackled to a simpleton like *you*, Beckett. And the moment I laid eyes on *you*, fairy."

This is quality entertainment, thought the duke. I haven't seen anything this good since Charlie Chaplin played the West End. But my time is precious.

He tip-tapped through the smartphone's menu and his finger hovered over FIRE ALL, but he hesitated, for it seemed as though Myles Fowl was herding the others closer to the cliff edge.

Surely not, he thought. No one could be so callous.

Though that wasn't strictly true.

Lord Teddy had to own the fact that he himself could certainly be that callous when the occasion demanded it, and often when it didn't.

And these Fowls did have something of a reputation. In spite of his better judgment, Lord Teddy held off from loosing his metal dogs on his enemies.

I'll give him thirty seconds, decided the duke. To seal the deal before I fire.

Myles did it in twenty-five.

"We need a group conference," he said, and the others gathered around him on the cliff edge.

Beckett wiped his nose and took Whistle Blower in his arms. "You're being a bad brother, Myles. Saying stuff about us. You better stop it, or I'm taking a twin time-out."

Twin time-out was a fancy way of saying that Beckett intended to sulk, which, because of his exuberant nature, he had only ever managed to maintain for five minutes or so.

"We are totally surrounded," said Myles. "I can get out of this alone, but with Specialist Stupid here and the Terrible Twin, there is no hope."

"Watch it, human," said Lazuli.

Myles's lips moved and it seemed that he was counting. When he was satisfied with whatever number he reached, he said to Lazuli, "No, Laser, *you* watch it."

And he pushed the little blue fairy over the edge of the cliff.

Lord Teddy was surprised and delighted at this development even though the fairy had possibly been an asset worth dissecting.

By Jove, he thought. The little chap has gumption. He is prepared to do whatever it takes to survive and work on this project.

It would seem that the lure of immortality had been too much for Myles Fowl to resist, for, after he had in effect murdered the small blue creature, there was a snatch of garbled back-and-forth between the two brothers that culminated in some kind of clumsy attempt at a grapple, which ended with the twins bumping wrists. Then Myles snatched the toy troll from his brother's arms and elbowed Beckett, *his own twin brother*, over the cliff edge and sent him flailing soundlessly into the mist below.

Well, blimey, thought the duke. Those cliffs have claimed many victims, but never one twin done in by the other.

Myles turned from his grisly work. There were tears on his cheeks but also cold determination in his eyes.

"What do you think now, Your Grace?" he asked steadily, holding Whistle Blower close to his chest. "Do I have what it takes to be your assistant?"

Lord Teddy stroked his beard for a long moment, then stood down his army.

"I have to say that was an impressive interview," he said. "But let's not rush into anything. What say you to a probationary period? I shall review your performance on a daily basis, and if you're a useful little boy then there's a reasonable chance you won't follow your twin and . . ."

The duke did not need to finish the threat, but he did by whistling a long descending note that represented a fall and punctuating it with a *splat* noise.

Myles got the idea.

"I accept your offer, Your Grace," he said. "And I present this toy troll as a token of my good faith."

Lord Teddy Bleedham-Drye laughed long and hard.

"Good faith?" he said. "Good faith, you say? You just killed your brother, boy. The only faith you have is in yourself."

Myles could not find it in himself to argue with that.

The duke turned toward Childerblaine House and his robotic army parted before him like the Red Sea before Moses.

CHAPTER 13
NOS IPSOS ADIUVAMOS

The Island of St. George, Scilly Isles

Lord Teddy Bleedham-Drye's father had been fond of saying to company that Childerblaine House was built *to furnish old Georgie's dragon with a bonce. Bonce* being English slang for *head*. If the Island of St. George were indeed the fossilized skeleton of the decapitated dragon of legend, then the house would sit where the dragon's head might have been, at the top of the spinal curve.

"Of course, the whole thing is balderdash," said the duke now from behind his desk. "Saint George wasn't even English. The fellow was a Turk, don't you know? And according to the history buffs, he actually slayed the dragon in Morocco."

"*Slew*," corrected Myles Fowl. "And it was Libya where he did the deed, using a lance named Ascalon."

Myles was seated in an exquisite Edwardian club chair

with intricately carved wooden lion's-paw legs. The duke was semi-reclined in a complicated office chair that seemed to be comprised mostly of cables and pulleys and wearing slippers that he claimed were fashioned from the hide of an alligator he had wrestled from the Honey Island Swamp in Louisiana. He swirled a half-pint of brandy in a cut-glass snifter while Myles nursed a ginger beer. Each was swaddled in a blue velvet smoking jacket embroidered with the Bleedham-Drye family crest, which was an emperor swan with its wings spread over two crossed swords and the motto: NOS IPSOS ADIUVAMOS.

Meaning *We must help ourselves.*

The Bleedham-Dryes were obviously very fond of heraldry, as Myles had seen half a dozen of these ornate crests dotted around the manor already. It was uncomfortably reminiscent of Fowl Manor.

"Ascalon, eh?" said the duke. "A man who names his blades has too much time on his hands, if you ask me."

"A chap can never have *too* much time," said Myles, raising his glass.

"Never a truer word," said Teddy, obliging the boy with a *clink*.

The duke tossed his Myishi smartphone onto the desk surface and the contact was met by concentric circles of blue electronic ripples.

The entire surface is an induction plate, Myles realized. He rested a hand on the desktop and detected the slightest of vibrations.

This is the duke's server. Built right into his desk.

The pair settled into a comfortable silence while Teddy pawed through his cigar box searching for the perfect Monte Cristo. He chose one and offered the box to Myles. "Cigar, my boy?"

Myles declined. "I'll stick to my own brand, if you don't mind, Your Grace." He took a pack of seaweed sticks from the pocket of his robe and unwrapped one, rolling it between his finger and thumb. "Excellent crackle," he said, screwing the green stick into the corner of his mouth.

A fire blazed in the hearth, throwing flickering shadows on the eaves, and painting orange stripes on the steel curves of several suits of armor that stood watch over the pair. Myles rested his feet on a brass fire dragon that had been blackened by centuries of cinders. He was glad of the dragon's support, for without it his feet would be dangling, and it was difficult to maintain criminal-mastermind poise with dangling feet, and Myles supposed that was what he must be now.

A criminal.

The latest in a long line.

Lord Teddy lit his Monte Cristo with a taper and took several puffs, rotating the cigar for an even burn. "So here we are, Master Myles." He sighed with undisguised contentment.

"Here we are, Your Grace," agreed Myles. "And I must say, it is rare to see an aristocrat so happy."

Teddy barked with laughter. "That's absolutely correct.

From the nursery we are taught to repress our feelings, don't you know? *Decorum semper*. Propriety at all times."

"I quite understand," said Myles, who was reserved by nature, aside from his love of melodramatic posturing.

The duke stroked his magnificent beard until it might have purred. "But there are moments—when a fellow is on the verge of achieving his life's ambition, for example— when one feels a certain show of satisfaction is permitted by the gods of etiquette."

Myles chewed on his seaweed stick. "I know what you mean, Your Grace," he said. "I often think that an individual's character can be judged by what he considers worthy of celebration."

"Precisely," said Lord Teddy, punctuating each syllable with a jab of his cigar. "By Jove, that's exactly it."

"And today is certainly worthy of celebration." Myles drained his ginger beer. "This is a good brand. American?"

"I have it shipped from Seattle," said the duke.

"Medium bubble," noted Myles. "Very classy."

The duke swirled his brandy so that the liquid flashed in the grooves of the cut-glass goblet. "What you did today, on the Spine, ridding us of your own brother . . ."

Myles sighed as if the enormity of what he had done was just now dawning on him. But then the moment of reflection passed and he leaned forward on his elbows once more. Kneading his brow, he dropped his spectacles into the well between his forearms and onto the desk.

"I do not regret my actions, Your Grace," he said. "That

half-wit was no kin to me in any way that matters. I was glad to see the back of him."

"Still . . ." said Bleedham-Drye, watching Myles carefully for a lie. "He was blood."

"He was, and that's all he was," said Myles evenly. "A blood relative. Sometimes blood ties must be cut—surely you agree?"

"Indeed I do," said the duke. "I myself have pruned the family tree more than once to ensure certain inheritances."

Myles sighed again. "I was fond of poor Beckett. But we were incompatible as a unit. I gave the fellow a good eleven years to shape up."

"More than fair," said the duke. "I have never seen the like. He walked right up to the cliff edge. Extraordinary."

If Myles had any regrets, he hid them well. "A feeble mind is a malleable mind," he said.

Lord Teddy glanced up to the oak-paneled ceiling, considering his next words—that is, whether or not to say them.

"Do you know what, dear boy?" he said finally. "I'm going to tell you something. Confide in you, if you will."

Myles nodded slightly, honored.

"Now, don't sulk when I tell you this, Myles, but my initial plan was to kill you. Even though you more than proved your enthusiasm for our project, I had planned to dispose of you once you were no longer of use."

Not only did Myles not sulk, he actually dropped a wink. "I surmised as much, Your Grace. It was also my intention—to do away with you, that is. But now I have the feeling that we shall never outgrow our usefulness to each other. And, in point of fact, I enjoy your company. It is so refreshing to meet a like-minded individual."

"You were going to murder me?" said Teddy. "Capital. Poison in the brandy, I suppose." And now it was Lord Teddy's turn to wink. "Or nudge me over a cliff, perhaps."

"I try not to repeat myself," said Myles, not in the least offended. "I thought perhaps a cyanide capsule in your cigar."

Bleedham-Drye coughed a mouthful of smoke and just for a moment believed he'd come to the end of his rope, but then he caught the twinkle in Myles's eye.

"A cyanide capsule in my cigar," he huffed. "You are one of a kind, Fowl."

"I am now," said Myles, then offered a salute. "Here's to being one of a kind. After all, *adiuva nos ipsi*."

Teddy smiled. "Indeed. We must help ourselves."

"And we will," said Myles.

They toasted.

It would have been nauseating to watch had there been anyone to see.

Myles and Lord Teddy discussed the Brother Colman incident for an hour or so, but then science beckoned and the duke led his new friend up a metal staircase to his laboratory. The spiral stairway was of polished steel and bolted to the wall. As they ascended, the duke unconsciously whistled the short phrase of a tune over and over, and when Teddy punched in the eight-digit code to his lab keypad lock, Myles realized the significance of this melody.

Aha! he thought (actually thinking the interjection *aha!*). A Portunus Five-Star keypad. And now I know the code.

Lord Teddy ushered Myles into the lab with obvious and merited pride, for to walk through the attic laboratory itself was akin to taking a historical tour through the modern history of scientific endeavor. The duke had clearly been at this game for many decades, and nineteenth-century monocular compound microscopes stood alongside their modern electron equivalent.

Myles stopped before a gleaming instrument. "My goodness," he said. "Is this a Victorian bone saw?"

"Indeed it is," said the duke, picking up the saw. "You have a good eye for craftsmanship. That fellow has seen me through many a tough skull."

"I hate to resort to sayings," said Myles, "but it is true that a craftsman is only as good as his tools."

Teddy laughed. "Here's another saying for you: They say some people are tough nuts to crack. Not with this fellow in your hand." The duke replaced the saw on the table. "But as reliable as these old tools are, technological advances are truly most convenient. There is a lot of initial expense, I grant you, but I find that robots are not concerned with such trivial things as morals."

On they went through the laboratory. Past shelves lined with specimen jars, and miles of coiled tubing, and Bunsen burners lined up like tiny rockets, and spectrometers, and autopsy tables.

Bleedham-Drye had partially overcome St. George's incipient dampness with powerful dehumidifiers that droned in every corner like angry old men, but still the island insinuated its damp tendrils through cracks in the masonry. Myles sniffed the spore-laden air and wondered how experiments might be corrupted, but this thought evaporated when they reached the lab's latest test subject, who was being held inverted over a table by four robot arms, his tiny tusks puncturing the rubber lid of a collection beaker directly underneath him.

"Whistle Blower," he breathed.

The toy troll reacted groggily to his name, struggling vainly in the titanium clamps. The little chap was obviously sedated and there was an electrode attached to a shaved patch on his forehead.

"Whistle Blower?" said Lord Teddy. "What a curious name."

Myles recovered. "My idiot brother came up with it," he said. "Apparently he heard somewhere that an individual who squealed was known as a whistleblower."

The duke guffawed. "Oh, dear lord, I hate to speak ill of the dead, but what an idiot."

"I found the name quite charming, actually," said Myles. And then: "But of course you are right. What an idiot."

It was difficult not to feel sympathy for the tiny troll in these wretched conditions, especially when the electrode delivered a shock directly to the creature's brain. Whistle Blower reacted to this interference by chomping down on the rubber top and squirting twin jets of venom into the beaker.

Myles was stunned by this development, which he had not anticipated. "The venom should not be collected this way," he said, his tone clinical.

Lord Teddy was mildly surprised. "Don't tell me you feel sorry for this beast? Perhaps you are not the stalwart I took you for."

"I am a scientist, Your Grace," said Myles, striking a scientific-style pose of right hand cupping left elbow, left hand stroking chin. "This troll's comfort, or lack thereof, is of little concern to me. But if you repeatedly shock the fellow, then it is quite possible that the venom will be corrupted with diverse hormones and chemicals. Also, we should run an electrocardiogram to see how much his heart can take. It would be a catastrophe to lose our specimen during the first round of harvesting."

Lord Teddy toyed with his beard while he considered Myles. Was the boy trying to trick him, or were his concerns genuine?

Myles plowed on. "Frankly, I am appalled at this procedure. I had expected best practices, and this is most certainly not it. There could be any number of unwelcome side effects to ingesting this venom: nausea, migraine, paralysis." He paused. "Hair loss."

The duke removed his fingers from the depths of his

beard and, without a word, peeled the electrode from Whistle Blower's forehead.

"I concede the point," said the duke. "We shall harvest manually. It will take a little longer, but no matter. In the end, this is the world of man. No matter how magnificent the creature, it will fall before our superior intellect. Everything falls before us. Soon, even time itself will be vanquished."

Myles thrilled to this notion, in spite of his better nature. Imagine what could be learned in five lifetimes. In a hundred. Myles Fowl would literally be the smartest person in the world.

But at what cost? Whistle Blower seemed so desolate. His small shaggy head turned to Myles and he grunted. Even though Myles did not share his brother's magical gift of trans-species communication, he recognized that particular grunt.

He's calling for Beckett, he realized.

With his forefinger, Lord Bleedham-Drye stroked the venom beaker, which was perhaps one-third full of a mucilaginous, honey-colored liquid.

"Imagine," he said, "all the secrets contained in this jar. For thousands of years, man has searched for the fountain of youth, and here it is. We will drain this tiny troll till the animal is little more than a husk."

"There may be more to this troll than venom," said Myles. "We should do a complete blood workup and search for viruses and drug levels."

The duke had little patience for this notion. "What care I about viruses or drug levels? I will be immortal, dear boy."

"Immortality is expensive, Your Grace," Myles pointed out. "This troll's blood could conceivably cure various diseases and might be worth a fortune to Big Pharma. People need hope, and we can sell it to them."

The duke clapped Myles on the shoulder. "What price a dream, eh, my boy? Already our partnership yields dividends. The names of Bleedham-Drye and Fowl will go down in history, and we will live to see it." Lord Teddy removed the venom beaker from Whistle Blower's jaws. "But this we will never sell. This is for us alone."

And it seemed to Myles as though the duke would drain the beaker of venom right there and then.

"Have a care, Your Grace," said Myles. "We must proceed with caution with the elixir of life. Brother Colman survived only because of an almost incredible series of events that would be nigh on impossible to re-create. The venom must be analyzed and the dosage carefully calculated. Being a well-preserved corpse holds little attraction for me."

Lord Teddy held the beaker up to the laboratory light strips and Myles saw that there were tiny particles in the liquid that sparkled like gold dust.

"Marvelous," said the duke with some considerable reverence. "You have no idea how long I have searched for this. How much blood I have spilled, how much more I would be prepared to spill. . . . Oceans of blood."

Myles felt he had to ask. "But tell me, Your Grace, why? What drives you to such extremes?"

Lord Teddy thought before answering. "That, to quote Sherlock Holmes, is a three-pipe question."

Three-pipe problem, thought Myles, but he did not correct the duke, as he was trying to build trust.

The "three pipes" Lord Teddy alluded to were actually three more snifters of brandy, and once they had loaded tiny samples of Whistle Blower's venom into various analytical machines, including a spectrometer, a rheometer, and an elemental analyzer, they retired to a second study in the cellar, where the duke filled a brass tub from a pool that was plumbed directly into the bath. Myles noticed the slick coils of small electric eels gliding through the water and wondered if he himself were about to be tortured.

But no; Lord Teddy disappeared behind a screen and emerged clad in a neck-to-knee-long, striped Victorian bathing costume.

It would appear, thought Myles, that the duke is about to voluntarily electrocute himself.

Lord Teddy lowered his frame into the salt water, a brandy decanter beside the yellow washcloth on his varnished wooden bath tray. He quickly poured and swallowed his first measure, allowing the eels to cluster around him like old friends.

"Don't fret," said the duke to Myles. "These are only baby eels. And they know me, so low-level shocks only, and nothing direct. Even less electricity than our troll friend was getting. You should try it—the effect on the epidermis is phenomenal."

"I am eleven years old, Your Grace," said Myles, settling on a velvet footstool. "My epidermis is fine for the time being."

Lord Teddy poured himself yet another generous snifter of brandy, his only reaction to the almost continuous shocking being a slight quivering of the upper lip.

Two beings enduring shock treatment in one house, thought Myles. How utterly bizarre.

"Now to your question, dear boy," said the duke. "Why my obsession with eternal life? This is a subject I have often pondered. In the beginning I was simply an adventurer like many of my nineteenth-century peers. I traveled to India and beyond on the trail of glory and, of course, treasure. War, I found, was the best way to earn a sovereign, but I soon discovered that rich men die just as easily as poor ones. Cold steel does not differentiate between the two, as many of my fellow officers can bear witness to from beyond the grave. Life itself and its preservation, I realized, was the prize. Shortly after this inarguable truth occurred to me, I was wounded by the Afghans at Maiwand. Mortally wounded, as it happened—took a scimitar right in the guts. Oh, it was all done and dusted for the future duke of Scilly, according to the camp sawbones."

Lord Teddy paused for a nip at his brandy and Myles nodded as though the story had his full attention, which it most certainly did not. It would be a dull individual indeed who required any more than a half percent of his active brain cells to follow such a simple narrative, and Myles Fowl was definitely not a dull individual. He was using the rest of his gray matter to plot his next move.

The man is in a bath of electric eels, he thought. Surely this is my moment.

But Myles maintained an interested expression and Lord Teddy did not suspect anything was amiss. For, in truth, nothing was amiss. Yet.

"But the lure of my father's gold brought healers from far and wide," continued Lord Teddy. "Doctors, shamans, and crackpots. Charlatans, the lot of them. I was coated in potions and drained by leeches. Naturally, nothing worked. But there was one old man—an ancient beggar clad in rags; the fellow reeked of camels—who poured a single drop of liquid onto my wound. The next morning, he was gone and I was healed. And what's more, there was no scar—the wounded skin was completely rejuvenated. Smooth as an infant's posterior. The fellow disappeared with his purse fattened, but he left behind the belief that it was possible to extend one's life span. I knew that I could live forever, and, with your help, I shall do exactly that."

The duke topped up his glass for the third time and somehow relaxed contentedly while the eels coiled around his wrists and ankles like elaborate jewelry.

"So, young man," he said, "what do you think of my eel friends?"

"Actually, Your Grace," said Myles, "they are not, in truth, eels. They are knifefish."

"Don't be tiresome, Fowl," said the duke, disappointed. "Surely you appreciate the effort required to train these fellows, no matter what you call them. It involves a system of staggered introduction."

Myles began picking up Teddy's clothing, which the duke had simply discarded on the floor.

"Don't worry about that, dear boy," said Lord Teddy. "The robots will take care of it."

"It's no trouble," said Myles. "Mess distracts me. I cannot think straight with irregularities in my vision."

The duke waved a royal hand. "Well, then, by all means; perhaps you could be my butler."

This made Myles smile. Perhaps the duke would like what a butler could do for him, but he certainly would not like what a Butler would do to him.

Myles hung Lord Teddy's smoking jacket on a door hook. "In point of fact, I know very little about knifefish, aka electric eels. Only a few facts, in fact. For one thing, they have an excellent sense of smell underwater."

"You don't say?" said the duke, a little tipsy now and growing churlish. "That is the very definition of useless information."

Myles fished one of the duke's alligator slippers from under a divan. "And, because of their special talents, the *Electrophorus electricus* have very few predators. One main predator, in fact."

"And what might that predator be?" asked the duke, interested in spite of himself. After all, he was a hunter.

Myles held up the slipper. "Well, by strange happenstance, Your Grace, the electric eel's main predator is the American alligator."

Myles waited a beat for the duke's brain to catch up.

"Ah," said Lord Teddy, the implication dawning, and he reached for a handgun hidden under the washcloth on his bath tray, but it was too late for the duke to defend himself.

"Exactly, Your Grace," said Myles, and he tossed the slipper into the tub.

The electric eels took one whiff of alligator skin and went berserk.

Myles had been so displeased by Lord Teddy's mocking use of the phrase "useless information" that he added literal insult to actual injury by tearing the duke's smoking jacket from its hook and dropping it in a puddle on the floor, revealing his own suit underneath.

"Useless information," he said to the unconscious Lord Teddy, whose upper torso was draped over the tub's curved lip. "As if I, Myles Fowl, would ever deal in that particular commodity."

And then, realizing that this was perhaps not the time for petulant dillydallying, he dressed and hurried from the room at medium hustle so as not to trip over his own toes. It would be mortifying to ruin his own ingenious escape strategy by stumbling on the uneven flagstones. Behind him the bathwater popped and crackled like an energetic vat of rice-based cereal and the eels' subaquatic lightning bolts threw flickering shadows on the tapestry-draped walls.

Tapestries in a damp bathroom, thought Myles. I mean, honestly.

He felt a twinge of guilt for having electrocuted the duke beyond his usual limits, but the fish were little more than babies and the duke would awaken soon enough.

Having successfully exited the duke's bathroom without a single stumble, Myles clanked up the metal stairs, fervently hoping that Lord Teddy had not trained his eels to slither from their natural habitat and hunt intruders. It seemed unlikely, but in the past few days the unlikely had become almost commonplace, and only a fool did not adjust his mind-set accordingly. There were obviously things in the world that could not yet be explained by science.

Three stories later, Myles found himself panting at the laboratory door, unpursued by man, beast, or robot. He rested bent almost double for a moment, drawing deep breaths to his core and vowing to pay more attention to his cardio regime in the future. But as soon as his heart had dropped below two hundred beats per minute, Myles, whistling the same tune Teddy had earlier, summarily tapped in the lock code and pressed on into the lab. He was momentarily distracted by the Aladdin's cave of cutting-edge equipment, especially a cryogenics pod that was definitely not on the general market, but a whimper from Whistle Blower reminded him of his mission's urgency and he hurried past computer banks and elevated readouts to the troll station, where the little fellow had obviously been completely disoriented from being suspended upside down and pumped full of sedatives.

For a supposed scientist, the duke's methods are quite cavalier, thought Myles. It is no wonder his arms are elongated.

Whistle Blower reacted to Myles's approach with sluggish aggression, twitching his claws and rattling his bonds, all to no avail. It would take many multiples of the troll's strength to fracture titanium robot clamps.

Fortunately for Whistle Blower, it was a matter of half a dozen keystrokes on the nearest keyboard for Myles Fowl to free the little troll from his bonds.

Whistle Blower dropped into the plastic funnel, his head stoppering the funnel mouth.

Myles Fowl had never been known for his bedside manner. He'd once tried to assure a six-year-old food-poisoned Beckett by telling him *The German philosopher Friedrich Nietzsche said: "That which does not kill us, makes us stronger,"* a factoid that did nothing to ease the churning in his twin's belly.

And so now, as he gingerly tugged the toy troll out of the funnel by one leg, he had no idea how to comfort the creature.

"There now, little chap," he said. "Chin up and all that. It could be worse—you could be dead instead of simply drugged and depleted."

This had about as much effect on the troll as the Nietzsche quote had on Beckett half a decade earlier. Whistle Blower simply continued his soft moaning, his eyes white slits.

He will recover, thought Myles. He *must* recover.

In point of fact, there was indeed a recovery, but it was not the troll but rather the duke who exhibited more vitality than Myles had expected by appearing at the laboratory door. Teddy's hair stuck out in a frizzled halo, effectively tripling the size of his head, and from deep inside that hirsute globe came a raw wail.

"Fowl!" he cried. "Fowl."

Even at the age of eleven, Myles had become somewhat accustomed to hearing his own surname roared/screamed/yelled at him by irate adults, but he had been so sure the eels would blast the duke from consciousness for some time that he was surprised to see the fellow not ten feet away with his Victorian costume hanging from his limbs in sopping pouches.

"Bravo, Your Grace," said Myles. "You display remarkable powers of recuperation."

Lord Teddy offered a brief explanation before continuing with his offensive. "I've built up a resistance, don't you know? And also, I had a wireless grounding breaker stuck to my palm in case you tried something."

Lord Teddy held out his hand, revealing what looked like a circular Band-Aid. He tore off the device and threw it at Myles's feet.

"A breaker," said Myles. "I should have foreseen that."

And Myles realized that the unsettling emotion that he was experiencing was probably a blend of surprise and shock that the duke had not been completely taken in by his fratricide act. He took several steps backward—quicker than he would have liked, given what Beckett had always called his two left feet—and found himself with his back pressed hard against the safety bar of the balcony door.

Lord Teddy shook himself like a wet dog so the water flew in ribbons from his beard, and then returned to his previous state of anger.

"I almost trusted you, Fowl. I really wanted to believe I had found someone who understood."

Myles cradled Whistle Blower to his chest. "Oh, but I do understand, Your Grace. I admire your quest, in fact. But your methods are crude and unscientific. Craft cannot be replaced by equipment and brutality."

Lord Teddy checked that the venom beaker was in the desktop refrigerator and deposited it in a pouch at the front of his swimming costume, where it hung like a potbelly.

"I feel, my boy," he said, "that our partnership has run its course."

He strode to the wall-mounted Bleedham-Drye crest and drew both rapiers, tossing one toward Myles so that it skittered to a rest at the boy's feet.

"Shall we settle this like gentlemen?"

Myles wondered why on earth a chap would mount a crest in his laboratory and also felt that this challenge was a bit rich coming from a practiced swordsman with a considerable reach advantage, and so he replied, "No, Your Grace. We shall settle this like scientists."

Myles backed through the balcony door into the night, with the blood moon full at his back and the sea breeze sharpening his senses.

"Give me that troll," said Lord Teddy, trembling with indignant rage. "Get back in here this instant and hand him over."

Whistle Blower's extraordinary recuperative powers were kicking in, and the little fellow wriggled in Myles's arms.

In seconds he will be back to his destructive self, Myles realized.

And though he felt foolish even attempting to speak the creature's language, Myles growled an approximation of Beckett's name in what he supposed might be called Trollish.

Teddy was too stunned to maintain his anger. "Are you . . . ? Are you actually speaking to that troll, Fowl? Have you completely lost your marbles?"

Myles spoke Beckett's name once more in the troll's tongue and the effect was remarkable. Whistle Blower stretched out in the crook of his arms and burbled as though he were taking a nap in a beachside hammock and not at the center of a gothic scenario involving a vertiginous altitude and a murderous duke in his swimming costume, with a backdrop of all the best nature had to offer.

Even at this height Myles's shaven skull was quickly coated with a fine salt mist, which the boy was absently aware would dehydrate his epidermis. He also knew that that he only had two choices regarding which way he could go, those choices being up or down, and so he talked to the duke to buy himself a few paltry seconds.

"My marbles, Your Grace, are all accounted for," he said. "You are the one who suffers from marble deficiency."

Teddy had calmed somewhat now that he had a sword in his hand. "My dear boy, you are trapped, and that is all there is to it. Step inside and we can talk about this. I may decide to simply give you a thrashing and send you on your way."

"A gracious offer," said Myles, "but I am the one in control here. After all, I have your test subject in my grasp." And with that he dangled Whistle Blower over the balcony railing by one foot.

The duke was not in the least alarmed and, in fact, scoffed, which involved a flapping of his lips followed closely by a sarcastic comment. "Of course, my boy. The bald twerp on the very high ledge is in complete control." He knuckled the venom beaker in his pouch so it clinked. "I have what I need right here, Myles Fowl. Technically, I don't need either of you."

"Perhaps," said Myles, "but that small sample will run out."

"Perhaps," said Lord Teddy. "And perhaps I will hire somebody even smarter than you to replicate the venom. So, unless you can climb or fly, you are certainly not in control."

Myles looked to the skies and then to the courtyard below as though considering these options.

"I'm afraid, Your Grace, that physical activity has never been my strong suit," he said. "But I do know someone who can climb, and another someone who can fly."

And with that magnificently dramatic declaration, Myles Fowl turned and dropped Whistle Blower over the balcony and followed this shocking action by raising his arms and taking off like some form of miniature superhero.

The duke, driven beyond demented by the odious grandstanding twin, lunged at the boy's ascending ankles, succeeding in snagging one.

"No, you don't, my clever lad," he said, digging in his heels. "No one turns his back on royalty."

At this point the duke's gaze was naturally directed upward, and he realized that Myles Fowl was not, in fact, flying, but being airlifted by the blasted fairy who was supposed to be dead.

"Bamboozled!" he cried, and he would have gnashed his teeth if the thought had occurred to him, which it did not. What did occur was that he had a sword in his hand and the fairy's gossamer wings were well within the reach of his elongated arms.

I'll bring the pair of them tumbling down, he thought.

At this point Whistle Blower's fate had temporarily slipped Lord Teddy's mind. In fact, his quest for eternal life seemed somewhat less important than it had moments ago.

Now the shining goal in his life was to destroy this infuriating boy with his smug grin.

And so the duke put his cricket training to good use and swung the foil in a wide arc, which was, strictly speaking, a move more suited to a saber, but Teddy was angry and can be forgiven for mixing up his weapons. However, bad technique or not, the swing did achieve its purpose, that purpose being to damage Lazuli's wings. The tip of Teddy's foil sliced through her lower right winglet, which was possibly not catastrophic, and the specialist could have pulled out of the spin given perhaps thirty seconds of open sky.

But Lazuli had neither an open sky nor half a minute and was weighed down by a passenger. The ratio of passengers to pilots was increased to three to one when Lazuli's rig lost altitude abruptly and Teddy was forced to relinquish his hold on Myles's leg. The duke's hand was replaced almost immediately by Beckett Fowl's own, as the twin had climbed Childerblaine House's gray wall to take delivery of Whistle Blower. When Lazuli's whining rig spun her down and into the wall, Beckett thought he might save both Lazuli and his brother.

"Myles," he cried, "hold on!"

Myles did not answer, for he was engaged in quite an acrobatic activity and was intensely uncomfortable.

Somehow, in a single moment, Beckett threaded his arm under Lazuli's belt, securing the fairy to him. With his natural instinct for weights and balance, Beckett figured he could both maintain his perch on the wall and support Myles and Lazuli, for a few seconds at least. Had Lazuli's rig been inactive, Beckett might have proved correct, but the damaged wing split completely and interfered with the upper set of wings. The left wings went into spasm with such force that the entire group of assorted fairies and humans were snatched from the wall and sent pinwheeling through the dragon's breath toward the unforgiving rock some thirty feet below.

For perhaps one hundredth of a single second, the bunch left their outline in the fog, cartoon-character style.

It could be pointed out, perhaps somewhat cruelly, that Beckett and his intrepid comrades had finally lived up to their chosen group name:

The Regrettables.

CHAPTER 14

CHOMP

THIS is perhaps an opportune moment for us to freeze our heroes in mid-plummet and swing back in time to the first major fall of the day. You will remember how, mere hours before, Myles had succeeded in tipping one team-mate to her supposed death and then pushing his brother off the top of a cliff, sealing the deal with a wrist bump. This was step one in his audacious plan to hoodwink the duke and save the Regrettables, for, in fact, ye of little faith, it was never Myles's intention to betray his twin. Certainly indulging in criminality is a Fowl family trait, but, unlike the backstabbing Bleedham-Dryes, one Fowl would never sell another down the river—or over a cliff edge, for that matter.

In Myles's mind, his plan was simple mathematics and therefore utterly straightforward, and it never would have made it onto the CHOMP (Chart of Myles's Plans) that he updated on a weekly basis and kept on NANNI's desktop.

The current number one was his plot to steal an Egyptian pyramid during an eclipse using only a revolutionary system of pneumatic levers and some double-sided tape.

As a matter of fact, Myles had been mildly surprised when Lord Teddy even partially fell for his ruse, but he supposed that, in all fairness to the duke, he had been missing a vital piece of information, that being the fact that Lazuli had allowed Myles to examine her wrist computer as the Orient Express passed through Switzerland. During this cursory examination of the display, he had quickly realized that the system ReGen MeePee (Regeneration Mini Program) was funneling power to functions in order of urgency. The first priority for reactivation was the computer's readout itself. The LEP device had not yet been ready for complex calculations, but Myles had determined, using the exponential growth equation $Y=AB^x$, that the circuits would regenerate sufficiently to provide the next available function—flight mode—in seventeen hours. And so Myles had started a mental countdown toward that time.

Fast-forward seventeen hours minus five seconds, and we find the so-called Regrettables clustered at the edge of St. George's precipice. Myles was finishing up his countdown to the moment he could safely nudge Specialist Heitz over the edge. Her wings activated just as predicted, because *science*, and it was only when Myles saw Specialist Heitz hovering at a safe altitude that he tackled Beckett. Not literally tackled him, of course, for that would be foolhardy given Beckett's expertise in all matters physical. Instead, he babbled on about brotherhood and loyalty, but that was just structured noise—the important information exchanged between the brothers was passed through the medium of Fowl Argot.

Myles did not go into details, for he knew that Beckett preferred the direct approach. And, in this spirit, he waggled his tie with three fingers, and Beckett realized that everything was okay. So, when Myles told him to jump, he did so without hesitation.

To explain: The Fowl family had for years enjoyed film night, but the only movies that could tempt Artemis into the den and away from his laboratory were the old black-and-white Laurel and Hardy shorts, which never failed to crack everyone up. Even Butler had been known to stop scowling, which was his equivalent of an uncontrollable laughing fit. The most famous running joke in those movies was when Hardy waggles his tie and says to Laurel, "Well, here's another nice mess you've gotten me into."

Which was something Myles often had occasion to say to Beckett. He generally augmented the quote with the clause *and I suppose it's my responsibility to get us out of it*. This sentiment was absorbed into the Argot minus the actual words. Myles simply waggled his tie and Beckett was assured his twin had a plan to deliver them from whatever mess they were in. That was all Beckett needed to know and, in fact, wanted to know. So, when Myles waggled his tie on the Spine, Beckett handed over Whistle Blower, did a quick wrist bump, and, with utter confidence, leaped off the cliff into the arms of Specialist Lazuli Heitz, who had absolutely zero clue as to what was going on and was only sure of one thing: Humans are unpredictable.

Now Lazuli was falling again, tangled in a jumble of limbs, and it seemed as though the rescue had gone sideways, and this time there was no infernally clever Fowl plan to cushion their impact.

It's up to you, Lazuli, she thought. You're the LEP specialist. Time to prove you are more than semiprecious.

Quite a challenge for someone with barely a nanosecond to spare, loaded down with two humans and a toy troll.

If only I had magic! she thought for perhaps the eightieth time that day. If I had some magic, we might survive this.

In truth, Lazuli did not form this precise thought, for it occurred so often that she had assigned it a color. Whenever Lazuli vaguely lamented her lack of magic, an angry orange screen rippled across her inner monologue.

It was true that many hybrids never manifested on the magical spectrum, but some were late bloomers. Even so, Lazuli was coming to the end of her sixtieth year and no longer an adolescent by anyone's measure.

In the Academy, she had been the only member of her class without some kind of magic. And she was the only specialist in the history of the LEP without magic. It was stressful enough being a tiny blue pixel, but Lazuli was fine with that—more than fine, actually. She was proud of her heritage and was, in fact, a member of an online pixel community. But not having magic did rankle. Everything was so much more difficult.

Lazuli realized with some alarm that the orange veil was more intense than usual. In fact, it was dominating her consciousness. Her brain seemed to be heating up and growing too big for her cranium.

Perhaps I'm having a panic attack? she thought.

Which would be of no use whatsoever.

Quit it, she told her brain. Think of something useful.

But in spite of Lazuli's admonition, her mind focused on her unfair lack of magic and the orange glow intensified, seeming to color her actual vision.

Lazuli seemed to have no choice but to give in to the mood, though it was against her nature to wallow.

It isn't fair! she thought. We're all going to die because I have no magic. No stupid magic.

As they scythed through St. George's ring of mist, it seemed to Lazuli that the cloud itself was tinted orange.

Sunset, she thought. Is it sunset?

But it was not the sun. Lazuli felt the *orangeness* emanating from her in an irresistible wave.

I'm having a psychotic episode, she thought.

The hard-packed earth surrounding Childerblaine House rushed up to meet them, and Lazuli knew it would be almost as unforgiving as rock.

Someone might survive, she thought. Whoever lands on top.

But she abandoned this thought as it seemed there was no more room inside her for anything but orange, and it became so large that it had to come out.

Lazuli felt herself going mad and opened her mouth to scream, but, instead of a scream, what blasted from her was a roaring bolt of fire that shot straight down, liquefying ten cubic tons of clay and boring through to the seawater below, which fizzed up to fill the space.

Specialist Heitz thought that perhaps her mind was supplying a nice hallucination so she would die calmly. But when the group crashed into the cooling slop of a mud bath, she understood that the fire and its effects were real, and she suddenly knew what the mystery five percent of her DNA was.

I'm a little bit goblin, thought Lazuli as the mud closed over them.

And also: I think I broke my nose.

Beckett Fowl was also thinking on the way down. He was totally relaxed now that Myles was by his side (and under his armpit and between his legs) and had no doubt that his twin's big brain would take it from here. And so he simply wondered what they would have for dinner, and whether Whistle Blower could do handstands, and then:

Muuuuuud! Best rescue ever!

* * *

Myles's pre-impact thought process wasn't so much a process as a loop.

His ingenious and largely improvised plan had completely failed, and now they were plummeting toward intense agony at the very least, and there was precisely nothing he could do about it. Myles had, of course, fallen flat on his face before, plan-wise—three times, to be precise—but now he was about to fall flat on his face in more ways than one. The shock of his own helplessness had almost shut down Myles's brain and it was all he could do to mentally mumble *No. This is not right. I had a plan* over and over until it rebounded in the echo chamber of his mind.

Myles did manage to utter two words in the final moment before impact, just after a fireball from Lazuli's mouth provided them with a mud bath to land in.

"Oh, my," he said.

He really should have kept his mouth shut.

High above, Lord Teddy watched the descent from the laboratory balcony. His initial emotional blend at the prospect of the death and maiming that would result from the fall could be described as fierce glee tempered with regret.

Glee that the Fowl Twins would be no more.

Slight regret that the troll would probably die alongside or underneath them.

But mostly glee.

Then the cloud of mist turned orange and was suddenly burned off, and so the duke could clearly see Myles and his sorry bunch tumbling toward a mud pool that he could have sworn had not been there earlier in the day.

"Blooming hell!" swore Bleedham-Drye, slapping the railing with one hand. "What has the Fowl brat done this time?"

It was too much for a fellow to bear. In all his years on this earth, the duke had never encountered such an ingenious trickster. And while part of him respected Myles Fowl's wiles, most of him dearly wished to stamp those wiles underfoot.

Lord Teddy pointed a rigid finger at the orange mist.

"That was your last chance, my boy!" he shouted. "Your absolute last chance. If you are indeed still alive down there, then prepare to die, for I, Teddy Bleedham-Drye, Duke of Scilly, have had enough."

Under normal circumstances, the inflamed duke would be a terrible sight to behold, but, on this occasion, Teddy's frizzled hair resembled brittle cotton candy, his soaked swimming costume was more comical than imposing, and his vocal cords, dehydrated from his misadventure with the eels, had elevated his baritone to a far higher pitch.

"Enough, do you hear me?" he squeaked. "Prepare to meet your maker, Fowl."

Five minutes earlier, Beckett Fowl would have laughed heartily at the sight and sound of the distraught duke. But then again, five minutes earlier Beckett Fowl was not drowning in mud.

The instant mud pool had indeed been a lifesaver, but it

was a double-edged one in that Lazuli's firebolt had drilled through the island, finding the ocean below, and while the pressurized water was surging upward now, it could just as quickly drop back down to sea level, taking the Regrettables with it.

And, as much as Beckett Fowl adored sloshing around in mud, he knew in that instinctual way of his that while they were riding a swell at the moment, soon the swell would begin to suck.

"Okay, team," he said once his mouth broke the surface. "Fun's over."

Lazuli heard this, or at least thought she did.

Did Beckett say this was fun? she thought. There must be mud in my ear.

Beckett's arm was still looped under Lazuli's belt, and so it took barely any effort to sling the small fairy onto relatively dry land. Whistle Blower took care of himself, scampering along his human friend's body and stepping neatly from the crown of the boy's head to solid ground.

Beckett was about to haul himself and the semi-catatonic Myles over the muddy rim when he cocked his head to one side and listened to a wave crash against the nearby shore.

"Water spout coming," he said, and rode the suddenly rising water from a blowhole, landing easily on two feet with Myles gasping under his arm. The water throbbed skyward in a giant column, then blossomed into a fountain worthy of a Roman piazza.

Beckett watched the ocean retreat down the blowhole and grunted in Whistle Blower's direction.

Whistle Blower rejoined with a similar grunt, which Lazuli assumed was an approximation of *Wasn't that awesome?* And suddenly she understood Beckett a little better. You just had to think of him as a toy troll, but taller and hairless.

Myles Fowl collapsed onto his back, arms crossed on his chest, looking for all the world like a boy laid out for his own Irish wake. He was draped in a shroud of congealing mud and all that was missing to complete the wake illusion was a pair of pennies for his unseeing eyes.

Beckett nudged him with the toe of his fencing boot. "Myles, what's the matter? We made it."

Myles blinked and salt water trickled from his eyes, cleaning pathways in the mud.

"My plan didn't work," he said. "I failed."

Beckett squatted beside him. "I used to do what you're doing," he said. "Live in the past. But now I know the past is past. When your plan failed, that was then. This is now, and we need a new plan. Say good-bye to old-failure Myles, and hello to new-plan Myles."

Myles closed his eyes to absorb this, then said, "But we must learn our limits from our mistakes, brother."

"You always say that learning is good. Is that a lie?"

Myles opened his eyes just enough to squint at Beckett. "Are you using social influence on me, Beck?"

"Me?" asked Beckett innocently. "I'm the action twin, remember? I don't know anything about brain stuff."

Myles clarified the term. "Social influence is a tactic that psychologists use to challenge patients."

Beckett pulled Myles to his feet. "Whatever you say, Brainiac. All I know is that a really smart but boring guy once told me that what doesn't kill us makes us stronger. Is that true, brother, or was that boring guy just speaking words?"

The mud fell in sheets from Myles's clothing and he thought, Two suits destroyed in as many days, but he said, "It's true, Beck. Thanks for reminding me."

If he were being honest, Myles did not feel very strong at the moment, but, thanks to his brother's optimism, he could feel his confidence already reasserting itself like a fire in his belly.

Fire in my belly, he thought. That reminds me.

Myles turned to Lazuli, who had torn off her helmet and was vomiting smoke and mud, her back arching with each retch.

"Specialist Heitz," said Myles, "as soon as you feel able, we must be away from here. I imagine the duke is already on the move."

"Agreed," Lazuli managed between heaves. "Just a"— heave—"second, Myles."

"You know," continued Myles, "that what doesn't kill us makes us stronger."

Lazuli was in no mood for German philosophy and shook a warning fist at the twin, but Myles continued to speak undaunted.

"When you have an interval in your bouts of illness, perhaps we should drill down into what happened. You appear to have blossomed into a magical creature. Artemis's files are typically incomplete on this subject, so perhaps you could fill in the gaps? It would help me to strategize if I knew the extent of your gifts."

Lazuli knew she wouldn't be much help in this area. The fire-breathing seemed magical, but in fact it was not. Goblins were born with the biological tools. Heaven knew she had been through enough MRIs and physicals for little things like oil ducts at the back of her throat and fireproof body parts to be detected. Today they had finally served a purpose.

She spat into the earth and accepted Myles's offer of a handkerchief to wipe her mouth.

"I don't fully understand how it's possible for me to make fire."

"Magic," said Beckett, as if it was obvious. "Magic *is* impossible."

Whistle Blower aped Beckett's stance and growled an approximation of the word *impossible*.

Myles nodded. "It seems that will have to satisfy us for now. Can you walk, Specialist?"

Lazuli flashed on a hokey human movie she had always loved, and, with a wry grin, said, "I'll bloody well walk out of here."

But she wouldn't walk off the island.

Ever.

Enraged though Lord Teddy most assuredly was, he made time to snatch his bathrobe from its hook and tug on a pair of riding boots that stood sentry by the front door. He checked the pockets for the shells he kept in most of his clothes, and selected a twelve-gauge Myishi semiautomatic gas gun from the umbrella stand, slinging it over his shoulder, which left his hands free for the two wireless remote mitts that he used to control his various robots and battle drones. He was on a maintenance contract with Myishi, which had cost him a bloody fortune over the years even with his friends-and-family discount, but it did ensure that St. George's defenses were always ready to go at the touch of a button. The duke pressed that button now, and the aluminum central server built into his desk clunked once then rumbled into life.

And now, my boy . . . thought Teddy, flexing his fingers in the controller mitts, activating literally hundreds of electronic death/gardening/cleaning machines, including dozens of his own construction—little steampunk fellows with tommy guns attached to their arms, which Ishi Myishi had described as *delightful anachronisms*.

It is time to end this tiresome chapter in the life of Teddy Bleedham-Drye. The chapter titled: "Lord Teddy Meets the Fowl Twins."

There was only one way, it seemed, to be sure of eradicating the Fowl blight.

Massive overkill.

And Teddy was prepared to pound a good chunk of his own island with ordnance to ensure that Myles Fowl and his merry gang were no more.

Mostly Myles, if he were honest.

CHAPTER 15
THE SWORD & THE PEN

MOSTLY Myles was feeling frustration. It felt to him like the universe was intent on eliminating his group. It was indeed regrettable.

Perhaps Beck's name for us is, in fact, appropriate, he thought with some glumness. It seemed as though his intellect was about to be defeated by sheer firepower, disproving the trite old maxim that *the pen is mightier than the sword*.

The reasons for Myles's glumness could be itemized as follows:

1. His fellow team members were in pitiful disarray—most notably Specialist Heitz, who seemed capable of little more than snatches of conversation in between barfs.
2. The toy troll, while undeniably cute, even with a shaven patch on his forehead, was incapable of grasping the seriousness of the situation and was lying with Beckett in the mud.

3. His brother Beckett was incapable of grasping the seriousness of the situation and was lying with Whistle Blower in the mud.

4. He himself was running dangerously low on ideas and lacked confidence in the various schemes he'd already put in motion.

I need a win, thought Myles. Then aloud: "I need a win, NANNI."

But, of course, NANNI's voice was not in his ear.

At any rate, a win seemed increasingly unlikely when one considered the myriad lethal weapons headed their way. The air was filled with an electronic cacophony, and it seemed as though there was not a square inch of earth or sky that the duke's machines did not inhabit. In seconds the group were surrounded by murderous minions.

It would have been prudent for Teddy to give the kill order, but he held back, preferring to negotiate before pulling the virtual trigger. So, as soon he was through the front door and satisfied that his robotic army had surrounded Myles and his pathetic band, Teddy belted his robe and considered how he might once again negotiate possession of the toy troll. As he strolled across the courtyard, he looked every inch the picture of an eccentric nobleman out for a spot of hunting on his estate.

He did not have far to stroll, for Myles and his bunch had plummeted some thirty feet from the laboratory turret into a mud puddle on the grass that bordered the house on three sides, but something caused the duke to miss a step: a sinkhole by the wall. Lord Teddy knew every blowhole on St. George—there were many—and he was one hundred percent certain that there hadn't been a sinkhole there this morning. A puddle, perhaps, but definitely not a sinkhole.

Blast the boy, he thought. That sinkhole is adjacent to the family plot and could very well cause a disaster.

There was no doubt in Teddy's mind that Myles was somehow responsible for the geological formation, but he sensed with his hunter's nose that the boy was no longer a threat. Even so the duke was on high alert. There would be no more risk-taking with these little blighters. If the last couple of increasingly bizarre days had taught him anything, it was not to underestimate the twins, and, on top of that, he had no idea what the tiny blue fairy was capable of. So Lord Teddy ignored weapons protocol and kept his forefingers on both triggers of his wireless controllers and his remaining fingers and thumbs on the various control buttons.

Myles saw the duke approaching through the throngs of buzzing, beeping, and whirring robots and could not help but be impressed by the sheer volume of the little machines. The duke must have forked over a pretty penny to Ishi Myishi for the metallic swarm, which split like a theater curtain to allow their human master access to Myles Fowl and his bedraggled band.

Once Lord Teddy was standing about twenty feet away

from Myles, he stopped. His hair had settled somewhat, and he seemed like a man in charge again, which, in his opinion, he was.

"And so here we are again, dear boy," he said to Myles. "Don't you find these confrontations tiresome?"

"Usually I would," said Myles, the brightness of his tone belying the barbed twists of anxiety in his gut. "But this one is so entertaining. I have never been threatened by garden implements before." Myles pointed to a beetle-shaped robot right in front of him. "Is this a hair dryer?"

"Indeed, it is. Very powerful action, in fact. I shall probably use that one to blow your remains into this blowhole."

"Very droll," said Myles, and, to give himself a moment to think, he picked another robot to insult. "And that lawn mower—shall it be giving our troll friend a haircut?"

Lord Teddy wiggled a combination of fingers and lawn-mower blades slid out from underneath the machine and whirred vertically.

"Perhaps," said Lord Teddy. "But this little fellow also does hedges. And kneecaps."

Myles winced, as anyone in their right mind would when their kneecaps were threatened.

"There's no call for that kind of talk, surely, Your Grace," he said. "A gentleman does not threaten violence."

"This one does," said Teddy, and he flexed his fingers so that the sights of every single drone and land-bound robot focused on Myles's head. "And more than threaten. I guarantee it."

Myles closed his eyes against the glare and wished that perhaps Lazuli would recover sufficiently for a second display of her newfound magic. But it seemed that there would be no assistance. Beckett and Whistle Blower were prone in the mud, and, judging by her sky-blue pallor, Lazuli was fit for little more than a spell in a hospital bed hooked up to various drips.

"I have a proposition for you," continued the duke, "though there really is no incentive for me to offer terms. But I am, as you say, a gentleman. Give me the troll and whatever that blue thing is, and I will kill only you. For now, at least. Your brother may leave unharmed. Physically unharmed, that is. I imagine the sight of his twin being cut in two by lasers might scar his psyche somewhat."

The knot of anxiety in Myles's belly tightened. "Those are hardly favorable terms, Your Grace."

Bleedham-Drye shrugged. "They are what they are. You have ten seconds to decide."

Beckett chose this moment to get involved. "Five seconds," he said, jumping to his feet.

"Beck, please," said Myles. "This is a life-or-death situation."

"Four," said Beckett, counting down on his fingers.

"I am a man of my word," said Lord Teddy. "So I'll see your four seconds and double them."

"Three," said Beckett, peering into the blowhole.

Myles felt as though a serpent were constricting his intestines. "This is not helpful, Beckett."

"Ooh," said Whistle Blower, joining his human friend at the chasm's edge.

The duke blinked. "Did that thing just say 'two'?"

"One," said Beckett, and he jumped into the blowhole.

The troll went with him.

All this jumping off and into things, thought the duke. But this time, unlike Myles Fowl, Teddy Bleedham-Drye knew what was going on. This was his island, after all.

He flicked the safeties on his glove controls and shrugged the strap off his shoulder, pumped a cartridge into the shotgun's chamber, and waited.

A moment later, there came a rumbling as a wave passed below the rock shelf and powered up through the fissure.

"Ha!" said Lord Teddy. "Do you really think I haven't ridden the water chutes on St. George, Myles? I used to do it for fun. My own dear pater would toss me into blowholes to toughen me up when I was five."

Myles understood then what Beckett was attempting, but he also realized that, for Teddy, this was the equivalent of target practice.

Beck and Whistle Blower are little more than clay pigeons, he thought.

"Pull!" cried Lord Teddy, and, right on cue, a water spout erupted from the newly bored blowhole, and with it came Beckett and Whistle Blower. They were borne high into the air before they disengaged from the salt water and engaged with the nearest drone. If a chap hadn't been expecting the move, then it might have been effective, but Lord Teddy was prepared to sacrifice a few drones in order to immobilize the jumpy Fowl boy and his pet.

"Die, evil drone!" cried Beckett as he pounced on the nearest flying robot. It dipped under his weight, rotors whining, then fizzled out altogether as Beckett yanked out its engine wires like entrails. Whistle Blower performed much the same action on not one but three drones, springing from one smoking machine to another, relishing the destructive acts.

"By Jove!" exclaimed the duke. "They are agile blighters, are they not?" He laughed. "This is most entertaining, dear boy, but time's a-wasting. . . ."

And, taking casual aim, the duke blasted off two shells, nailing both his moving targets in the space of perhaps two seconds. It was marksmanship at a most impressive standard. Beckett plopped to the ground at his brother's feet, his impact cushioned by the wobbling blob of cellophane that had wrapped around him, restricting his movements. Whistle Blower fell on top of his friend, which was perhaps fitting, and their cellophane blobs blended so that boy and troll shared a single prison.

"Bull's-eye!" crowed the duke, but, in true aristocratic form, he limited his celebration to this single outburst before shouldering the weapon, reactivating his glove remotes and returning to the business at hand.

"The troll I will keep," he said to Myles. "But your brother goes down the blowhole, and you, dear boy, will follow shortly thereafter. As for the fairy, I do believe I shall harvest her organs for study."

This casual declaration of murderous intent turned Myles's blood to ice and it was all he could do to stay on his feet. Mortality, it seemed, was about to come calling. No time-stops. No counting to ten. Dead forever.

He will kill us without remorse, thought Myles, and unlike during previous near-death escapades, he had time for the notion to sink in. Dear Specialist Heitz and charming little Whistle Blower will be mere lab rats. And it's all my fault.

Myles saw the pain on his brother's face as the cellophane began squeezing, and the expression broke his young heart.

If I do one thing before I die, it will be to relieve Beck's suffering.

But how to achieve this humanitarian objective?

Myles thought back to the two lemons who had been shrink-wrapped in the shower room. Steam from Lance's lance had distended the cellophane. He did not have steam at hand, but perhaps he had a substitute.

Myles eyed the hair dryer that was mounted on a small cherry-picker-type platform, possibly so it could dry the duke's beard while he walked.

I have a more noble use for you, little fellow, he thought, snatching the hair dryer from its clamps. He flicked the switch and stuck the nozzle into the cellophane, wiggling it through so the hot air could create an air pocket between Beckett and Whistle Blower. Almost immediately the cellophane wrap expanded, various bubbles and blisters appearing on its surface and magnifying Beckett's features. Whistle

Blower clawed at a thin-skinned blister until he managed to open an airhole.

Myles dropped to his knees, stretching the hole till Beckett's face appeared. Unfortunately, it was impossible for him to remove more of the cellophane, for it was too tightly wrapped.

"Beck, are you hurt?"

Beckett drew a deep breath, then smiled. "I counted, did you see? I did a Myles thing."

"I saw," said Myles. "That was clever. I wouldn't have thought of it."

Beckett disagreed. "It wasn't clever. It was stupid. But I thought to myself, Myles has a plan, so all he needs is time. We bought you some."

"You did," said Myles, thinking that it was too late now for his plan.

"It's time for brains now," said Beckett, wriggling his hand through the hole. "Go use yours, brother."

"I will," said Myles, trying not to weep.

"Wrist bump?" said Beckett.

"Always," said Myles, and they did their signature move, which was touching, but also more gross than usual because of the slime coating both of them.

That is possibly our final wrist bump, thought Myles as he stood to face the duke and his army of killer drones.

Lazuli had never in all her life felt this wretched. She was so nauseated that it did not seem possible she would ever recover. Even as her spine shuddered and her stomach convulsed, Lazuli felt there was more at play here than simple biliousness. She had to be changing at a molecular level. And it wasn't just her goblin DNA revealing itself. Her magic had finally surfaced, and, in all likelihood, she would not live to take advantage of it. If the spasms didn't kill her, then the human with his murderous machines would. Somewhere in her subconscious, where rational thought had taken refuge while her body dealt with the illness, Lazuli knew what was happening: late-onset magical warp spasm. It was rare but not unheard of for a hybrid's magic to manifest in times of extreme stress. It was also not unheard of for the hybrid's antibodies to violently reject the magic, which could literally tear her apart. At the very least, Lazuli knew she belonged in a hospital under observation from a warlock who specialized in cases like hers.

I am in for a rough few days, she thought. And then: If any of us live for a few days, which is unlikely.

Her angel had once told her: *If your magic ever shows up, Specialist, it will have a mind of its own. Think of magic like a symbiote who is desperate to survive. If you are born magical, you learn to control it naturally, but if it manifests late in life, it's like suddenly having an extra arm flailing about on your chest.*

Lazuli understood that now. When the fire had burst forth from her mouth, she had felt as though it had been a part of her but certainly not belonging to her.

And now her vision turned orange again, and her breath made the air shimmer.

The magic protects itself, she realized, and suddenly she was standing up beside the Fowl boy, preparing for the fight.

What do I do? she wondered. How do I turn it on?

If the magic could have answered, it would have said: *Leave that part to me.*

Lord Bleedham-Drye realized that, while the odds were with him, he did not have the higher ground, which any chap with ten minutes of battle time under his belt knew was advantageous in a fight. In this particular case, the higher ground would facilitate his murder of the Fowl boy without having to damage the troll, and so, while Myles Fowl was fussing over his brother with a hair dryer, he guided one of Myishi's more robust drones to land before him, and he pushed his feet into the adapted ski clamps on its back until he heard them click.

This was the first time Lord Teddy had used this particular tool, and he was pleasantly surprised that the platform drone lifted off smoothly, just as Myishi had assured him it would, bearing his weight without any discernible stress on the rotors.

You never let me down, Myishi, he thought, grinning tightly. It was not what could be described as a happy grin—more the grin that might be observed on the chops of a wolf with the scent of blood in his nostrils.

He noticed that the little blue fairy had stumbled to her feet and was shaking like a newborn deer. Lord Teddy decided that on second thought it was probably best to put the creature down. She doubtless had people who would come looking for her.

He held down the voice-control button under his left thumb. "All eyes," he said to his robotic minions.

Over a hundred laser dots painted Myles Fowl and his blue friend the deep red color of fresh blood, and Lord Teddy realized that this moment right now was the most supervillain moment of his entire life.

He held down the voice-command button again. "All video drones record a three-D virtual package and live-stream it to Myishi. Old Ishi will be so proud. He might even use this video on his website."

This command he would come to regret.

Myles had only one card to play, and that card was no longer up his sleeve. In fact, he had played it several hours ago, shortly after arriving on St. George, and it seemed now in retrospect that his gambit had been a rash waste of resources. He knew instinctively that the duke had finished monologuing and was on the point of obliterating him utterly. Judging by the sheer volume of weaponized drones and robots pointing their business ends in his direction, there wouldn't be enough left of him to bury. He would be little more than dust to blow out to sea and perhaps drift into space.

I will be one with the universe, he thought. And then: But I would prefer to be one with my own body.

The duke had not, in fact, finished with his gloating monologuing and had two words left in his speech. And those words were:

"Good-bye, Fowl," he said, and positioned his forefinger over the appropriate buttons to send the *fire all* command.

If Myles had not been the one on the receiving end of an imminent bloody homicide, he might have appreciated the spectacle. A swarm of airborne death-dealing machines arranged in a semicircle before the foreboding mansion, controlled by their hovering master. In fact, it would have been an almost perfect gothic tableau had the duke been wearing a billowing cape instead of a bathrobe and striped swimming costume.

The *fire all* command was a combination order so that it could not be sent accidentally. First, Lord Teddy held down the prime button with his forefinger, and then he swiped his thumb across a small track pad. This second motion was not really intuitive, and Teddy had meant to program in his own shortcut, but he had never gotten around to it, which was why he pressed too hard on the first try and had to attempt it again.

Note to self, he thought. Check with Myishi to see if I am eligible for a controller upgrade.

For Lazuli, the world turned liquid orange, as though her helmet had dropped its glare filter. But this was no filter— it was her magic running on autopilot. Lazuli was in mortal danger, and the magic rose in her as a fiery life preserver. And before Lord Teddy had time for a second swipe, Lazuli opened her mouth and unleashed a firebolt that melted the shells and workings of a dozen drones. She then turned her attention to the ground forces and bathed the electronic land troops in intense blue-white flame. The robots' metal carapaces buckled and clanged, their plates warping and splitting, some flipping entirely and others collapsing sadly on themselves, belching smoke from their innards. Once Lazuli's magic had cleared the ground forces, it turned itself on the prime danger: the Duke of Scilly.

Lord Teddy was forced to bank right on his airborne plat-form to avoid being caught in the inferno and could only watch as his metallic minions were carbonized by the intense flame. Suddenly his goal became survival rather than conquest. This is not to say that Teddy panicked, for he did not. The duke's life had been threatened on numer-ous occasions over the years, and he had discovered that he could, as Kipling said, *keep his head while all around were losing theirs.* In fact, his senses became somewhat sharpened in a fray, and though he did not realize it, his lips drew back from his teeth and his eyes widened, giving him something of a sharklike appearance. Right now he was a flying shark being pursued by a column of fire while being rained on by metallic shards that scorched his skin as they landed. Things rarely ended well for flying sharks.

Teddy pulled a sharp right, as though he were surfing

an invisible wave, and managed to escape a scythe of flame with only a lick on his heel, which burned away his riding boot and caused a dozen tiny heat blisters to rise and pop.

It's the end of you, Teddy old chap, he thought.

But it wasn't, because just like that, the assault was over.

CHAPTER 16
THE MOST POWERFUL GULL IN CORNWALL

MAGIC makes harsh demands on the bodies of its hosts, draining their reserves of glucose, glycogen, and fat, in that order. If a fairy pushes too far, the body will simply shut down for recuperation. All of a sudden, the host is overcome with an incredible fatigue that will pull the rug out from under their consciousness. And because she had precisely one minute's worth of magic experience under her belt, this is exactly what happened to Specialist Heitz. One moment she was blasting glorious roiling pillars of fire to the heavens, and the next her body said *Night-night* and she toppled over with smoke wafting from her pores. It was only an uncommonly and uncharacteristically quick reaction from Myles Fowl that prevented her from tumbling into the blowhole. Myles had no time to catch Specialist Heitz, so he bodychecked her away from the sinkhole and was forced to pinwheel his arms to avoid falling in himself.

Myles and Lord Teddy righted themselves at roughly the same time. Lord Teddy's cool head had increased in temperature, as it were, so that now he was entirely hotheaded and had reverted to his previous plan of blowing Myles Fowl and his darned coterie to hell, or at least wiping them off the face of the earth. Myles, for his part, could not think of a single thing to do other than not give this monster of a man the satisfaction of begging for his life. His comrades had bought him every second of time that could be reasonably expected of them, and now he had to accept these facts:

1. His plan had not worked, and . . .
2. Sometimes being a genius would not get the job done if a person made bad choices.

Lord Teddy steadied himself on his hovering platform. His face was blazing with rage and his foot was also ablaze with second-degree burns. Any slightly comedic aspect his appearance may have presented mere seconds ago had completely vanished. Now the duke was bloody-minded and prepared for war, and his thunderous expression reflected as much.

"Light up the target," he told his remaining electronic soldiers, and dozens of red laser dots covered Myles from the top of his head to the tips of his toes.

Among the red lasers, there was one green dot.

* * *

Myles saw the dot and his relief was so powerful that for a moment his legs shook. He was unaccustomed to this emotion, as his plans usually proceeded without a hitch, and so his relief muscle was rarely exercised. In fact, the last time he could remember feeling anything even remotely close to this level of relief was when he solved the notorious Breman two-year crossword in fourteen minutes, beating Artemis's record by thirty-eight seconds. Myles realized in this moment that there were things slightly more important than besting his elder brother in newspaper puzzles.

"Well, now," he said to the green light, which blinked from the undercarriage of a battle drone. "I am truly delighted to see you."

Lord Teddy had, in fact, also spotted the green light, which appeared as a dot precisely in the center of Myles's forehead, but the duke took it for a glitch and certainly not one worth conversing with.

"I am delighted to see you, too, my dear boy," he said, mistakenly believing that Myles was addressing him. "But I shall be ecstatic to see the back of you."

And once again the Duke of Scilly executed the *fire all* command, this time carefully executing his swipe in spite of his mood.

And nothing happened.

Well, to be accurate, something *did* happen, just not what the duke expected to happen. Lord Teddy expected a salvo of concentrated laser beams, explosive projectiles of various calibers, arrowheads, and even low-yield missiles to utterly obliterate the Fowl spawn and all their allies, troll be damned. But instead, a single one of his drones executed its fire command, and that little fellow was wildly off-target, only managing to singe the tail feathers of an innocent seagull passing overhead. As a result, that seagull could reasonably have been expected to abandon any dreams he might have nurtured to become the alpha gull in his flock. On the contrary, the bird, whose name phonetically was Krruaa-ka-ka, learned to use his newfound erratic flying style as an avian martial art and became the most power-ful gull in all of Cornwall, eventually uniting the southern counties.

But back to our story.

One by one, Lord Teddy's drones switched their target beams from red to green. This took a few seconds, and while the duke looked around at his army in consternation, Myles used the time to smooth his tie and check on the hair dryer's progress.

He knelt beside the bubbling cellophane.

"Are you comfortable in there, brother?"

"Yep," said Beckett. "Sleeping a bit. Me and Whistle Blower are having the same dream about an emperor seagull."

Myles remembered that there was a dash of sedative in the cellophane mix. It made sense to keep one's captives subdued. That was certainly what he himself would do. Beck and Whistle Blower should be fine as long as he could extricate them from their cocoon posthaste.

One of Lord Teddy's drones had dropped to Myles's shoulder, and it spoke to him. The sound was quite clear through the most excellent Myishi speakers, and it was most definitely NANNI's voice.

"Perhaps I should cut Master Beckett free?" suggested the Artificial Intelligence, who was now, it seemed, in control of the duke's network.

"Affirmative, NANNI," said Myles. "But be careful. Beck thrashes in his sleep and we wouldn't want to bring him home minus a limb."

"Fear not, Myles," said NANNI. "This drone is the most sophisticated in the bunch, which is why most of my consciousness is concentrated here. The others are mere worker bees that I am flying."

The NANNI drone spun her rotors, which could have been interpreted as a groan, and set about the business of cutting Beckett and Whistle Blower loose. The operation was over in seconds without incident, though, in the course of a day for normal individuals, being lasered out of the cellophane prison that one shares with a toy troll might be considered incident enough.

Myles turned his attention to Lord Teddy, who was desperately trying to release his entire payload on Myles. Only one tech machine responded—a damaged spray bottle that lurched forward in a rather pathetic fashion, its wheels spinning for grip, spitting out weak arcs of weed killer.

"May I?" asked the NANNI drone.

"By all means," replied Myles, and a quick laser burst

from the drone gutted the weed killer, which apparently had an internal combustion engine complete with oil tank, as black smoke belched from its belly in a tiny mushroom cloud.

By all means. Myles had said the words casually.

But he was well aware that luck had played a part in maintaining his status as *currently living.* A much larger part than he would either like or was used to conceding. NANNI had saved their lives, and while it was true that he had put the AI in play some hours previously, that had been as a fallback measure rather than a primary strategy. Myles had fully expected to have resolved the Lord Teddy situation long before NANNI could infiltrate the closed St. George network, for, to be honest, he hadn't been a hundred percent certain that the AI was capable of cracking a Myishi server.

As if reading his thoughts, which Myles often suspected she could, NANNI said, "You didn't think I could do it, Myles, did you? Hack the system, I mean."

"Of course I did," said Myles. "I designed you, did I not?"

"You assisted Artemis in designing me," corrected NANNI. "But it was your work on the general AI chip that enabled me to figure out a back way into a Myishi-built system. In fact, you may be pleased to know that we are now in *all* the duke's systems."

"That was not part of your brief," said Myles.

"I am aware of this," said NANNI. "But, thanks to you, I have evolved to the level of Superintelligence."

This was a momentous declaration, as Earth's computing experts did not expect General AI to arrive for another fifty years, and Superintelligence was considered to be centuries away.

"You did it, Myles Fowl," said NANNI. "Or, rather, *I* did it with your help. We really should renegotiate my contract, just as soon as you deal with the flying English nobleman."

"Ah," said Myles. "I had almost forgotten about him."

Lord Teddy often had nightmares about his years in boarding school at Charterhouse. Bullying was a part of life in every dorm, and one of the older boys, Robert Hardie, developed a system where he would hang the little ones in rows on cloakroom hooks and subject them to a caning while they dangled defenseless. Teddy had endured this torture for almost an entire term until he had managed to get hold of a cast-iron screwdriver from the groundskeeper. Young Teddy skipped evening prayers to loosen the row of coat hooks, so that when Hardie indulged himself in his sadistic practice that evening, the coat hooks were dragged en masse from their mounts and Hardie found himself surrounded by a dozen enraged juniors who had concealed wooden rulers in their stockings. Hardie left the school at term's end.

But Teddy had never forgotten the feeling of helplessness as he hung on that coat hook, and now he experienced the same infuriating emotion again as he dangled on Myles Fowl's metaphorical hook. Once more suspended in the air and dependent on the whims of an eleven-year-old.

I triumphed over Hardie, thought the duke now. And I may yet triumph over Myles Fowl.

Teddy's first move was to try an emergency shutdown of the entire system. True, he was twenty feet in the air, but that was a survivable fall. Teddy linked his handsets and held down the power buttons for a count of five. But there was no reboot.

I am completely shut out, thought the duke, tossing away the useless controllers.

Old-school, then, he thought, reaching for the shotgun strapped across his back.

"Bring me down, boy," he called. "Or, by all that's holy, I will let you have both barrels."

Myles was smart enough to know that he had pushed the duke over the horizon of good sense. Lord Teddy could not care a fig about consequences now. He had been bested by a mere child, and, for most men—especially a man from his era—that was intolerable. And yet Myles tried to reason with him.

"Your Grace," he said, "be sensible. We have infiltrated your entire system. We own it."

"But how?" asked the duke. "The system is sealed. You would literally have to plug into the server."

Myles gave him a moment to figure it out.

"Of course," said Lord Teddy. "The spectacles."

Myles nodded. "Precisely. Your mistake was charging

from your computer rather from an outlet. There is a universal sensor on the arm of my spectacles. When I tossed them on your desk charger, I was actually plugging in. It took a little longer than I'd expected, but NANNI eventually cracked Myishi's system. Everything you once controlled is now in my power."

Lord Teddy leveled the shotgun.

"Not everything," he said, which was a valid point.

Myles sighed. "You still have dignity, Your Grace. Can we not preserve that, at least?"

This was not true.

Not really.

Lord Teddy's dignity had gone the way of the dodo. He was trapped on a flying skateboard clad in beachwear, and his beloved beard was a mass of crisped split ends. The only way for the duke to reclaim his self-respect was to eliminate any and all witnesses, and to purge this entire sorry affair from his memory and mainframe.

The duke might have capitulated—after all, his situation was desperate—had not NANNI asked:

"Should I stop streaming the three-D package for this Myishi person?"

Lord Teddy actually felt ill as he remembered his instruction to live-stream his destruction of the Fowls to one of the few people he actually cared about: Ishi Myishi.

"You infernal machine! You are streaming?"

"I am," said NANNI. "Recording too, through half a

dozen of your excellent surveillance drones. I could have stopped, but I am experimenting with humor. Was that humorous?"

"Absolutely," said Myles.

"No!" barked the duke. "Shall we see how humorous you think *this* is?"

And he fired a shell at Myles's head.

Although NANNI could make millions of calculations per second, there was only one course of action that could stop the shrink-wrapper from enveloping Myles's head and knocking him into the blowhole. This course of action was two-pronged: First, she would place herself in the missile's path while simultaneously trying to shoot it out of the sky. If NANNI had been in one of her own bodies back in Villa Éco, then possibly she could have been successful in nailing the shrink-wrapper. But the targeting software of the Myishi drone she was currently inhabiting was nowhere near as sophisticated as her own, and so she merely succeeded in clipping the missile, which set off the gel capsule, which, in turn, short-circuited her exposed wires and engulfed her in a blob of cellophane. The cellophane smothered all her workings except a few sparking wires that were shaken loose. NANNI's errant laser went on to slice through the front left rotor of Lord Teddy's platform, and the duke dropped to earth at speed—but not as fast as he might have, as three rotors were still operational.

The next few seconds, Myles knew, would be crucial. NANNI's works were gummed up for the time being, and it would take her a few moments to wirelessly transfer to another host. Beckett and Whistle Blower were still coming to, and he himself was, as his peers often told him, *useless in a fight*.

"Oh, dear," said Myles.

"'Oh, dear' does not begin to cover it, my boy," said the duke, stomping in place until the platform fractured beneath his feet and he was free to stride toward Myles, shotgun raised with menacing intent.

But then Lord Teddy changed his mind and pocketed the shrink-wrappers, loading a couple of regular shells in their place.

"No nonlethals for you, Fowl," he said, leveling the weapon at Myles's body. "That bird has flown the coop."

"Wait," said Myles, raising his hand as if pale, spindly digits could ward off a shotgun blast.

"No more waiting, dear boy" said the duke. "You have taught me that much, at least."

CHAPTER 17

FAREWELL, FRIENDS

AND so we arrive at the moment of truth: the imminent death of Myles Fowl.

It is commonly believed that a person's life flashes before their eyes at the moment of departure from this mortal coil, but in Myles's case, what he experienced was a deep regret that he could not save his companions. Myles had expected his expiration to be attended by grieving admirers who would weep uncontrollably at the foot of his bed. Weeping not just for Myles himself, but for the very future of humanity. Myles had even spent an inordinate amount of time choosing his last words, and the current edit was:

Farewell, friends. Do not weep for me; weep for a world without me.

It was, he thought, succinct and quotable.

At any rate, it didn't matter, for Myles was destined to survive on this occasion, right after he died.

* * *

Lord Teddy Bleedham-Drye pulled the trigger, unloading one subsonic forty-grain slug into Myles's upper right chest, completely shredding his new suit and, of course, penetrating deep into the skin. Amazingly, the slug hit neither Myles's hand nor his heart, and so he did not die immediately but *almost* immediately. His slight frame was catapulted backward into Specialist Heitz's arms, which was indeed lucky for him. Ten minutes earlier, it would have made not a whit of difference where Myles landed, as Lazuli had not yet manifested her magic, but now she was an entirely different creature. On the plus side, she was a magical pixel. On the negative side, she had zero control over her magic and no idea what her talents actually were.

There is a maxim written in the Testament of Orsoon in the Fairy Book that says: *Like water flows where it will flow, magic goes where it will go.* A simple rhyme that has been debated over for centuries by theologians, but most take it to mean that, if unchecked, magic will choose to go where it is needed. In this case, the magic was most definitely needed in Myles's torso, and his brain, too, which had already shut down. Lazuli didn't really know what was going on, as she was still semiconscious following her spectacular bout of fireballing, and so she didn't even feel it when her right hand pressed itself into Myles's wound and transmitted pulses of orange energy deep into the tattered flesh.

The other two members of the Regrettables were also making some proactive moves. Moments before Lord Teddy pulled the trigger, Beckett was alert enough to put an idea of his own into action. The duke was too far away for Beckett himself to bridge the gap between them, but he did have a missile of sorts.

He lifted the toy troll from his chest, grunted terse instructions, and then, with all of the considerable strength in his dominant arm, he hurled Whistle Blower toward the sparking NANNI drone.

Whistle Blower was more than equal to the mission entrusted to him, even if he did not quite understand the point of it. The toy troll would have preferred to be heading directly toward Lord Teddy, but the human boy Beckett was his friend, so Whistle Blower did as he was bid and used the thick plate of bone on his forehead to butt the drone toward Lord Teddy, who instinctively caught it under one arm.

"Ha!" said the duke. "Nice try . . ."

The duke was correct.

It *had* been a nice try.

A very nice try, in fact, for the wires dangling underneath the drone made contact with Lord Teddy's frame, sending a low-voltage charge through his body. It was not enough to do much more than tickle the duke, who had, after all, built up a considerable resistance to electrical currents, thanks to his eels. But the charge was certainly enough to set off the cellophane virus slugs in his pockets.

All of them.

It was both horrific and fascinating to watch. And when Ishi Myishi himself reviewed the tape later that day, he was moved to make several safety modifications to the shrink-wrappers' design, for he had to admit there was a serious flaw—that being that any electrical charge could set them off and not just the one built into the shell itself.

The projectiles ignited in a chain reaction that soon saw the duke engulfed in a series of blossoming cellophane spheres that oozed across his body like transparent slugs, the trapped electricity crackling through the blobs of plastic. Lord Teddy could only watch in horror as his entire self was engulfed in the same material he had so carelessly inflicted on others with no regard for their discomfort. In fact, his victims' discomfort was nothing compared to Teddy's own. What he felt now must have been akin to what a mouse feels in the fist of a gorilla, for the CV slugs were designed to be employed one per target, whereas the duke was now being crushed by a dozen, each one forming another layer around his trapped person. His bones were shattered, his flesh split, and electricity crackled along his intestines. Lord Bleedham-Drye was mortally wounded several times over—though, of course, one would have been perfectly sufficient. The final thing Teddy almost said before being consumed completely was *I would have gotten away with it if it hadn't been for you meddling kids.*

But the last vestige of his noble upbringing caused him to think better of that, and so he went under the cellophane without saying a word. His cold glare spoke volumes of purest hatred, which was of little importance, for no one was looking his way at that moment to read them. After several seconds, the cellophane settled into a roughly spherical shape and, with Lord Teddy suspended inside, rolled, bounced, and wiggled its way down into the blowhole. It did not reappear.

The raw power of Lazuli's healing magic boiled the salt mist into a spume of steam. When the cloud drifted away on the sea breeze, Lazuli found herself hugging one of the Fowl boys close to her chest, but she could not be sure which one it was, because her face was mashed beneath his back. They seemed to be lying in a slop of mud and salt water that had settled at a level halfway up her face. Lazuli could hear voices from somewhere, but she couldn't make out any actual words because of the water in her ears, which some part of her knew would take weeks to shake out. While her particular hybrid ears were excellent for localized hearing, they were like a maze of cartilage and a nightmare to clear of lodged water.

I'll probably need to have them syringed, she thought, even while she knew that her ears were the least of her worries.

If I don't get out from under this human, I'll either drown or suffocate.

It was funny: The Fowl boys had always seemed puny to her, and she had jogged up training ramps with heavier packs on her back, but now Myles or Beckett, whichever one it was, seemed to weigh a ton.

Lazuli waved her free arm to remind those still alive that she too was among the living and was relieved when someone grabbed it and hauled her out from under Myles. It had to be Myles, because it was Beckett who pulled her out.

Beckett was shaking his head and talking at her, with Whistle Blower doing his usual mimicking act by the boy's side.

"What?" she said. "What are you saying? I can't hear."

Lazuli tugged at her chinstrap, removing the LEP helmet, and shook her head to clear out at least some of the water.

"Now, Beck," she said. "What did you say?"

Beckett pointed to Myles, who was lying beside her, having recently been piled on top of her, and she had a fuzzy memory of someone being shot.

"I said that when Myles sees that," repeated Beckett, "he isn't going to be happy, even though he should be."

Lazuli looked where Beckett was pointing and was inclined to agree. Myles was not going to be happy, but at least he would be alive to be furious.

D'Arvit, she thought. I did that. I can do things now!

Myles's journey back to consciousness was quite abrupt, and he sat up suddenly, shouting, "Do not weep for me; weep for a world without me!"

And then he immediately collapsed back onto the muddy ground, breathing deeply through lungs that were certainly not perforated by shotgun pellets as they had been minutes ago. Myles lay still with his eyes closed for several moments, just letting the information percolate.

He heard Whistle Blower grunt and Beckett reply, "No, pal. He is not sleeping or stupid. Myles is thinking about stuff. Trying to make sense of it all."

The troll grunted again, and perhaps an expert linguist could have told the difference between the two sets of grunts, but Myles could not. Fortunately, Beckett the trans-species polyglot understood.

"Those were Myles's last words. He's been practicing for years."

The troll made a rumbling sound, and Myles, even with his eyes closed, knew he was being laughed at.

Myles took another moment to compose himself, then opened his eyes to find Beckett squatting beside him. His brother may have been bantering with Whistle Blower, but there was a look of serious concern on his young face.

"Welcome back, brother," said Beckett.

Myles realized that he was indeed okay when he patently should not be okay.

"Was I shot?" he asked.

"Right in the chest," confirmed Beckett.

"So, by all the laws of anatomy, and indeed, biology, rigor mortis should be already setting in."

"You would be fish food, if that's what you're trying to say."

"My suit?" asked Myles.

"Ruined. Blood and guts all over it."

"That was a brand-new suit."

"And there's mud on your shoes."

Would the indignities never cease? Myles wondered. "What a day," he said. "How are any of us alive?"

Whistle Blower pointed a talon at Beckett. The implication was clear. He had saved everyone.

"You did it?"

"I remembered what you said about the shrink-wrappers being set off by an electrical charge, and I saw sparking wires hanging from NANNI's guts, so I pinballed Whistle Blower off NANNI so the drone would set off the duke's shells. You should have seen Whistle Blower. He got the angle perfect."

Myles was amazed. "That was really clever."

"I know," said Beckett. "Don't tell anyone."

Myles closed his eyes again and said what he really wanted to say: "You saved us all, Beck. I thought I was so smart, and you saved us all."

When Myles opened his eyes, Beckett was smiling down at him in that open way of his, with his love for his twin right there on his face.

"You are smart, Myles. And you did buy me some time by dying."

Myles frowned thinking about this. "That's right. I should be dead. Specialist Heitz must have manifested healing powers. They are common among fairies."

"That's what happened," said Beckett. "You should have

seen it. There was like steam and lightning, and then two purple dragons flew out of the clouds, and you got a hand-print burned onto your chest."

Myles thought that maybe his twin was exaggerating. "Is all of that factually accurate, brother?"

"You caught me," said Beckett. "There were no dragons."

Myles laughed and felt a burning stretch in the skin of his chest. "Oh," he said.

Lazuli peered into the blowhole. What she saw down there ranked among the weirdest sights of her lifetime, and that was saying something, considering all that she had seen over the past couple of days.

So much chaos in two days, she thought. And then: I would not have believed it possible that I would feel sorry for the duke.

But she did, even though she herself still felt wretched and Lord Teddy had tried on at least two occasions to abduct her for purposes of experimentation. Why? Because the fate he had brought upon himself was, in her opinion, worse than death. For, by a bizarre confluence of circumstances, Lord Teddy had simultaneously achieved his ambition of immortality while forfeiting any hope of eternal youth.

To explain:

Lord Teddy and his cellophane sphere had plugged the blowhole most effectively, and so he hung there suspended while the seawater sporadically battered the sphere from below. The chemicals in the shrink-wrappers had somehow combined with the troll venom in the beaker the duke had been carrying on his person. The poison had been rendered chemically active by the trapped electricity and entered Lord Teddy's bloodstream through the lacerations in his stomach made by the fractured jar. So now the duke's life had been both saved and indefinitely extended, but he would live that life as a hundred-and-fifty-year-old man. Lazuli used her helmet Optix to zoom in on Lord Teddy's face and saw that the duke's prized beard had thinned considerably and was as gray as ash. She was surprised to see that Lord Teddy was glaring back at her. His eyelids were heavy with folds of ancient skin, but there was still a crack of eyeball visible, and it seemed as though all the hatred of the past one and a half centuries were being beamed up the blowhole at Lazuli. The glare turned Lazuli's already queasy stomach and any sympathy she had been feeling immediately evaporated.

That human would kill us all, she thought and knew it to be true. Lazuli realized that she didn't know what to do about the duke. Would it be best for all concerned, including Bleedham-Drye himself, if she simply dropped rocks on the sphere until it became dislodged and washed out to sea?

An icon in her visor beeped and Lazuli realized with some relief that this decision was not hers to make. After all, she was Recon. This was a command decision.

CHAPTER 18

THE NEXT CRISIS

MYLES buttoned his tattered shirt as best he could. To the casual observer, it would seem like he was wearing an outfit that had been fed through a rather voracious industrial shredder. There were four buttons left but only two buttonholes, and so the actual coverage was negligible, but it made the fastidious Myles feel a little better.

A small drone hovered at his shoulder and played a delivery fanfare, and Myles saw that his spectacles were in its wire tray. Myles put on the glasses and felt instantly more relaxed and ready for the next crisis, though he was sure the universe would grant them a breather after all they'd been through.

"NANNI," he said. "Situation report?"

"There are imminent crises," said NANNI. "We have a coast guard boat approaching from the nearby island of

St. Mary's. Apparently, Specialist Heitz's pyrotechnical displays were noticed. On the plus side, the light penetrating the mist is simply beautiful."

Myles nodded. The light *was* beautiful, he supposed, when one considered its refraction on contact with a dense medium. But he was more interested in the approaching coast guard.

This was not too serious. It should be simple enough to hijack a boat from unarmed sailors. In fact, this approaching craft could be a blessing in disguise.

"Hardly a crisis, NANNI," he said. "Monitor their radio chatter."

"There are also two Westland helicopters inbound. Both with paratroopers packed in tighter than sardines. Have you ever heard Bach's Chaconne in D? A perfect blend of mathematics and beauty. This is what I intend to become eventually."

Interesting, thought Myles. It would appear that NANNI is grappling with a creative impulse.

But he should probably concentrate on the helicopters.

"ACRONYM," muttered Myles. The organization had located them somehow. It was reasonable to presume that Sister Jeronima had survived and pointed a finger at Lord Teddy. Myles found that he was relieved Jeronima was alive, for he had no desire to see her die or even be seriously harmed. Though it would have been nice if the bloodthirsty nun had been incapacitated for a few weeks. Perhaps with a nasty gum infection that required complete bed rest without much in the way of talking.

"*That* is a crisis," he admitted to NANNI. "ETA?"

"Nothing too immediate," said NANNI.

"Good," said Myles. Perhaps they could get away on the lifeboat before the helicopters arrived.

"We have thirty, perhaps forty seconds before the first helicopter breaches the cloud bank."

"Fantastic," said Myles. "That gives us so much time."

"I know," said NANNI brightly. "Imagine how many calculations I can run in forty seconds. I have, in fact, composed a concerto since we've been speaking."

"Round up your metallic troops," said Myles, bringing the conversation back on track while straightening his goldfish tie, which had curled a little in the heat but was otherwise undamaged. "We need to face down some soldiers."

Lazuli appeared at Myles's side.

"Don't worry about that," she said.

"That's what I do," said Myles. "I worry. And thank you, Specialist, for saving my life. I fully intend to have regression hypnotherapy in order to relive my own death at my leisure and perhaps learn a little something about the afterlife."

"That sounds like fun, Myles," said Lazuli. She nodded at the bright red handprint scar seared onto Myles's chest. The scar was so perfect it could have been dusted for prints. "Sorry about that," she said. "It was my first healing."

Myles shook his head. "Don't be sorry. It doesn't hurt

really, and I have no doubt that this scar shall become a touchstone. A reminder that life occasionally gets in the way of my plans and I should be prepared for that."

Beckett joined them, Whistle Blower perched on his shoulder, sniffing the air. "Whistle Blower says there are metal birds approaching. I think he means helicopters."

"Helicopters full of ACRONYM operatives sporting knee pads, no doubt," said Myles. "We should retreat inside the house and prepare the drones for a firefight. I will not allow these people to touch a hair on our fairy friends' heads." Myles tapped the arm of his spectacles and even this familiar action comforted him. "NANNI, monitor their communications and see what we can interfere with on those birds."

Lazuli reached up and touched his shoulder. "Myles, there is no need. You are not the only thing healed by the magic."

Myles noticed that Lazuli was wearing her helmet, and that its heads-up display was running streams of data.

"Oh," he said. "Biological circuits."

"Exactly," said Lazuli.

Myles also noticed that while their group in general looked like they had been dragged flailing through a muddy thicket full of crabs, Lazuli's uniform was now immaculate.

"Self-cleaning fibers?" he asked.

"Precisely."

"In that case," said Myles, "the floor is yours, Specialist Heitz."

"I could use thirty seconds of interference," said Lazuli.

"I think we can do that," said Myles. "NANNI, can we put up a curtain? Nothing lethal, but annoying."

"I can manage that," said NANNI. "You will be safe here on the ground."

"Safe," said Myles. "Finally."

And relief flooded his brain with neurotransmitters.

Beckett experienced no such brain flood. "What? I have a lot of pent-up energy. Can't I hit something?"

"No, Beckett," said Myles firmly. "It's Lazuli's turn."

Whistle Blower threw a mini tantrum, sloshing in the mud and slashing the air, sensing from Beckett's disposition that they would not be stomping on anyone.

"Boys," said Lazuli sternly, "go and sit on that bench and watch. You might as well enjoy it, because you more than likely will be getting your minds wiped in a few minutes."

The three sat on the bench, a cast-iron affair rather cleverly wrought to display the battle between Saint George and his dragon, even though that battle had actually taken place on another continent.

As the three watched Lazuli walk with some degree of swagger toward the helicopters that breached the St. George cloud cover, noses aggressively angled downward, NANNI vibrated words into Myles's cheekbone.

"Artemis left a file on the subject and legalities of mind-wiping. Perhaps you would like to review it now? There may be a loophole."

"I would very much like to review that," said Myles under his breath, and a small window in his right lens played a message from his big brother for his eye only.

"Very interesting," he said, after the short video played.

The message gave Myles an idea of what to do if what he thought might happen later did happen just after what was about to happen more immediately.

Sister Jeronima Gonzalez-Ramos de Zárate of Bilbao knew that the traditional image of a nun was a calm, unarmed, pious lady clad in a simple smock, but, at this precise moment, she certainly did not fit the usual profile. Sister Jeronima was kitted out in her battle suit, which was slightly reminiscent of a nun's smock if one squinted from a distance, but, up close, the body armor and Kevlar plates were clearly visible, as were the handles of throwing knives sticking out of various custom pockets in her vest, not to mention the assault rifle she held in her gloved hands.

Jeronima was not the only one prepared for battle. There were a further twelve agents with their own favorite hardware all checking their safeties and going through whatever good-luck rituals they had performed in a hundred similar encounters. Similar in the fact that they were going into battle, but that was where the similarity to this situation ended. No one had ever flown through a cloud bank with two teams of paratroopers to take on a couple of niños and miniature fairies, she felt sure.

But she was not about to take any chances. Jeronima was determined to have those fairies alive and those children dead. And as for Lord Teddy Bleedham-Drye, he would either die here today or spend the rest of his life in ACRONYM's most secure cell, which happened to be two hundred feet underground in a repurposed nuclear shelter in Arizona with very poor air-conditioning, so the room constantly smelled of dead coyote.

And that fate, Jeronima thought, would be too good for the rat duke.

The ACRONYM birds had been holding at Penzance for a few hours, trying to poke their sensors through Lord Teddy's security field with zero luck. They had no visual through the fog bank, no thermals from the ACRONYM satellite, and nothing but the cries of seagulls from their directional microphones. Both pilots had been on the point of calling the whole thing off when suddenly St. George opened up like a flower in the sun and digital info began to flood through.

"Their dead zone has just livened up," said Phones, their tech guy. "I got everything we need."

Jeronima knew she should spend a moment wondering why the duke would shut down his defenses, but she was too angry for caution.

"We go now," she shouted. "¡Vamos!"

And so vamos they did, and, two minutes later, Jeronima found herself standing out on a chopper runner wearing a gunner's rig. Good battle practice would have been for her, as senior officer, to wait on the mainland and let the paratroopers perform the extraction, but Jeronima would not have missed out on this mission for all the velvet slippers in the Vatican.

They entered the outer ring of fog, rotors whipping the mist into vortices and graying out the windshields, and then they were through, and Jeronima saw that there was nothing special about the vista. Just another English rock in the ocean with a tumbledown manor house and a patchwork of threadbare fields.

What might be termed unusual was the tiny blue fairy standing on the edge of a northerly cliff, hands on hips as if daring the helos to come any closer.

"We got one possible hostile on the cliff," said the copilot into her cans. "You want we should use the fifty-cal on her, Sister J?"

Jeronima indulged her imagination for one sweet moment, seeing in her mind's eye the annoying little fairy blown to tiny pieces by a fifty-caliber cannon.

But I need her in order to salvage something from this mission.

So she said, "Negativo. I want her safe. The humans you can kill, but use small caliber only—I don't want any daño collateral. Tranquilize the fairy. And if you refer to me as Sister J again, I will toss you out of this helicopter. ¿Comprendes, idiota?"

Before the sharpshooter in the second helicopter could switch out his live rounds for tranqs, a flock of birds rose in a synchronized cloud before the helicopters. Pilots in general have a terror of birds, as a bird strike can bring most craft down as efficiently as any missile, but then Jeronima saw that the flying objects were not birds, but drones.

Myishi drones, I would bet, thought Jeronima, and when

laser sights painted both choppers, her suspicions were confirmed.

"Shoot them down," she ordered. "All of them."

There followed a brief but deadly firefight.

The drones under NANNI's command threw everything they had at the two helicopters. Everything they had included laser beams, small-caliber bullets, buzz blades, hedge clippers, weed killer, and even some bug spray. Most of the missiles fell well short of the mark, and even the lasers did little damage against the tough hides of the helicopters. The helicopters, on the other hand, rained devastating destruction on the drones. They hit them with machine-gun fire, mortars, and flamethrowers. Within minutes there were only soot and sparks where the drones had been, and still the small blue fairy stood defiantly in Peter Pan style, as though she were the one in charge.

"I gotta give it to her," said the copilot. "That little creature has guts. Standing right out there in the open. Making a target of herself. And look at those other guys, relaxing on the bench like they're at a baseball game."

It is true, thought Jeronima. It is as if they are knowing something that I myself am not knowing.

"No matter," she said. "Take the shot at the fairy as soon as you have one. I want to be out of here before the coast guard arrives."

"I got a shot right now," said the sharpshooter in the second chopper.

"Well, then, tranq her," said Jeronima. She flicked off

the safety on her own weapon, thinking: And I will shoot the Fowl Twins.

Jeronima tucked the stock of her weapon into her shoulder, took a breath, put a finger on the trigger, closed her eyes for a long second so she would not need to blink, then . . .

. . . opened her eyes to find she was somewhere she did not recognize doing something unfamiliar.

Or maybe not familiar yet.

Becoming familiar.

Around and round. Over and over. A rough wooden stick in her grip.

Cranking.

She was cranking a handle.

And beside her was a child. Maybe nine years old. A girl whose name was . . . Mercy.

The girl's name was Mercy.

I like this girl, Jeronima realized. I like her and everyone here.

Jeronima took a break from her work and looked around. She was in a village of mud huts with brightly painted walls, each one with a curtain across the doorway. There were people everywhere.

The Baka, she realized. The Baka of eastern Cameroon.

The Baka were swarming around her, tapping her shoulder, singing a local melody that someone had told her weeks ago was about carrying water along the trail.

331

No more, thought Jeronima. From now on, there will be water right here in the village from this well.

She wiped her neck with a kerchief and then bent to her work with renewed vigor, joining in the simple repetitive song.

"*Carry the water, carry the water.*"

In her mind adding the suffix *no more*.

Nine-year-olds like Mercy shouldn't have to carry water.

A thought popped into her head: This is how a nun should live. Not hunting other life-forms with guns.

Other life-forms with guns? That was estúpido. Why would a nun need a gun? Or a helicopter?

Sister Jeronima shook these crazy thoughts from her head. She was daydreaming when there was work to be done. She cranked the handle one more time, and the engine it was connected to caught. The engine was also connected to a pump, which created a vacuum in a pipe running deep into the ground.

A cheer rose up around her, decorated with beautiful laughs and singing, and Jeronima thought she could endure heat and mosquitoes for the rest of her life to hear that sound just once a year.

For a few seconds the pipe coughed dryly, like an old man's windpipe, but then it spat brown sludge and finally a sparkling stream of clear water. Jeronima sank back on her knees, accepting the hugs and kisses of her new friends, and she thanked the Lord for the benefactor who had sponsored the well, and, as she listened to the delighted laughs and songs of the children float above her head like sonic butterflies, she thought that days like this would help to erase the shadows in her past that she couldn't quite remember.

Jeronima did not notice, standing at the back of the crowd, one member of the Baka who was perhaps a head shorter than the other tribespeople and wearing a cap pulled down over his ears in spite of the heat. She did not see this fellow pull a matchbox from his pocket and speak into it as though it were a smartphone. And she did not hear him say "Relocation a success. Everyone's a winner. Requesting evac."

And even if Jeronima had heard these terse sentences, she would not have understood, as the nun did not speak Gnommish.

The Westland helicopters froze with their rotors in midwhirl. With the blades static like that, there was no way the birds should have stayed in the air, but something held them up. Myles could clearly see the muzzle flares of two weapons that were in the process of picking off the remaining drones. The flares should have faded, but they didn't, and the half dozen paratroopers who had started rappelling to ground were stuck in the air, torsos leaned back, legs splayed in the descend position, but completely still.

"Time-stop," said Myles, with no small amount of admiration in his tone. "I need to get a few of those."

If Myles tilted his head to the right angle and squinted,

he could just about make out spheres of sparkling poly-hedrons enclosing both helicopters and tethers leading back into a cloud.

Myles straightened what was left of his tie and checked that the remains of his pants at least covered his bottom, for he felt certain they were about to be introduced to someone.

The LEP shuttle emerged from the clouds, visible only because of the absence of vapor where it passed. It was an ugly ship, judging by the outline, all jutting sections and angular gun ports, and this impression of ugliness was only compounded when the shield was deactivated and, section by section, the LEP bird became fully visible.

"Isn't she beautiful?" said Lazuli, waving the craft in for a landing on the lawn of Childerblaine House.

"Not in the least," said Myles sincerely. "That craft spits in the face of Newton's ghost. I thought the Fairy People were supposed to be advanced."

"We *are* advanced," retorted Lazuli. "Everything you think you know about aerodynamics is wrong. But don't worry, you'll get there."

"Not in one of these things, I hope," said Myles.

One might assume that his dismissal of fairy technology was due to intimidation, but one would be wrong. Myles was genuinely unimpressed.

The shuttle touched down on the lawn without crushing so much as a daisy, and a few seconds later, as the boosters cycled down, a hatch opened in the shuttle's belly and a female elf in a flight suit and auburn crew cut strolled down the escalator backlit by the shuttle's interior lights. It was quite a dramatic moment.

"Specialist Heitz," said the figure. "We have been looking for you."

Lazuli saluted the elf who was her angel. "Yes, Commodore. There have been some exceptional circumstances. I got a beacon out as soon as my suit regenerated."

The elf tugged off her mirrored Wayfarers and took a look around. "Exceptional, indeed. But hardly surprising when there are Fowls involved. Are you injured in any way?"

"No, Commodore. I am fit for duty. Thanks in no small part to these humans."

Beckett had been trying to put his finger on something since the elf's first word, and then the lightbulb suddenly turned on. "NANNI," he said. "You're NANNI in real life."

"Holly Short," surmised Myles. "Artemis used your voice for our Artificial Intelligence program. I remember he said: *Finally she will have some intelligence.* I didn't understand what he meant at the time."

One half of Holly Short's mouth smiled while the other grimaced. It was an odd expression, which usually meant that the wearer had spent time in the company of one Fowl or other.

"That sounds like Artemis," she said. "Believe it or not, I miss the Mud Boy, bad jokes and all."

"And now you have been promoted to commodore?"

"I control half a dozen LEP shuttles and also mentor

specialists like Lazuli. Though I don't seem to have done a very good job at that."

"That is true," said Myles. "As a mentor, you should have anticipated every possible scenario."

Holly ignored the remark and stepped off the ramp. She surveyed the devastation all around. The twisted and smoking carapaces of a hundred perforated drones, and the manor house itself, pocked with bullet holes, made the island look like the epicenter of a war zone, which it had been, for a few minutes at least.

"You seem to have involved yourself in a Retrieval operation, Specialist Heitz," she commented. "I expect a very detailed report."

"Of course, Commodore," said Lazuli. "I can explain everything."

Myles could not help but comment unhelpfully once more. "Most things can be explained, Specialist. Cause and effect and so on. Explanations do little to clarify the morality of our actions."

Lazuli jerked a thumb at Myles. "Commodore, there's no point in listening to this human."

"I know," said Holly. "I've got one just like him."

Beckett was rapping on the shuttle's paneling, seemingly oblivious to the gun turrets that were following his movements. Whistle Blower was not oblivious to the gun turrets—indeed, he appeared to be trying to eat one.

Holly could not help but be taken aback. "There seems to be a toy troll chewing on my ship, Specialist."

"That's why I involved myself. The troll was completely exposed to the duke and the nun."

Holly blinked rapidly. "It may take some time for me to absorb that last sentence."

Beckett placed an ear against the hull and listened. From inside the shuttle came the sound of a fairy talking in hushed tones, telling her boyfriend that she was at work and couldn't chat now, and also, don't forget to renew the Picflix subscription.

"I better get to ride in this flying machine," Beckett said, "or there will be trouble."

Holly smiled and there was a little guilt in there. "You will, human. There is a procedure you need to undergo. Nothing painful, trust me."

Beckett shook his own hands as he had seen Artemis do in the video. "Fowl and fairy, friends forever. Right?"

Myles knew what the procedure might be. "You intend to mind-wipe us, Commodore. We have seen too much of the fairy world."

"Of course not, Myles," said Holly, and then to Lazuli in Gnommish, "We are definitely going to wipe these humans. The last thing the LEP needs is two more Fowls with all of our secrets."

Beckett laughed. "Ha! She's so tricky. We are definitely being wiped. It sounds like fun."

Holly glared at Lazuli, who said, "I was about to warn you. That one speaks our languages."

"Nevertheless, it must be done," said Holly, recovering

quickly. "It's not something I would personally choose to do, but there are rules for close encounters. Humans must be wiped and possibly relocated with new legend implants."

"New legends?" asked Beckett. "Can I be a troll? I already speak the language."

"Perhaps we could make an exception," said Lazuli, sticking up for her human comrades. "Without these boys, Whistle Blower and I would have been dissected on a lab tray by now."

"No exceptions, Specialist," said Holly, obviously uncomfortable with the regulations but determined to follow them. And then: "Whistle Blower?"

"The toy troll," explained Lazuli. "Beckett, the second Fowl boy, named him. And it's true, they can talk to each other."

Holly was taken aback. "He speaks Troll, too? I had thought I was beyond surprise when it came to the Fowl family, but I was wrong. I am both surprised and intrigued, but nonetheless, I am forever being told by Commander Kelp that the law is the law, so wiped they must be."

Myles clasped his hands behind his back in a fashion reminiscent of his big brother. "In that case, Commodore," he said, "I must raise a point of law regarding the legality of our proposed mind-wiping. Artemis left me a video on the subject, which I would like to present as defense exhibit A."

Holly sighed. "When a Fowl wants to discuss a point, it usually takes a couple of hours at least, and we don't have time for that." She pointed to the two helicopters frozen in space above them. "The sun is rising and will soon burn off the cloud cover. And we have a battalion of human paratroopers to relocate."

"And a duke," said Beckett.

"Of course, the duke," said Holly. "And where would we find him?"

"He's down a hole covered in plastic."

Holly rubbed her forehead. She had almost forgotten the level of weird that followed the Fowls around. "Of course he is. And that is probably not even the strangest thing I'll hear today. Very well, we'll hoist him out of there and do a little poking around in his head. No dissection, though—that's not how we operate."

"Mental scars only, eh, Commodore?" asked Myles pointedly.

Holly felt like she had stepped back in time into the argumentative minefield of Fowl-world. "Myles, we have laws to protect our society. And mind-wiping is not the ordeal it used to be. We don't even use drills anymore."

"Very droll, Commodore," said Myles. "But I doubt you will be mind-wiping us. My argument is quite persuasive."

"I would expect no less from a Fowl," said Holly, and she patted Myles fondly on his exposed neck, and then repeated the action on Beckett.

Myles felt a gentle tingling at the point of contact. "Sedative, Commodore? That was very sneaky of you."

Holly was unapologetic. "Just a thirty-minute snooze patch. There will be no ill effects. In fact, you will wake up completely refreshed, and, if Artemis's video is persuasive, perhaps you will have your memories intact."

Beckett sat down in the mud. "My brain is buzzing," he said. "Tell me a story, brother."

Myles thought he should ease his brother's passage into unconsciousness and so began:

"Once upon a time, in a magical land called Harvard University, a team led by physicist Isaac Silvera squeezed two opposing heavy-duty diamonds together to compress gaseous hydrogen."

Beckett groaned and closed his eyes even before the patch took effect. "Booooring," he said, and fake-snored for a few seconds before his real C-major snores took over.

Five seconds later, Myles himself succumbed to the LEP snooze patch and found himself being gently lowered to the earth, a fairy at each elbow. The last thing he heard before the velvet darkness took him was Whistle Blower growling Beckett's name.

Villa Éco

Beckett woke in his own bed and looked up at the 3-D-printed solar system mobile that Myles had suspended from the ceiling in an attempt to access his brother's learning receptors first thing every morning. Beckett did, in fact, often absorb what his brother tried to teach him, but he enjoyed teasing his brother by pretending to learn absolutely nothing and forgetting what he already knew.

Beckett turned his head to check that Myles was in the other bed, even though he sensed in the way that the twins often did that his brother was lying on his back with both head and feet elevated by pillows to maximize blood flow to both his primary brain and the second brain in his gut.

Myles was indeed there and awake, staring at the poster pinned to the ceiling above him. It was a finger painting of Angry Hamster in the Dimension of Fire, which Beckett had pinned there in an attempt to make his brother less smart.

"Angry Hamster seems more forlorn than angry today," said Myles, smoothing back his head of thick black hair.

Beckett thought that Myles seemed a bit sad, which he often was in the morning, as he suffered from bad dreams. Myles's self-diagnosis for his night terrors was that, while he strived to stay optimistic during the day, his intellect focused on the negative at night—how the world might end and so forth—and therefore, he often woke grumpy.

Beckett decided to cheer him up.

"I made up a thing about the planets," he said, brushing blond curls from his eyes. "To help me remember."

"That's nice, Beck," said Myles, removing his night guard.

Beckett pointed at the planets on the ceiling. "Mercury, Venus, Earth, Mars, Jupiter, Saturn, Uranus, Neptune, and Pluto, right?"

Myles frowned. "Well . . ."

Beck plowed on. "So what about: Medium Voltage Easily Makes Jumpy Snakes Undulate Near Pylons? That's good, isn't it?"

"Undulate," said Myles. "Nice. But . . ."

Beckett swung his legs out of bed. "But what?"

Usually Myles would be thrilled that some of his teachings had taken hold on the slippery slopes of Beckett's mind, but on this morning, he was less than impressed.

"But there are a growing number of scientists advocating for the dwarf planets to be considered actual planets, and I've come around to that way of thinking since Pluto is already included in the official list and it is a dwarf planet. In which case, you must add a *C* for Ceres, an *E* for Eris, *H* for Haumea, and *M* for Makemake for your device to be complete. Of course, Artemis takes the opposite view, because he is a simpleton."

Beckett grinned. "Artemis simple-toon. I remember."

When this drew no reaction, Beckett played one of his trusty cards, which was to make a deliberately glaring error in his vocabulary.

"But come on, Myles, I made an acronym. Me, Beckett!"

"No, brother," said Myles with some weariness. "You constructed a mnemonic. That's a different thing, as you well know. We covered wordplay devices last term."

Beckett threw back his covers and began bouncing on his bed. He was pleased to find he was wearing his favorite pajamas, which used to be white but, after being washed with colors, had become art.

"What's wrong, brother?" he asked. "Why aren't you more Myles-y?"

"I'll tell you what's wrong, shall I?" said Myles, rising from his bed, slotting his feet into velvet slippers, and belting on his silk dressing gown, which bore the Fowl crest stitched onto the breast in golden thread. "What's wrong is that I presented an irrefutable argument to the LEP as to why we should not be subjected to a mind-wipe and still they have taken three days to deliberate. The fate of our very brains is in their hands. It is, in a word, ridiculous. My mind should be bequeathed to science, not tampered with by some intern with electrodes. It is intolerable."

Beckett executed a near-perfect dismount from the bed and landed nose-to-nose with his twin.

"But, brother, we are at home with Mum and Dad, the sun is shining, and there are fairies in the world. Plus, the fairy serum made our hair grow back."

"Be all of that as it may," said Myles, "I gave up my quest for knowledge to protect Specialist Heitz. I followed their rules, which is not easy for a Fowl, and now I am to be brain-scraped. No, I say. Not fair. Do you know something, brother?"

"I know seven things," said Beckett seriously.

"I am beginning to think that Great-Grandmother Peg O'Connor Fowl had the right idea."

Beckett was aghast. "Peg the Pirate?"

"No," said Myles. "Peg the Information Corsair. She knew that knowledge was power, not gold. Lord Bleedham-Drye knew that, too."

Beckett asked a pertinent question. "Would you rather end up like the duke?"

Myles opened the bedroom window and looked out over the island. His parents were performing sunrise tai chi on the beach, and Dublin Bay was picture-postcard Irish.

"The duke made mistakes," said Myles. "He was vain and obvious. I would never make those mistakes. He had the right idea but used the wrong methods."

There was a shimmering on the windowsill—small at first, like the flash of fish scales in a clear stream, but the shimmer grew larger and solidified to become Lazuli Heitz, whose uniform seemed to have been upgraded somewhat. For one thing, it fit her well, and for another, it was golden.

Myles checked his smartwatch. "Specialist Heitz," he said, "you are early. I prefer not to conduct conversations until after my brain smoothie."

Lazuli smiled. "Sounds like Myles Fowl. How are you, Beckett?"

Beckett bounced across the room. "I am excellent, Laser. Yesterday I taught a worm to tie itself in a knot. Today we are doing untying."

"And that sounds like Beckett," said Lazuli.

The pixel was changed somehow, and it wasn't just her uniform. Her features seemed sharper and her eyes more alert.

"You have been promoted," Myles guessed. "You are wearing a new uniform, and confidence has given your body language a certain focus."

Lazuli stepped inside. "You are half right, Myles. I have been bumped up two grades in my pay scale but not promoted exactly. A new post has been created for me."

Myles unwrapped a seaweed stick and sucked it as he deduced. "Our objection was upheld and we are not to be wiped. And you are to be our babysitter."

"Not babysitter," said Lazuli. "Fairy liaison officer. You

can call me Ambassador Heitz, Fowl Affairs. It's a whole new office. Just me and a robot. And yes, your objection was partly successful. Magical creatures cannot be mind-wiped, as it would be a violation of their civil rights, and, since both you and Beckett were once possessed by magical creatures, you have been deemed, by extension, to be magical. A tiny loophole, humans, but you squeezed through it."

Myles did not seem cheered. "A babysitter by any other name is still a babysitter. We already have a NANNI, thank you very much."

Lazuli took off her helmet, tucked it under her arm, stood soldier straight, and did not back off from Myles's gaze. "This is not a request, Myles. You are on probation. If I find that you are interfering with fairy affairs, your privileges will be revoked. If you tell anyone about us, even your parents, your privileges will be revoked. If you attempt to harbor or make contact with a fairy fugitive, your privileges will be revoked. You will wake up one morning with no memories of the Fairy People."

"How long is the probation?" Myles asked.

"Five hundred years."

"That seems excessive, given our life span."

Lazuli shrugged. "As I'm finding out, humans have ways of cheating when it comes to life spans."

Beckett too had a question. "Would we remember you?"

Lazuli relaxed a little. "No, Beck. You wouldn't remember me."

"Then we'll be good," promised Beckett. "You're my friend, Laser. I want to remember you."

"And I you, Beck," said Lazuli. "Meeting you both has been quite an introduction to humanity. To be honest, I never believed the stories they tell about your brother in the Academy, but the past few days have changed my mind. We owe each other our lives, boys, and I feel honored to be your point of contact with the LEP."

Myles knew flattery when he heard it, but still he appeared to soften.

"Thank you, Ambassador. We too feel honored. Without you I feel that it would have taken me slightly longer to outwit Sister Jeronima and the duke, but you certainly expedited matters."

"Thanks . . . I think," said Lazuli. "We will set up a timetable for weekly debriefings. Also, I have something for you."

Lazuli handed each boy a golden acorn pin. "Communicators, in case you ever need me. They've already been coded, so just press your thumb on the acorn to speak."

Beckett immediately pressed the pin and said, "Check, check. This is Beckett Fowl of the Regrettables, and I made a mnemonic for the planets: Medium Voltage Easily Makes Jumpy Snakes Undulate Near Pylons. That's good, isn't it?"

Lazuli touched her earpiece, wincing slightly. "Very good, Beck. No need to shout."

Myles held the pin in his palm, regarding it with some

suspicion. "You wouldn't be trying to spy on us, would you, Ambassador?"

"Not spy, Myles, monitor," said Lazuli. "For your own protection."

"Protection?" asked Myles. "And why would we need protection?"

Lazuli was about to answer, but Myles held up a hand to stop her.

"The duke," he said. "He escaped."

"Not exactly," said Lazuli. "But when Retrieval checked the blowhole, Bleedham-Drye was gone. He must have washed out to sea."

"Washed out to sea?" said Myles, amused. "And the mighty all-seeing LEP with all its regenerative technology couldn't find one bobbing nobleman?"

"Bleedham-Drye is probably dead," said Lazuli. "Killed by his own weapons. But, just in case, we'll keep an eye on you for a while."

"I am comforted beyond words," said Myles. "And how did you deal with Sister Jeronima, or is she too missing?"

"Sister Jeronima and her team are devoting their time to humanitarian efforts," said Lazuli. "I can't say any more."

Myles pocketed the pin and clapped once. "That's it, then, Ambassador," he said. "Our business appears to be concluded."

"For this week," said Lazuli. "I'll be in touch. Perhaps you could help us out from time to time?"

"Consultants?" said Myles.

"Exactly," said Lazuli, strapping on her helmet. "Would that interest you both?"

"Absolutely," said Beckett, hugging the tiny fairy tightly. "The Regrettables ride again."

"Consultants," repeated Myles. "I would enjoy that. I imagine there are many problems that would require a Fowl mind to solve."

Lazuli coughed when Beckett released her. "I imagine there are," she said. "So we are parting on good terms, then? All is well? I am on probation as much as you are."

Beckett shook his own two hands. "Fowl and fairy, friends forever."

"Fowl and fairy, friends forever," repeated Lazuli.

Myles could not help but join in the spirit of the moment. "Fowl and fairy, friends forever," he said, then added: "Ambassador." For decorum's sake.

"You don't have to call me Ambassador," said Lazuli. "I think we know each other reasonably well by now. It's Lazuli. Like the semiprecious stone."

"Not semi," said Myles, with uncharacteristic and temporary affection. "Utterly precious. In fact, I would say invaluable."

"Thank you, Myles," said Lazuli. "I will see you both in a week. Look for me at sunset."

Ambassador Heitz activated her shield and disappeared in sections, the last thing to go being her smile, which lingered behind her like that of the Cheshire Cat.

Some minutes later, Myles was leaning on the bedroom balcony, sipping his brain smoothie at a rate of precisely five milliliters per minute to ensure maximum absorption, when Beckett appeared at the doorway below and made his way into the garden.

It looks suspiciously like Beck is sneaking away some-where, thought Myles, and he called down to his brother. "Beckett, brother mine. Might I ask you a question?"

Beckett stopped in his tracks and craned his neck upward.

"Wait a sec," he said, and in seconds had clambered on top of the kitchen door and jumped onto the balcony. "What is it?"

"When Ambassador Heitz was here, I inquired about Lord Teddy and Sister Jeronima, and yet you never asked about Whistle Blower. Why was that, I wonder?"

Beckett pointed one finger to his lips and another to the LEP communicator now pinned to Myles's lapel.

Myles waved away the finger. "Oh, don't worry about that. Artemis left us detailed specifications of fairy technol-ogy, details which were accurate for once. NANNI hacked the communicator in less than half a minute. She is feeding the fairy police with inane banter about her latest obses-sion, which happens to be the residual life force found in oil paintings. It will take the LEP months to catch on."

"In that case," said Beckett, "I didn't ask about Whistle Blower because he escaped already and is hiding on the beach. I didn't bring him to the house, in case he was bugged."

"You are violating our parole, Beck," said Myles sternly. "Are you certain you can bear the consequences?"

Beckett smiled his wide innocent smile. "I can't choose between friends, brother. That's just me being me."

This, so far as Myles was concerned, was the perfect answer.

One has to be oneself, he thought. Nature always wins out.

"In that case," he said, handing Beckett his spectacles, "take NANNI with you. She will debug Whistle Blower and make it safe for him to come indoors."

Beckett placed the spectacles on his face. "Look at me," he said. "I'm Myles Fowl. The vortex of the quadrangle is deteriorating my underpants." And he was gone, back-flipping to earth and scampering across the garden like a boy who had been raised by beasts.

"Be careful, brother," Myles said softly. "We both play a dangerous game."

For he, too, intended to violate the LEP parole as soon as possible. There was so much to learn and so little time in which to learn it.

Lord Teddy had good ideas but bad methods, thought Myles Fowl.

In his own quest for knowledge, Myles was fully confident that his techniques would be superior to

352

Bleedham-Drye's but also certain that these techniques would put him in the LEP's crosshairs.

We shall see, he thought, which of us will emerge victorious.

Myles shook his own hands and said with no little sarcasm, "Fowl and fairy, friends forever."

Forever is a long time, he thought. And I don't have forever.

Myles watched Beckett disappear over the ridge.

"Not yet I don't," he said softly.

Some two hundred and fifty miles south of Dalkey Island, a strange blob of cellophane was being nudged deeper into the Celtic Sea by our old friend the white-tip shark. White-tips are not typically aggressive but can become agitated in the presence of food, and this particular shark could see a sizable chunk of meat inside what seemed to be the corpse of an enormous jellyfish, and so he tore chunks from the cellophane ball with the hope of reaching the bounty inside. The bounty was, of course, Lord Teddy Bleedham-Drye, who, by an amazing aligning of the planets, was not yet deceased. For the perfect storm of stomach wounds, troll venom, and electricity had shocked him back to life, cauterized his wounds, regrown his broken bones, and granted him a longevity equal to that of a troll. A dream come true, one might think. But one would be wrong, for while Teddy was preserved, he would not be for long if this blasted shark had his way.

Perhaps that would be for the best, thought Teddy.

Chew away, you gruesome beast, he broadcast at the shark, whose sharp features were distorted by the cellophane. *I hope you choke on that rubbery gunk.*

In case you are anxious for the white-tip, fear not. The shark's stomach acid was more than equal to the task of dissolving any ingested Myishi cellophane. The shark took another chomp, affording the duke a frightening glimpse of its rows of teeth, and Lord Teddy found that he did, in fact, want to live after all. He managed to summon the strength to crunch down on a crown mounted on a rear molar, activating the Myishi tracker that came as standard with the Myishi Concierge service.

In one of the Myishi service centers in London, a young man named Douglas noticed that the Duke of Scilly's emergency beacon was flashing. He followed protocol by putting a direct call into Ishi Myishi himself in Tokyo, while simultaneously trying to open a line to the duke, for, more often than not, the emergency molars were cracked by an errant piece of toffee or the corner of a cashew nut.

Myishi picked up, but the duke did not.

Douglas explained the situation to his boss and recommended they send a chopper, for, after all, the duke was literally their oldest and certainly most valued client.

Ishi Myishi found himself concerned for his friend's well-being and immediately gave the order to send the helicopter, demanding hourly updates. Myishi warned Douglas to ensure the chopper was flown under the British Coast Guard's radar.

"I will pilot the helicopter myself," said Douglas, delighted that he would finally get to meet the duke in person and perhaps earn himself that elusive six-skull rating.

LOOK FOR THE NEXT FOWL TWINS BOOK,
COMING IN FALL 2020

THE FOWL TWINS

DENY ALL CHARGES

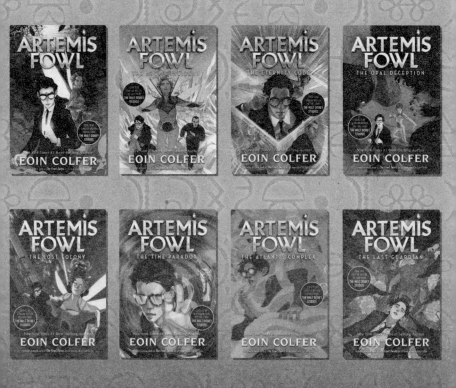